BETWEEN THIS ONE AND THE NEXT

BETWEEN THIS ONE AND THE NEXT

A When Souls Collide Novel
— • book one • —

by

GINNA MORAN

SUNNY PALMS PRESS

ISBN 978-1-942073-92-5 (soft cover)
ISBN 978-1-942073-96-3 (eBook)

Cover design by Silver Starlight Designs
Cover images copyright 123RF

For Inquiries Contact:
Sunny Palms Press
9663 Santa Monica Blvd Suite 1158
Beverly Hills, CA 90210, USA
www.sunnypalmspress.com
www.GinnaMoran.com

For Malory Knezha, my soul sister, friend, and confidant. Our journeys don't always align, but I'm so thankful for all the times we cross paths.

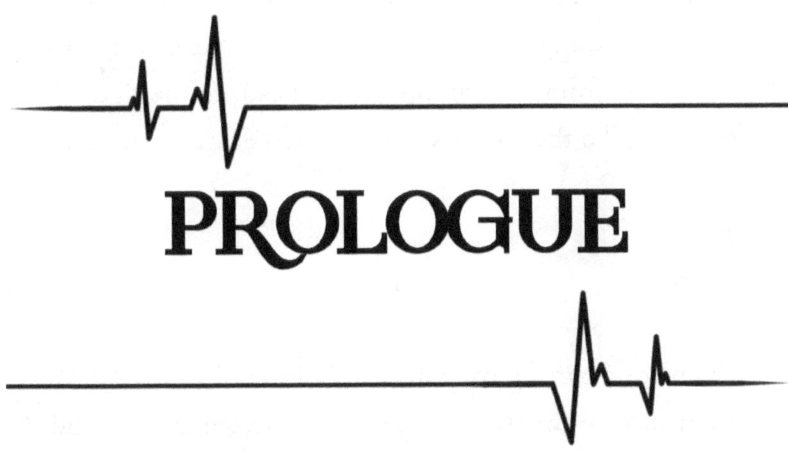

PROLOGUE

TIME OF DEATH: ELEVEN FIFTY-NINE P.M.

YESTERDAY, I DIED.

It's the only memory I have outside the chain-link barrier I'm imprisoned in now, and it's the memory I want to forget the most. I don't know where I was, only that the stars glittered above me through the moonlit, snow-covered trees. My teeth chattered, shaking my shadowed surroundings until I blinked in and out of the horrible reality I found myself in.

One moment, I was digging my nails into the frozen ground beneath me. The next, nothing but stars. Stars unlike the ones I saw overhead. They weren't distant sparkles of light. I was among them, one of them, hovering in a world filled with everything and nothing. A world I was pulled from when pain exploded behind my eyes, dragging me back to the snow, to the blood running from the wound on my head, to the figure lurking feet away. To the seconds that counted down to my death.

Five.

Four.

Three.

Two.

"Time of death," a woman said. "Eleven fifty-nine P.M."

I returned to the stars, to the place between this life and the next. The place I wish I were now instead of within this small room, remembering my death over and over again.

Time of death: Eleven fifty-nine P.M.

But that's not the only thing I remember.

"Time of life," the woman said when I opened my eyes and gasped what felt like seconds later. "Twelve fifty-nine A.M."

I remember my new life. My only life. I don't even think I was really living before. If I was, I don't know. It doesn't matter.

Because yesterday, I died.

And today, I'm more alive than ever.

CHAPTER 1

SUBJECT FOUR

"NO!" A HIGH-PITCHED scream rips through the musty air from the other side of the chain-link barrier.

Shadows bounce around the room, and a figure emerges from a pitch-black hallway to stand in front of the glass—no, clear plastic—door of the girl's cage next to me. She scrambles to the far corner, locking her doe-like, brilliant green eyes with mine.

"Please, not again. Not me. It should be the new girl this time." The thought slithers into my mind, and I tilt my head to the side. It was neither my thought nor voice in my head. Gaping at the girl, I study her, expecting her to say something to

me, but she doesn't. She flicks her gaze to the plastic door where the figure stands on the other side messing with a few items I can't see on a rolling tray.

I don't know how long I've been in this room, but it couldn't have been for more than a day since I've only fallen asleep once on the thin blue mat under me. And where I was before I woke up here? I have no idea. All I can remember is small fragments of things and feelings. Like the cold. The way the stars shone through the gnarled, wintery branches of the trees. I remember a figure. I remember the pain. The announcement of my death, and how I went from staring at the stars from the ground to floating among them. Then, I remember waking up here with a dull ache in my shoulder from lying on my side for too long.

"Please step forward, subject three," a stern, feminine voice says from the other side of the girl's door.

"No. Not today. Take the new girl or Avery instead," the girl says.

"Oh, God, shut up, Gemma. You're going to make it worse for all of us." I stiffen at the sound of another foreign voice in my mind.

Swiveling, I shift to glance behind me to the partitioned room two over from mine. I've been too scared to really look around until now. I meet the gaze of a lanky girl with long legs pulled to her chest, tight curly hair tied in two knots, almost like ears on top of her head, and a gaze dark enough to have me shifting away.

"I will not ask again, subject three. Step forward," the

masked figure repeats.

It's not until I hear the sound of a chain clanking against metal that I turn back to look at Gemma's room. The plastic door swings open, and Gemma rises to her feet, turning her back toward the figure to stare at the sink and concrete wall making up the backside of all our divided rooms.

The figure steps into the dim lighting, and my heart pounds so hard in my head that I press my cold fingers to my temples. A petite figure—a woman—wearing jeans, a blue shirt with a loose fitting jacket over it, a medical mask, protective eyewear, and a surgical cap reaches into the pocket of her jacket and pulls out a metallic canister.

"No," Gemma says, thrashing her head back and forth. She presses her hands against the concrete wall, and the lights flicker above us. It's like I'm here one second, and then gone, and back again. "Stay away!"

Curling my knees to my stomach, I try to pull in on myself, wishing I could disappear. A scream rips through the air again, and the chain-link barrier rattles all around me. The figure reaches out for Gemma. With one hand, she grabs onto Gemma's long, wild red tresses and spins her around. Gemma scrambles back, hitting the wall. The woman sprays the contents of the canister directly into Gemma's face.

"Please, let this be it. Let it be over. I can't do this anymore." Gemma's prayer swirls through my mind, and tears drip onto the thin mat underneath me. With a thud, Gemma falls to the floor, her eyes rolling to the back of her head, and a sigh sounds out from behind me, coming from the other girl—Avery? If on-

ly someone would tell me my own name, maybe I could figure out what I'm doing here and who this woman is. Who Gemma and Avery are. It feels like none of this would be happening if I could just remember something, anything, before waking up here.

But my head's too foggy. It throbs the moment I try to focus on anything but what's unfolding in front of me.

A shadow falls across my face as the woman shifts and bends down to touch her fingers to Gemma's throat. She glances from Gemma to her wristwatch. "Time of death: Nine twenty-five P.M."

Locking her gloved hands around Gemma's ankles, the woman drags the dead girl from her room and hoists her up onto a gurney placed against the wall near the pitch-black hallway on the other side of the metal and plastic barrier that keeps me locked away.

Avery releases another small breath from behind me, and I roll over. I peer at the empty room between us before turning my gaze to her. Her lips hide in a thin line, but she doesn't meet my stare. Her focus remains on the woman outside our doors. The sound of a chain clanking against metal draws my attention away from Avery, and my chest tightens when the woman swings open the plastic door to my room.

"Subject four, step forward," the woman says.

My lip quivers, but I don't resist. Fear rolls through me in waves, and tears burn my eyes and trickle down my cheeks. I'm too frightened to resist or put up a fight, so I hold my arms over my chest and take a few wobbly steps forward. It's the first time

I've really moved since waking up, and my muscles throb with the movements.

"Where are we going?" I ask, my voice only coming out a whisper.

The woman locks her fingers to my shoulders and pushes me from the room first without letting me go. "I'd like you to push the gurney," she says instead of answering my question.

She motions to a doorway on the far side of the long, concrete room. The stale air makes it harder to breathe, but I do as the woman says and push the bed with Gemma's body forward, trying my best not to look at her blank, open eyes.

The woman stays behind me. "To the corridor on the right."

I don't know if she thinks I'll suddenly try to fight or what, but I don't know what else to do. I don't want to die. Again. If I even had really died. *But it's the only thing I remember...*

"Good. Leave her here and enter the first door on the left and close it behind you," the woman says.

I hesitate. "Please, tell me what's going on. What is this place? Who are you? Who am I?" All the questions fall from my mouth at once. The edges of my vision shadow, panic sneaking from my stomach to my chest to wind around my heart so tightly that I lean against the cold concrete wall for support.

"Enter the room," the woman repeats.

It's not until I peek at her from over my shoulder that I get a close up view of the metallic canister she aims directly at me. Stumbling away, I cover my face with my hands and swivel on my bare feet to the heavy door on the left.

A sob wracks my chest, and I heave a few deep breaths, forcing myself to stroll toward the door until I'm standing in front of it. It's pitch-black through the glass window. I lace my fingers around the cold handle, gripping the knob until the woman clears her throat.

Taking another shuddering breath, I crack the door open and step forward. Freezing air engulfs me, sending goosebumps up my arms and down my legs. The chilly air stings my eyes, making me sniffle. The moment the door clicks closed, I press my face to the window cutout, my warm breath fogging against it.

The woman stares at me through the door for a moment, and I hear her turn the lock. She then slides the window covering over, blocking my view, surrounding me in freezing darkness. I don't move from my spot, panic rushing over me. Fear claws at my back, and a strange sensation crawls over me like I'm being watched, like someone else's presence lingers nearby, maybe even in the same room. I'm too terrified to turn around and look, my mind automatically assuming a monster lies in wait to eat me alive.

I bang on the door. "Don't leave me in here!" My hands throb the harder I pound my fists, and I end up kicking the door with my foot, sending pain radiating through my whole body. But I don't care. I'd rather break my foot than stay another second in utter darkness with the fear threatening to kill me.

"Let me out!" I scream again.

A hissing sound cuts over the thudding of my hands on the

metal door, and I freeze. Spinning around for the first time, I face the dark room and strain to see something, anything, but no matter how long I'm in here, my eyes don't adjust.

"This is caretaker Sienna Clarke." The woman's voice echoes through the room from somewhere to my right, but I can't see her. "I'm now recording subject four, death number one by blunt force trauma to the temporal lobe."

Blunt force trauma? Hearing the woman confirm my death sends uneasiness through me. How would she know that? Was she the figure I saw? Was she the one who murdered me? Was I even murdered? So many questions fly through my mind.

"Subject four, please state your name, age, and birthplace," Caretaker Sienna says.

I don't respond.

"Subject four, the faster you answer, the faster you will be released back to your room."

I lean my back on the door and hug myself. "I—I don't know."

"Subject four, please state what day of the week it is."

"I—" I close my eyes. It's a simple enough question, but the harder I try to remember, the more frustrated I get. "I don't know."

"Subject four—"

"Stop it!" I yell, cutting the woman off. "I can't answer any of your questions. I don't know what you want from me. Please, let me out."

The soft static that came along with the caretaker's voice disappears, leaving me in a silence so intense I'm not sure if I will ever hear again. My whole body trembles, and I do the only thing I can. I slide to the floor, pressing my back to the door, and just stare into the darkness.

I shiver, the cool temperature of the room seeming to drop with every passing minute. My chest heaves with every breath, and I'm afraid that because I couldn't answer any of the caretaker's questions she's going to leave me here to die alone and in the dark.

Unable to sit any longer, I get up and pace back and forth, running my finger along the wall five steps in each direction. The last thing I want to do is wander too far from the door, like I'll somehow get lost amid the nothingness if the caretaker returns for me.

I run my hand over my cheeks, my tearstains frozen streaks trailing down my face. Even my eyelashes are frozen from the air. It makes me cry harder.

"The longer you walk around, the longer it will take." The soft, masculine voice sneaks into my mind, pushing my own thoughts away. *"Trust me. Stop fighting."*

"Who's there?" I ask, stopping in place.

"Stop fighting." The voice is much softer, barely in my mind.

"Who are you?" I think to myself.

No one responds. I'm imagining things. My mind is playing tricks on me like the fear rattling my bones along with the chills.

A small gasp cuts through the darkness followed by more silence.

"Hello?" I call out. It feels like eternity has passed by, and I'd give anything to hear someone beside my own thoughts again, even if it was just my mind playing tricks on me.

"Subject four, remain in your current position." Like an answered prayer, or maybe a demonic summoning, the caretaker's voice erupts through the room again.

The sound of a lock sliding open resonates through the air, sending such relief through me that I release a long, shuddering sigh. But the door behind me doesn't open. A bright square of light erupts in front of me from another door, but I can't tell how far away it is and can't see anything beyond the bright light that somehow makes everything around me even darker.

The door swings inward next, and the caretaker stands silhouetted in bright light like a monster from—I can't remember. But she scares me.

Her tennis shoes squeak against the floor, and a blinding light blinks on in her hand, shining a beam over the metal floor and onto a body. I suck in a freezing gasp through my teeth, holding myself tighter without moving. My instincts were right. I wasn't alone this whole time, but I don't know if the person was alive when I entered. But I could feel it—him. The body is much too big to be a girl, broad shoulders, short blond hair, blue complexion.

I cover my mouth to stop the scream from ripping out of my throat. The world starts to spin, and I drop to my knees. Pain explodes in my legs and then in my shoulder as I fall to my side. Stars burst in my vision, sending spots dancing through the flashlight the caretaker shines in my direction. I open and close my mouth, gasping for breath that doesn't come. My heart pounds in my throbbing head, beating slower and slower. Pressing my cheek into the icy floor, I stare as the caretaker rises to her feet. She squeaks across the room in my direction, the light shining over the metal floor with a drain in the center of the room and nothing else.

She raises her flashlight, shining it directly into my eyes, and it's all I can see. I lift my arm, stretching out my hand to try to touch the light, but my muscles give out on me. I lie frozen, unable to move, unable to breathe, unable to do anything but watch the caretaker.

She does nothing but gaze at me from under her winter clothes, watching me stare up at the light, my thinly dressed body no longer able to stand the cold.

And then I hear the same masculine voice I heard—moments ago? Hours? I'm not sure—slither into my mind, but he's not talking to me. He's counting.

Five.

Four.

Three.

Two.

"Time of death: Nine thirty-five P.M.," the caretaker says.

"*Skye,*" the masculine voice whispers through my mind. "*You found me.*"

All I see are the stars.

CHAPTER 2

BETWEEN THIS LIFE AND THE NEXT

DARK. LIGHT. DARK. Light. The memory of my death dances in my mind. The freezing air. The metal floor. My frozen tears. The world flashing from dark to light to the rhythm of my fading heartbeat. And now, the stars.

They're everywhere, and I'm a tiny spark among the vast galaxy. My weightless body hovers in the glittering void, light dancing off my skin. I'm everywhere and nowhere all at once, and I don't ever want to leave.

"Skye," the familiar masculine voice calls. It's my name. I know it is. I can feel it deep inside me, embracing me in the peace from memories too far to grasp but so close I can feel them wanting to break free. Memories that remain lost to me. Ones I want so desperately to push away the one of my death.

I smile, joy erupting in my heart.

"Skye, you have to follow me. You can't stay here," the voice says.

"You know my name," I say.

"Of course I do. Don't you—"

"Who are you? What is this place?"

A deep groan echoes from my right. "Oh, no. No. No. What did they do?"

"Who?"

Something touches my hand, but I can't remember how to move in this world of stars.

"Please, we don't have time."

"But I don't want to go," I say, letting my arms dangle at my sides, shifting from the strange feeling consuming my hand. My hair drapes down as I'm suspended in the beautiful, endless galaxy.

"Listen to me," the voice says. Desperation lines his words, stealing some of my happiness away. "We have to go back, and I'm not leaving you behind. I'm afraid you don't remember the way."

The way? I ignore the boy's pleas. A familiar-feeling presence rises just to my right, but I don't move or look. I remain suspended among the beauty of the galaxy that promises nothing and everything. The world feels like home, like I've visited this place hundreds of times before yet I can only remember one instance.

"Skye, I can't lose you." It's not only the world that feels familiar, but I'm afraid to look at the boy next to me. I'm afraid of what he's saying.

"I'm already dead."

"It's never stopped us before. We're in the in between—between this life and the next one."

"But I like it here," I say.

"I know, but we made a promise to each other, and I don't intend to break it," the boy says. I search my mind for any memory, any little tiny moment I can grasp onto to explain the sudden tingles blossoming from my chest at the meaning of his words.

The world around me shakes, and something warm slithers over the coolness of my hand, lifting my arm up so it's no longer dangling behind me as I float on my back. A shock runs from my fingertips to my elbow, and then straight up my shoulder and neck and into my head.

It stirs something within me, something unexplainable. "What's happening?"

"I told you, we have to go," the boy says.

I shake my head. "No, I can't. Everything's so confusing. I don't know you."

"You do. It's me, Luka. Please, try to remember."

But I can't remember. I don't want to. Because every time I try to remember, something dark stirs within me, flashing my death over and over again. The bloody snow. The figure behind me. The stars through the trees.

"I—" The image of a man flashes into my mind. His ice-blue eyes crinkle in the corners, and he smiles. The image expands, taking over the view of the stars, and I'm now standing in a room with a view of a fountain cascading sunlit water in the center of a garden.

"Skye, my girl. Are you ready?"

"I'm really sorry, Skye," Luka says, pulling me from my memory.

"What for?"

"Please, forgive me."

"I don't understand." Like a jolt of electricity, a shock rushes through me, sending the world around me spinning. The stars dart through the air like a lightshow of fireworks, and pain explodes in my chest and head, stealing away the sweet peace the galaxy world brought me.

Five.

I hear the sound of humming lights.

Four.

A warm sensation slithers up my legs.

Three.

My heart beats.

Two.

I gasp.

"Time of life: Twelve forty-three P.M.," a familiar, feminine voice says.

Snapping my eyes open, I glare at the unfamiliar reflection of a girl in the shiny plastic lenses of Caretaker Sienna's protective glasses. Wide, steel-gray eyes blink at me, but they're not the caretaker's. They're mine. My reflection.

"Subject four, please state your name, age, and place of birth," Caretaker Sienna says, lifting a small penlight to shine in my eyes.

It sends a wave of dizziness through me, and I jerk my hands up to shield my vision. "Where am I?" I ask instead of answering her questions.

"Subject four, answer my questions," she repeats.

I squeeze my eyes shut, my mind hazy. The answers stick to the tip of my tongue, but I can't seem to remember how to turn the answers into words. The stars are the only thing I do want to remember. I wish I could close my eyes and return to the boy—Luka? Yes. Luka.

I try anyway, refusing to look at or answer the caretaker.

Something hard jabs my side, and I curl in on myself while releasing a scream.

"Subject four, answer my question now," she repeats.

"Skye. Your name is Skye. You're seventeen. You were born in California." Luka's voice sneaks into my head, revealing the answers that were in my memories all along. Like he's the key to unlocking what's hidden in my mind, his voice sends a few memories trickling to me. A bedroom with gray walls. A messy living room with clothes scattered across the floor. A swimming pool. Bright blue eyes. Hundreds of candles. A red door. Just small flashes of things that have no meaning to them, things Luka's pulled from me without my permission. *Where is he? Is he even real? Am I going crazy?*

I squeeze my eyes shut again, pressing my fingers to my temples. "My name is Skye. I was born in California, and I'm seventeen," I say.

"Death count number two appears to have triggered a

memory response," Caretaker Sienna says. "This is a good sign."

I have no idea who she's talking to, and I open my eyes to peer around to see if I can see anything. It's then that I notice a small, black box in her front pocket—not a black box—a cell phone. She's wearing an earbud in one of her ears.

"Will you tell me why I'm here?" I ask, remaining on the floor. I'm afraid of what she'll do if I move even an inch.

"Rise to your feet," she says instead of answering my question. "You'll return to your room for further evaluation."

"Evaluation?"

She ignores me. "Subject four, rise to your feet or I'll leave you here until the morning."

I turn my head and realize I'm lying in an all metal room with two doors, a tinted window, and a drain in the center of it. It's long and narrow like a shipping container, but it's ice-cold like a freezer. My breath puffs out in small clouds as I shift to my side to roll over to my knees. The icy, metal floor stings my hands when I press my palms flat against it and get to my feet.

Caretaker Sienna aims the metallic canister at me but doesn't attempt to spray. She knows I'm not going to try anything. Fear grips me as hard as I hug myself, still shivering. With a sweep of her hand, she motions me to head through the same door I originally entered in. The lights flick off the second I step into the polished concrete hallway, and I suck in a warm breath of stale air through my teeth.

Every part of me aches with each small step forward. The gurney with Gemma's body is no longer in sight, and I search around, trying to take in as much as possible, but there isn't much to see. We step back into the area with the divided rooms where I last saw Avery, and I pause in place. All the rooms are identical, each with a sink and toilet, a privacy curtain to cover the chain-link barrier, a potted plant, bookcases with a variety of reading material, a small crate of necessities, and a thin, blue mat to sleep on.

Avery hasn't moved since I rolled the gurney with Gemma out of here, and she doesn't smile upon my return, and now the room between ours has someone in it. I can't see what the girl looks like because she's pulled down the curtain from the barrier to use as a blanket.

Caretaker Sienna shoves me toward my section of the room, and I stand in front of it, staring at an information sheet attached to the door that I wouldn't have been able to see from inside the room. It has the name *Skye Stone* scrawled across the top with detailed information I assume is about me including my age, birth place, hair color, eye color, height, weight, allergies, and then an empty log with a place to fill in the date, time of death, and time of life in, which has two times of death and one time of life. Caretaker Sienna fills in the newest time of life before swinging the door open and nudging me in.

My eyes turn back to my name: *Skye Stone*. Something feels wrong about it. Skye feels like me. But Stone? No. I don't think that's right. I don't mention my feeling, though. I don't want to utter even a word more than I have to.

The caretaker locks the door behind me, and I hover in place, just glancing around my plain room.

"Aw, look who decided to stay," an almost whiney voice

says from my side.

My brows furrow, and I look at Gemma's room, my heart racing when I meet her vivid green eyes. She sits cross-legged in the corner with her blue mat folded a few times to create a thicker cushion beneath her.

"God, you look like you've seen a ghost," she says, smirking.

Turning my head, I peer over my shoulder, but Caretaker Sienna is already gone. Instead of answering Gemma, I drag my feet forward, ignoring her, and lie down on my mat with my back toward her. The figure next to me is so close to the barrier between us that the chain-link fence bulges into my room and over a sliver of my mat so I can't adjust it.

Long fingers hook through the links, gripping onto it, and if I couldn't still feel Gemma's eyes on my back, I'd roll over in her direction.

"What? Are you too good to respond to me?" Gemma asks. The chain-link barrier rattles behind me.

I still don't answer.

"Gemma, leave her alone. She just replaced your sorry ass in the freezer," Avery says. I can't see her over the lump of a body in front of me, but I'm thankful she says something.

"She should've resisted like me. Made things quick. But damn do I have a headache now." Gemma doesn't sound like the frightened girl I heard before Caretaker Sienna killed her with whatever poison she sprayed in her face.

I scowl without turning. "Why did *you* come back?" I ask, interrupting.

"What an idiot. She says that like we have a choice." The foreign thought invades my mind, and the chain-link rattles again. "Whoa! She speaks."

I cringe, staring at the long fingers of the girl under the curtain squeezing the links tighter. Something about her seems so familiar, I consider running my fingers over hers to get her attention but stop myself when she relaxes, though she never lets go of the barrier. I don't know if it's because she's in my space, but something about her calls to me.

"Tell me, new girl. What's your name?" Gemma asks, ignoring my original question.

The lights flicker, and I suck in a breath. I should've just kept ignoring her until she left me alone. But I couldn't help myself. "Why did you come back?" I ask again. "You prayed—"

"Skye, stop!" The voice comes sharp and fast into my mind, causing me to snap my mouth shut. My head pounds at the familiar intrusion, sending a dark haze dancing in my vision. It's the same voice that counted down to my death. The same voice that pleaded with me among the stars.

My whole body trembles. Tears slip from my eyes and pelt the mat I press my cheek against. Just remembering the stars makes the fact that I'm lying here, cold and afraid with no idea of what's going on, a million times worse. I shouldn't be here. I should be there where it's safe. I should be there where I have everything and nothing. Where I am everything and nothing.

"Hello? New girl?" Gemma's voice cuts through my racing thoughts. "Death mess up your head or something? I asked you your name." It's like my question to her went right over her head. She either purposely ignored me or maybe I imagined asking her. I don't know.

Confusion washes over me. I wonder if she's right and death did mess me up more than stealing my memories away. "It's Skye Sto—" *Knezha.* The name hits me hard and fast, drawing a memory of a wrought iron gate with a strange emblem welded onto it. KF. What does it stand for?

"You're not a Knezha," the masculine voice thinks to me, intruding in my mind. *"You're Skye Stone."*

"Stone," I answer, repeating the name the voice thinks to me, the name scrawled on my information sheet. *I'm blond with blue-gray eyes, five and a half feet tall, a hundred and thirty-five pounds. I'm seventeen years old, born on New Year's Day in Los Angeles, California, and have no known allergies.* It's like if I say them to myself, I can almost remember. Almost. But it still feels like a fact sheet about a girl I wouldn't be able to pick out in a crowd. If I saw my picture, I'm not sure I could even recognize myself.

The sound of sneakers squeaking on the floor cuts off the conversation between us, and I wedge myself closer to the chain-link barrier. Fear prevents me from looking, and I hold my breath, hoping if I hold it long enough I'll somehow transport myself out of here.

Fingers slide over mine, and it's not until I feel their warmth that I realize I'm gripping the barrier for dear life. I inhale a quiet gasp, forcing myself to stay frozen in my spot as I hear the chain clank outside my door.

Something scrapes across the polished concrete floor next

to me, and I bite down on my bottom lip, terrified my ragged breathing will give me away.

"Eat up, subject four," Caretaker Sienna says from above me.

"Hey, what about me? I missed dinner, too," Gemma says from her room.

Caretaker Sienna doesn't respond. I listen for the clanking of a chain and then the squeaking of shoes and don't open my eyes until I'm sure she's left us alone. I meet the serious gaze of a blond boy with dark eyes. I had assumed he was a girl since the rest of us are. His nose and mouth remain hidden under the curtain he pulled from his side of the barrier that would've been between us.

"This is all your fault, Gemma," Avery says from in front of me, though I can't see her past the boy. I don't even try.

We stare at each other without a word, our fingers still touching. I don't know if it's because we're not alone, or if it's because I can't find the words, but either way, I can't stop from blatantly staring at him with my mouth gaping, tear stains drying on my cheeks, and probably the reddest nose in existence. He doesn't look away, though. Doesn't even try, either.

"How was I supposed to know the monster would do this? She still got her experiments done," Gemma argues.

"Yeah, right!" Avery yells.

The chain-link rattles and the lights flicker. "Shut up!" Gemma screams.

"No, you shut up!"

A light bulb pops overhead, sending a shower of sparks

through Avery's room, dimming the light for all of us.

"You're so crazy, Gemma." Avery smacks her hands against the chain-link. "*I wish Caretaker Sienna would just take her away,*" she thinks, forcing her thought into my mind.

"Me? Look at you."

The boy lets go of the chain-link barrier and my fingers. He brings his index finger to his lips, motioning for me to not say anything, though I don't think I would anyway. There's no way I'm getting between Gemma and Avery. Their anger and frustration feels like it heats the already humid room.

"I wish you wouldn't come back," Avery says. "Life would be more bearable if you didn't."

"Don't you think I haven't tried?"

Another flash of light blinks through the air, and all the chain-link walls rattle around us.

"*Don't touch the barrier, Skye,*" a familiar, masculine voice says into my mind.

I automatically pull my hands to my chest.

Five. Four. Three. Two. One.

Gemma and Avery both scream, their voices ripping through the air. The whole room buzzes, sending the hair around my face floating. The girls hit the ground hard. The thud of their bodies dropping resonates through the concrete room. A wisp of smoke swirls into the air from the part of my mat touching the metal barrier. *Whoa.*

The hum suddenly stops, leaving me and the boy in silence. My eyes blur with more tears, and I'm afraid they won't ever stop coming. And I hate them so much. They feel stupid coming from my eyes. Unfamiliar.

"It's okay to cry, Skye." The boy's voice trickles to me like he knows exactly what I'm feeling.

It makes me cry harder.

What have I done to deserve this? What have they? The sound of rubber soles on the smooth floors sends my heart racing. I squeeze my eyes shut, like if I can just keep them closed long enough, I can pretend I'm somewhere else altogether. That this monster of a woman didn't turn the walls into an electric fence strong enough to kill anyone who touches it.

"Time of death: Eleven thirteen P.M.," the caretaker says.

I listen without looking as she removes both Gemma and Avery from their rooms. She bangs on my door and says, "Eat up, subject four. You need your strength for tomorrow." Tomorrow? I don't ask what happens tomorrow. I have an unsettling feeling that it'll be the same as today.

Caretaker Sienna talks to herself, commenting on Gemma and Avery's deaths. About their agitation. About how a breakthrough will be made. Her voice fades along with the squeak of her shoes, and I shiver.

"It's safe to open your eyes," the boy says from next to me.

I sit up and face him, curling my knees to my chest. "What is this place?"

"Your worst nightmare," he says without a smile. "Mine, too."

"How long have you been here?" I'm afraid if I don't spit out all my questions, I might never get them answered.

"For two hundred and twenty-three—I mean, twenty-four

deaths."

I grimace, my heart sinking into my stomach. "Oh, God. Two was bad enough."

"Two?" Disappointment lines his words, and I crinkle my nose. He says it like he was hoping I'd have died a million times more. "So, you don't remember anything?" It's not really a question despite the inflection in his voice. It's more like he's questioning his hope that I would.

"What do you mean? My name is Skye Stone. I'm seventeen. I was born in Los Angeles. I—"

"You don't really remember knowing any of those things, Skye Knezha." He groans without moving his lips. *"I was hoping to never hear you refer to yourself as that ever again."* I don't know why I didn't recognize it sooner, but his voice—it's Luka's voice. He's...

"Luka?" I whisper.

His eyes light up brighter than the stars from our galaxy world. "You remember me."

I tighten my hold on my bare legs, and a blip of sadness rushes through me. His hope hurts me. I don't know why, but something about disappointing his cute, pouty face gets to me. "You brought me back here. Why? Why wouldn't you let me go?" My curiosity turns to anger thinking about how he dragged me back to this place without my consent, thinking he was doing me some sort of favor by not letting me stay in the galaxy.

The light vanishes from his gaze, and he doesn't respond. He turns away and lies back on his mat with his back to me this time, like what I've said offended him. Like it's me who's in the wrong.

I bang my hand on the chain-link. "Hey, what's your problem?"

"You should eat like Monster Sienna said, and then you should try to sleep. She was right. You need your strength," he says instead of answering.

I huff a breath. I'm so sick of people ignoring my questions. "Did I do something?"

He sighs, turning to look at me with a much softer expression, his eyes no longer narrowed. "No, Skye. I'm sorry, it's just..."

"Just what?"

"Nothing. Never mind."

He's obviously keeping something from me, but exhaustion rushes over me, leaving me too tired to care.

I shift in my spot and glance at the tray of food behind me—a piece of dry looking chicken, an orange, a small bowl of salad, and a cup of multi-colored pills. Vitamins. Keep us healthy just to kill us. If I didn't know any better, I'd think we were at some human slaughter house. But of course, I don't know any better.

I watch Luka watch me in my peripheral vision. Using my fork, I cut the grilled chicken in half and hold out a piece to him. He takes it without arguing, and we take a bite of our pieces at the same time.

I gag and drop it on the tray. It's disgusting.

"What? You don't like it?" he asks, smiling.

I shake my head, handing him my piece through the barrier.

"You'll like the other stuff," he says, pointing at the salad and orange.

"How do you know?" I ask.

He shrugs. *"Because finding something to eat we both like was the bane of my existence until this place. You're a vegetarian."* The words come directly into my mind from his.

I blink a few times but hide my reaction the best I can. I don't respond to him. I can't. All I do is bring a bite of salad to my lips and stick it in my mouth.

"It's a hunch," he says, like he has to say something out loud even though we both know he answered my question telepathically with information about me I wish he didn't know for the sole fact that I didn't know it.

I scoot away from him, my nerves getting the best of me. I don't like feeling like I should know something, like I'm missing something.

You're missing everything, I think to myself. *This guy could be behind it. He made sure you came back here to this hellhole.*

The chain-link rattles from next to me, and I bring my gaze up to meet his dark eyes.

"You don't have to be afraid of me, Skye," he says into my mind.

"And why's that?" I ask, thinking back to him. I'm not even sure he will hear my thoughts, but I'm afraid to talk out loud.

"You might not remember, but we know each other."

"What?" I ask.

BETWEEN THIS ONE AND THE NEXT

"Yesterday wasn't the first time you died. The first time, well, it was sort of with me."

"Yesterday wasn't the first time you died. The first time, well, it was sort of with me."

CHAPTER 3

DEAD PROMISES

THE BOWL OF salad clatters to the ground, scattering the wilted lettuce, chopped up carrots and tomatoes, and soggy croutons over my bare legs and mat. I quickly scoop up the remnants, drop them back into the bowl, and turn my attention to Luka.

He tilts his head forward, concentrating on me for so long I shift uncomfortably. With his crinkled nose and pursed lips, it looks like staring at me causes him agonizing pain. Dropping the chicken I gave him onto his mat, he gets to his feet and paces in small circles. He's taller than I expect him to be, and through the half-buttoned backside of his hospital gown, his muscular back ripples with the stiff movement. A tattoo expands from his spine and over both his shoulders. I try to decipher what the tattoo is, but it's just two lines stacked over one another, the details hidden under thin cotton.

Spinning in his place, his gown shifts, exposing his boxers, and I avert my eyes to my shaking hands. It's bad enough being stuck somewhere I can't run from, but it's downright awful being stuck here next to a boy who looks pissed off at me because I don't know the things he knows. It's not like he's telling me anything, either.

He closes the distance between us as much as he can, locking his fingers to the chain-link. It rattles as he shakes it, startling me. I suck in air through my teeth, and he releases the barrier.

Grimacing, I can only imagine the thoughts running through his mind, but none of them trickle to me. He doesn't look like he's going to spill his secrets—at least not out loud. I'm not sure if I want to know.

He said he died with me. That I died before the two deaths I remember. But he's been here for a long time, and the other two girls didn't know me. I'm more confused than ever. I hate this. I hate everything about this.

Frustration scratches its way from my pounding heart and into my throbbing head. I can't stop the uncontrollable tears constantly burning my eyes. I cry, my chest heaving with sobs, and I lower myself to my side, pressing my aching shoulder into the mat while I pull my knees to my chest. I let my blond hair fall into my face to stick to my wet cheeks.

"Skye," Luka whispers, his soft voice almost as quiet as it sounds in my mind. "Don't shut me out, please."

"Leave me alone," I whisper. "This is too much."

"This is too much." With my words, a fragment of a memory breaks free from the darkness of my mind. The words hum in my ears, and I realize I'm saying them to a woman. Just seeing her face—her toffee-brown eyes, her full lips cracking open to show off her crooked teeth, streaks of gray through her curly hair, the deep wrinkles in her skin—sparks a heartbreaking sorrow through me. I know she's not my mother, but I miss her and love her how I imagine I would love my mother.

The woman disappears from my mind as quickly as she appeared, and I want so badly to remember her, to know about my life outside these chain-link walls. It's the lack of memories that makes it hard on me. My life feels pointless. Maybe it is. Maybe that's why I'm here.

"I know it's a lot, but I want to explain," Luka says, covering his mouth with his hand, obscuring anyone watching—if they're watching—from reading his lips. "But you're not letting me into your mind."

Whatever he said pulled the memory of the woman from my mind, and it's the only reason I focus on him. "What's the point? It doesn't change the fact my memory is missing or I'm locked in this room, and I'm just going to die again apparently. Next time, I'm not coming back." And I mean it. What's there to care about if I can't remember? Nothing is keeping me here. Luka might have forced me to come back from the galaxy world, but he can't stop me again.

"Please, don't say that," he whispers, pleading with me. "You promised me."

I open my eyes. "I don't know you, and you're scaring me. Maybe I knew you before or something, but I don't know you now. Whoever made that promise is dead, okay?"

He doesn't respond, and I think I've finally gotten through to him. I'd think if he meant something to me, I'd obviously feel something looking at him, but I don't. All I feel is tired and vulnerable...confused more than anything.

The silence between us could very well be the loudest thing I've ever heard, because it's hard to ignore. Luka's towering shadow begs for my attention, though I train my gaze at Gemma's empty room. Every small breath he takes, every time he shifts on his mat, even the mellow thump of his heartbeat, which I swear thuds louder than anything, attempts to get me to turn back over and let him explain.

Heat radiates from behind me, and the chain-link presses into my back when Luka finally lies down. His body sinks against mine, pressing into the barrier, but I don't move. I don't want him to know he's getting to me.

"Why won't you let me explain myself?" he whispers. "You've always been stubborn, but damn it, Skye. This is torture."

"I told you already," I mutter.

"You're scared."

"Yeah, and?"

"Of me?"

His question hangs heavy between us. Does he scare me?

Maybe. First he invades my mind, counting down to my death, and then he finds me in a world no one could randomly show up in—at least I don't think anyone can. The galaxy is mine. I know it. It's a feeling that burns deep within every piece of my being.

He sighs when I don't answer right away, and his annoyance is enough to force me to finally roll over to stare at his back. The curtain drapes over him, hiding even his head, and I wonder if I should yank down the one hanging on my side of the barrier, partially blocking my toilet and sink from Gemma's room. Maybe I should move it to hide me away from Luka, though I know he'd hang his back up if I asked—I don't know how I know, but I do. I feel like I know a lot of things but also know nothing at all—intuition? Instincts? Whatever it is, I'm relying heavily on them. And my instincts scream to shove my finger into Luka's back to get him to face me.

I don't get the chance. He turns over when I have my finger almost to the barrier, and I yank my hand back and hold it against my chest. He tugs the curtain from his face to look at me. Narrowing my eyes, I glare at him like I could burn a hole right through the middle of his cute face. I hate thinking it, but I can see why my supposed pre-death? First death? Post-death? Whatever. I can see why I probably liked him. Even with messy hair, tired eyes, and what looks like a fading bruise on his left cheek, he's attractive. Just having him look at me the way he is in this moment makes me uncomfortable, and not because I hate it, but because I like it. *"God, make him roll back over so I don't have to stare at his stupid, cute, jerk face anymore."*

He smiles. It's the first time he's given me one, and I seriously hate him more, or maybe I hate myself more for how much I want him to continue smiling at me the way he is. It's clear he heard my thoughts about him. "You could always turn around, you know."

I do just that. "I'm not afraid of you," I finally say to my discarded dinner tray, answering his question almost too late. But I have to get it out there, even if I'm lying. Because Luka terrifies me, and not because he knows things I don't. It's because I'm afraid he might make me remember, and I don't want to now. I thought I did, but the longer I sit in this cold room, the more I realize how even more soul-crushing this would be if I could remember who I was before I ended up here—if I knew what I'm now missing. I have it easy.

"You let me in," Luka muses, his thoughts entering my mind. The more I hear him in my head, the less unsettling it becomes. It's not sudden and invasive like when Gemma's or Avery's thoughts enter my mind, but Luka's more subtle, gentler. Like I've welcomed him in instead of him breaking down the door.

"No, I didn't," I say. *"I just don't know how to keep you out."*

"Oh, well, I'll teach you after we get things between us settled," he says.

"Why not now?" I ask.

"Because I know you'll lock me out, and we can't talk about this out loud. Monster Sienna can't know what you've acquired from death. She can't know we know we're linked," he says, sending fear trickling through me just thinking about the caretaker.

"I have so many questions," I think to him. I don't really try to do it, but I know he can hear me. It's almost like I can feel him—his soul—touching my mind. It's strange though, because I don't know what all I'm sending to him. My personal thoughts jumble around my dire questions.

"Let's start with something easy," he says into my mind.

"Like how I know you?" I ask.

His eyebrows jet up on his forehead. *"That's not easy, but I can see it's driving you as crazy as it's driving me that you don't remember."*

"Are you my boyfriend or something?" Heat blossoms in my cheeks at the thought. *"I'm sorry. I don't know why I'm assuming. All you said is that you knew me..."* Squeezing my eyes shut, I force my thoughts to reel back before my mind wanders into fantasyland where I can imagine wrapping my arms around Luka, burying my face in his chest, feel his lips...

The memory disappears.

The chain-link barrier clinks, and Luka's warm hand grabs mine and pulls it away from my chest so he can hold it. Something about him touching me, even just holding my hand, ignites something within me. I suck in a breath and open my eyes to meet his intense gaze.

"It's not so simple," he says.

I grimace. *"How do I even know what you tell me is true, anyway? You could be lying about everything, and I wouldn't know any different."*

"I knew your name, didn't I?" he asks.

"It's written on my door like everything else about me."

"You're an orphan," he says. *"According to you. Your dad is alive, but he abandoned you. Sorry about your mom."*

The new information washes over me in a tidal wave of confusion and anger. I hate that he can just drop some random fact about me, and there's no way I would be able to disprove the information.

"I think it's one of the reasons you're here," he continues. *"Monster Sienna wouldn't take someone who would be missed, and since I'm here..."* He sighs. *"She wouldn't have known that."*

"What about you?" I ask instead of turning away from his hypnotic gaze. *"Did I miss you? Is that why I'm here?"*

He doesn't react. It's something he can't answer because he doesn't know anything beyond what feels like he probably hoped I did. Blowing out a breath, I press my lips into a line and think, *"You're getting me sidetracked. Just spill how I know you already."*

"Like I said, we sort of died together. The exact day, exact second, exact moment."

"What do you mean sort of? And how?"

"I was murdered by my mom's boyfriend," he says. *"Suffocated. They say I was dead for a few minutes when my mom found me. They claim she resuscitated me, but you and I know that isn't true."*

"What does that even mean?"

"You showed me the way back from the galaxy world."

I don't question it. To me, how he's alive isn't important. How I died and met him is. *"And me?"* Did his mom's boyfriend kill me, too?

"I don't know," he finally says.

"I don't understand."

He scrunches his nose and mouth. *"You never got into the details."*

"But you said we died together."

"I said sort of *died together,"* he says.

"Okay, but I didn't tell you?" I'm annoyed with first death me for not telling him. It's something I definitely want to know.

He hums lowly. *"Nope. You said it didn't matter. And it didn't. Still doesn't."*

I hate to admit he was right about this not being an easy question. The more he reveals, the more confused I become. With my free hand, I rub my fingers over my temple. *"Just tell me how I know you then."*

"Well, like I said. We sort of died together—our hearts stopped at the same time, on our birthdays oddly enough. I didn't meet you until after that, though. In the stars."

"You were born on New Year's, too, and we died on New Year's?" What the?

"It's why we're linked, Skye. Call it a freaky coincidence, call it fate, whatever, but it is what it is. We found each other after we died, and it was you who pulled me back to life with you and showed me the way. It was you who appeared on my doorstep a few months later like a damn private investigator, begging me to come with you, and here you are again, showing up, even when you don't remember anything."

But what does it all mean? Who am—was I? It's like information overload, and I have no idea what I should ask next. If I should ask anything at all. And the link he's talking about? I'm not sure if I even feel it, if I'm even supposed to.

"Skye, I know you're overwhelmed, but we're going to be okay," he says. *"You're here now. If you're here, then—"*

I frown. "Nothing about this is okay!" My voice echoes through the room. I slap my hand over my mouth, my eyes nearly bulging from their sockets, then I think, *"How can you say that? Do you even know where we are? Why we're here? Why they keep killing us? Why we keep coming back?"*

He holds his face emotionless but squeezes my fingers in his. *"It's a feeling—one I didn't get until I heard your voice in my mind in the freezer."*

"Well, I don't have those feelings."

He chuckles.

"What?" I ask.

"It's not the first time you've said that to me," he says, a smile lighting his face.

Before I can comment, an ear-piercing alarm rings through the air, and then the lights flick out, leaving us in utter darkness. I tense, every muscle on my body tightening all at once.

"What's happening?" I ask out loud, my voice getting lost on the whine of the alarm.

"Grab you curtain!" Luka yells into my mind. *"Cover your mouth with it."*

Stumbling through the dark, I do what he says, ripping the curtain straight from the rod. The alarm cuts off, leaving my ears ringing, and a strange hissing noise sounds through the air.

I hold my breath, pressing the curtain over my mouth and nose. My heart threatens to spill from my chest with every thrashing beat.

"Don't be afraid, Skye. In a minute, Monster Sienna will return, and she's going to take me. I'll be back, I promise. Just do what you're told, and you'll be fine. They try to break what isn't broken, so don't give them a reason to hurt..."

His voice trails off from my mind, and I feel my way to the chain-link barrier, still covering my mouth. I lace my fingers with Luka's, holding his hand in the dark even though he doesn't grip mine back.

I hear the sound of tennis shoes before the lights blink back on, hazing my vision. Caretaker Sienna strolls in with a gurney and struts directly to my door first before messing with the chain and opening it wide.

"Looks like it's your lucky day, subject four. Rise to your feet. I need help with subject one's body," she says, motioning me forward. "I'm rather disappointed, you know. I was really hoping it would be you."

Me for what? I shiver at her words. I'm pretty certain Luka made sure it would be me awake instead of him, like he knew what the caretaker wanted.

I suck on my bottom lip to stop my burning questions from escaping and follow Caretaker Sienna's directions as she shuffles me out of my room. I wait beside her, and she unlocks Luka's door. His information sheet glares at me, and I read over it as quickly as I can. *Name: Luka Landon, age seventeen, born in Carlsbad, California, blond hair and brown eyes, six feet and two inches tall, one-hundred and ninety pounds, no known allergies.* Beneath his typed information sheet is a long list of dates with his times of deaths and revivals, some as short as a few minutes and one, from three weeks ago, that has him declared dead for almost five hours.

Caretaker Sienna swings the door open, cutting off my view of Luka's information sheet, and motions for me to head into his room first. Everything in it is identical to mine, except his houseplant thrives compared to the half-dead one on my bookshelf.

"Remove and hang up the curtain, subject four," Caretaker Sienna says, digging into her pockets.

I do as she says, just like Luka told me to do, and I grimace seeing Luka curled up on his side with his hand still stuck through the chain-links. I pull his arm back into his room, pretending like I had to adjust him to get the curtain free. I realize Luka is still alive and breathing.

I let out a soft breath while I reattach the curtain to the rod. Caretaker Sienna kneels down and touches her fingers to Luka's neck, checking his pulse, and then she straightens her back and shoves her slender fingers under his arms.

"Grab his legs," she says. "I hope you're strong, subject four, because if not, then it won't be your lucky day after all."

Surprisingly, I manage to hoist up Luka, straining just a little. His warm ankles bring feeling back into my icy fingers, and when I step backward toward the door, his hospital gown drags across the polished concrete as his backside hovers an inch over the floor. I don't look at him though. I can't. I hate that Caretaker Sienna makes me help her take Luka to who knows where to do who knows what.

After I help Caretaker Sienna lift Luka onto the lowered gurney, I cross my arms under my breasts and look around. There are only two exits from this room that I can tell. The one Caretaker Sienna always appears from and the one leading to the freezer she locked me in. And I happen to be closer to the dark corridor she enters in from.

Luka warned me to comply, but how can I knowing I can possibly escape? I'm currently free from my room with a gurney between me and the caretaker. This might be my only opportunity. The instincts that have been guiding me this whole time scream to just do it. Because what's the worst that can happen? They'll kill me? They'll do that anyway.

Do it, Skye, I tell myself. *Maybe this is why you're here. You can get help. You can save Luka and the others.*

With a quick intake of breath and a hard look at Caretaker Sienna as she situates Luka to her liking on the gurney, I summon all my courage. I thrust my hands out, pushing the gurney right into the caretaker and then spin on my heels and dash toward the dark corridor.

"Subject four!" Caretaker Sienna yells, but it doesn't stop me.

Ten feet into the dark hall, a light flicks on and then another and another, each one blinking on and off with my motion as I race down the cement hallway. A few cameras blink from above me, and I keep my eyes trained on the darkness in front of me, the lights allowing me to see only a few feet ahead.

I'm so focused on putting space between me and the caretaker I don't see the sudden drop of stairs. I trip, the ground slipping out from under me, and hit the slick floor. The air heaves from my chest as I slide on my stomach.

Lifting my head up, I peer at the hallway. A door with a push handle sits no more than a dozen feet in front of me. I force myself to my feet and rush in its direction. It's a metal door, familiar, like the type of door that would lead out of a building.

I gasp, my lungs working in overdrive and my side cramping, but I don't let the pain stop me from slamming my hands against the door. I expect nothing to happen. I expect it to be locked. What I don't expect is for it to fly open, leaving me falling onto the landing before a flight of stairs that heads up.

I don't stop. Using the rail, I climb them as fast as my legs can take me and turn to follow them up another flight.

"Subject four." Caretaker Sienna's voice echoes through the stairwell. I glance over my shoulder, but she's not there. "Don't move."

Ignoring her, I turn back to the landing, and my heart falters. Caretaker Sienna stands on the landing in front of a door, training her metallic canister on me. I rush through my options in my mind. I can turn back around and keep running through this maze of a place, or I can surrender and hope she doesn't spray me in the face with the poison. *Or fight. You can fight.*

Raising my hands in surrender, I take a step up to close the distance. Caretaker Sienna continues to train the canister on me, but she doesn't press her finger to the trigger.

Closing my eyes, I swivel my torso, aiming my elbow out, and knock the canister right from the caretaker's hands. Surprise widens her eyes behind her protective eyewear, but she doesn't have a chance to brace herself when I ram into her, knocking her back. I lock my hands onto her head, ripping her mask free with one hand and pulling the surgical cap off with the other.

I expect to see a monster underneath her medical gear, but she's only an ordinary woman, maybe in her thirties, with dark brown hair pulled tightly into a bun on her head.

"You're going to let me out of here." I grab onto the front of her jacket and shake her.

"I can't, subject four," she says.

"My name is Skye," I snap. "And you will. Don't think I won't kill you, 'cause I will."

"Please, Skye," she says. "You don't want to do that. I'm just your caretaker. I'm no one."

I hold her gaze for a moment, trying my best to see if I can get a peek into her head, but she's closed off to me. "Tell me what this place is."

"Just calm down and let me explain," she says.

But I can't calm down. Instead, I wrap my hands around her throat and shake her, hitting her head into the floor. Her hazel eyes widen, and she struggles under me, thrashing as something dark takes hold of me. The only way I'm getting out of here is if Caretaker Sienna is dead. I don't know what kind of person I was before, but right now, I'm the type of person who will do whatever it takes to survive. I don't want to die again.

Caretaker Sienna's eyes close, and she stops struggling. My breath heaves. Tears rim my eyes, before splattering across the caretaker's glasses. I swipe my hair from my eyes and then reach out to press my fingers to the caretaker's neck to check for her pulse.

It's there.

Before I have a chance to grip onto her once more, she jerks her hand out and stabs me with a pencil while slamming her other hand into my shoulder, knocking me back. The world spins around and around, pain exploding through my entire body as I topple down the stairs. My head smacks against the concrete landing, sending dark starbursts into my eyes. My shoulder screams, probably dislocated, and warm blood seeps from around the pencil and into my white and blue gown.

I struggle to breathe, hearing my heart pound in my throbbing head. The squeak of tennis shoes cuts through the noise of my own body failing me, and Caretaker Sienna blocks out the fluorescent lighting from above.

She watches me struggle, her hair disheveled and a splatter of blood—my blood—across her shirt.

The edges of my vision haze, and I know exactly what she's waiting for, because I'm waiting for it, too.

Five.

I can't move.

Four.

I can't breathe.

Three.

I can't see.

Two.

My heart stops.

"Time of death: Two forty-seven A.M."

CHAPTER 4

MEMORIES

"IT'S YOU OR them, my beautiful girl." The deep voice cuts through the darkness.

"I'll always choose me," I say.

"Because you're a Knezha. You fight. You never stop."

Haze swirls in my vision, the memory circling around me, threatening to strangle me. A blurry figure hovers in front of me, blue eyes opposite of Luka's dark ones peeking through.

Then the memory fades and a new presence arises.

"What the hell did you do, Skye?" Luka asks, his voice pulling my floating body in the direction I can sense him in, snuffing out the strange memory of the man completely.

I keep my eyes closed. "I died." My answer is incredibly obvious, and I know it's not what Luka was referring to, but how can I tell him I failed to kill the woman who has control over our lives? How can I tell him I tried to kill her in the first place?

It was the last thing I expected from me, and it scares me to think about how I was capable of murdering someone without putting much thought into it. I just reacted. My intuition took over and basically did it for me. I don't know what it means, though. Was I a killer before? A fighter? But for whom? What? I'm too afraid to ask Luka about it. I'm afraid he might think differently of me, even though I shouldn't care what he thinks at all. I shouldn't even be relieved to hear his voice, because that would mean he's...

Luka's silence doesn't go unnoticed. He refrains from replying to my automatic response, and I'm nervous I might have accidentally shared everything with him through my thoughts.

"What about you? Did that monster kill you again, too?" I roll to my side to face the direction I can feel his presence.

"You had a memory," he says without answering my question. "Of before."

"It didn't include you."

"I know."

"What did it mean?"

"Better not to think of it."

Hovering next to me, lit by the dazzling stars, Luka floats on his back without glancing my way. It's like we're both suspended in the galaxy by invisible wires without an escape that I can see. It's all stars. We're stars, two beings amid a world of peace that wraps around me to cloak the negative feelings pinching my soul.

"My past—I did something to deserve this, right?" I ask.

He doesn't respond.

"Luka, please, answer me."

"It doesn't matter," he finally says.

"It does."

"That past was not *our* past, and that's all that matters."

I reach out and brush my fingers from below his earlobe to his chin. My touch gets a subtle reaction out of him. He lifts his dangling arm and twines his fingers through mine and pulls my floating body closer to his.

And then the strangest thing happens.

Light explodes between us, flooding me with warmth and an emotion I can't put my finger on. A smile crosses my face, and I imagine digging a hole right in the center of me to bury the feeling within my soul for safekeeping, like it would be the end of my world if I suddenly lost it.

Luka's gaze meets mine, his own smile beaming brighter than the stars around us. The way he looks at me unleashes something familiar in my mind, and I imagine a green blanket sprawled on sparkling sand in front of white, foamy waves reflecting the sun's hot rays. Luka lies with his hands behind his head, stretching in front of me, his bare chest shining with droplets of ocean spray. He looks healthier, younger even, happy.

Reflecting in his sunglasses is a smiling girl, all squinty eyes, her blond hair cascading over her shoulders in beachy waves. Freckles splatter her cheeks and nose, and then her reflection obscures because she leans in too close to Luka. It's me, leaning into him, closing the space between us like the air is my enemy and I won't let it get in my way.

This is the type of memory I can survive on, one that fills the emptiness in my mind, snapping tiny fragments of who I am together to make me whole. This isn't a confusing moment with unfamiliar people from a past I can't remember or don't want to. It's a moment I want to multiply, replicate, guarantee that I'll have so many I could live in them for eternity.

"Skye?" Luka asks, pulling me from the memory. The girl reflected in the sunglasses swirls through my mind. It was definitely me. I don't need a mirror to know that Luka wasn't lying about knowing me. The girl fit the description of the girl on my door. Gray eyes, blond hair. But that girl looked happy. She looked carefree.

She looked far from being an attempted murderer like I am now.

I guess death changes people.

"Skye?" Luka asks again. "Come on, Skye. Say something." His soft voice pleads with me, and like that, the joy brought on by the memory dissipates. The indescribable feeling vanishes as well, leaving me with Luka and the stars, and the confusion I don't want.

"I can't go back," I whisper instead of telling him about the memory. There's no point. It doesn't change anything. He's still a stranger, who happens to know the girl I was, the girl who decided to abandon me to suffer in this new life filled with monsters and death and nothing to hold onto to keep me alive.

"I'll show you the way," he says.

"No, I mean it, Luka. I told you already," I say.

"Skye..." His voice trails off, and he looks at me with the saddest eyes. But they don't look sad because I refuse to return with him. They're more pitiful, like he feels sorry for me.

"You can't talk me out of it. I will stay here until I can't. Why don't you stay with me?" I feel strange asking, and with the way Luka crinkles his forehead, I'm sure he's never really considered it an option. Like it'd be too easy. Like whatever life we had is worth suffering for. Like it's worth dying and returning and dying and returning over and over again until we either die for good or get to finally live.

I scowl. Who's he to judge me? He might know me, but he doesn't know this version of me. "What?"

He continues to give me the look of pity, still holding my hand. "All promises aside, they'll eventually drag you back. The longer you fight, the more they want to get into your head. The more they take interest."

"Who?" I ask.

"The monsters. I've never seen their faces."

"Well, I have," I say. "And Caretaker Sienna isn't the Boogeyman. She's some average woman who thinks she holds the power."

He squeezes his eyes shut for a second before opening them again to stare at me, all brooding and serious, his brows low over his dark stare that threatens to rip me open to see what's going on inside my mind.

His look is all it takes to get me to say, "I almost killed her. I *thought* I killed her. But she tricked me."

"I told you to do what she said, Skye," he says like I somehow could ever forget.

"I didn't know I had it in me," I comment without explaining why I chose to ignore his words of warning in the first place. How I saw an opportunity and took it.

"And now the monsters know you do," he says.

Again, I ignore his remarks. "Who was I, Luka? Was I some awful person? Am I here because I deserve to be?"

If I'm here because I deserve a miserable life, that would mean Luka deserves such a fate, too. That, I can't agree with, even if I don't really know anything about him. Again with the intuition. But instincts can fail you. Obviously. I wouldn't be in the galaxy world if they couldn't.

He's quiet for a long moment. "It feels wrong to try to answer that," he finally says. "Like you said before, how can you trust me to tell you? I know the Skye you are to me, but I don't know the Skye you were to you."

"So, who was I to you?" I ask.

He releases a low laugh. "Trouble. A whole lot of trouble. I guess you haven't changed much, huh?"

"And you're annoying," I mutter.

"You've called me worse," he says, laughing louder.

His deep voice resonates through the galaxy, bouncing off each star, setting them aglow like bright flashes ignited by Luka's presence. This world isn't just mine. It's his, too.

I smile. I can't help it. His laughter is contagious and so familiar, like I'm experiencing déjà vu. As quickly as it comes, it disappears, and a blip of grief beats in my heart.

"Does it bother you that I don't remember anything?" I ask.

His smile fades, and I regret asking him my question. Something about his smile turns the fear and uncertainty into a minor annoyance, like his smile is capable of making me right with the horribly wrong world we're forced to return to. "It'd be nice if you did, but I won't hold it against you. Hell, it might be lucky for me. You won't be able to hold all the dumb shit I've done or gotten us into over my head anymore."

I pout my lip.

Slowly reaching out his hand, he brushes the pad of his thumb over my lips. I turn my head away at the warmth brought on by his touch. It jolts another memory within me. One full of anger and annoyance. Luka's back faces me, his fingers laced on his head, and I watch my arm lift up and grab onto his shoulder to spin him around. His lips move as he speaks to me, his brows knitted together, but I can't hear his words. The world blurs, like I'm shaking my head, and then he reaches out and rubs his thumb across my bottom lip. The memory feels as real as his hand felt a second ago.

I release a shuddering breath, the memory fading away. "I've upset you before, too." It's not a question, but a statement I feel the need to throw out into our universe.

"You're downright infuriating sometimes, Skye," he whispers. "Like when you don't listen."

I shift to look at him again and catch him still gazing at me. "I really thought I could escape."

"I know," he answers.

I hold his heavy stare. "I just wanted to get out of here and get help. I was trying to help you. Gemma and Avery, too. Now, I've probably made everything worse."

He presses his lips together. "Maybe. You're new, though. We've all tried to escape before."

"So, we can't really stay here?" I ask. "Because I want to."

"We've all tried," he says.

"Well, I haven't. Maybe I'm different."

"Maybe you are." He doesn't sound so sure. I'm not even sure.

"Will you try to stay with me?" Maybe it's the mysterious link Luka said we share or if it's because I like how every time I look at him, something familiar stirs within me—either way, if I do figure out how to stay, I don't want him to go back without me. It might be selfish of me, but he said I showed him the way out of this galaxy before. Maybe I can show him how to hold on.

"Skye..." His voice trails off.

Perhaps I'm reading him wrong. Maybe this supposed connection, the small blips of memory that keep coming to me in this world are all out of context. I don't know. He doesn't seem to want to tell me. But I can't help the pang of hurt.

"Whatever, I get it, Luka," I say.

"Hold on." He frowns. "I haven't even said anything yet."

"You don't have to, though."

He reaches out to me, but I turn away. His fingers rest on my elbow instead. "I want to stay with you, I do. But I don't want you to try to stay."

"And why not?"

He doesn't respond right away. It takes me glaring to get him to say, "I don't want to explain."

"So, you want me to go back and suffer?"

"Please, Skye. Knock it off. I don't want to have this conversation. Not here. Not when you're like this."

I pull away from him. "You know what? You can leave. I've changed my mind. I don't want you here. You're ruining my galaxy."

"I can't let you," he says.

Panic washes over me. "Don't you dare, Luka. I'll never forgive you. Is that what you want?"

"I'm sorry, Skye. I'm willing to risk it. The Skye I know wouldn't forgive me for letting her stay," he says.

"I'm not that Skye!" I yell. "She's dead!"

"And you're going to live."

He wraps his arms around me, heat rushing over me, burning away the sweet nothing of being amid the stars. Our souls touch, igniting in a lightshow that makes the stars look like fading pinpricks of soft light in comparison.

Suddenly, I hear my heart beating. Luka's, too.

Five.

No! My voice stays locked inside me.

Four.

My fingers tingle.

Three.

A clock ticks from somewhere.

Two.

I gasp.

"Time of life: Five forty-seven A.M."

CHAPTER 5

DAMAGED

PAIN EXPLODES THROUGH my entire body. My head throbs, forcing me to keep my eyes closed, and a burning sensation stretches across my torso, starting from a spot near my belly button and expanding around me like an invisible belt. I try to shift, but I either can't physically do it or something keeps me down. I'm too afraid to open my eyes to look.

I clench my jaw, holding my breath to listen to the sounds around me to figure out where I am before I take a peek. It's quiet. I can't hear any signs of life. No breathing. No shifting mats. No rattling of the chain-link barrier. I'm not in my room.

A light's on though. My eyelids tint red, and I'm pretty sure I'm alone because nothing shadows over me. I can't sense another presence either. Not like in the freezer where I sensed Luka.

I release my breath as quietly as I can through my nose and inhale again. I pick up on a strange smell, like lemons—no, something lemon-scented. It's familiar. Hand soap? Dish soap? Maybe a scented air-freshener trying to bring the outdoors in, because I know I'm not outside. Warm, stale air encompasses me, closer to how the hallway felt when I stepped out of the freezer, but I don't hear the hum of vents. I'm somewhere enclosed.

Pushing all my nerves to the back of my mind, I slowly open my eyes, trying to peek through my lashes. Bright light stings my eyes, causing me to thrash, but my chest hits something solid. The rest of my limbs are bound, too. Chains? No, straps. Rubber ones. They stretch a little but not enough for me to really feel around.

I force my eyes to stay open, hoping they'll adjust to the light, but it's like someone holds a flashlight directly over each of my eyes. It's not until then I realize I can't hear anything because something wraps around not only my eyes, but my head, covering my ears.

I scream. I think it's out loud, but I can't be sure.

Water fills my lungs, and I gag, thrashing. I'm drowning but still breathing as a memory surfaces, pulling me from the bright lights and bindings. The light dims, and I look up at the red-tinted bubbling water above me. Something holds me down, stopping me from gasping for breath. Fear squeezes my lungs, my vision darkening around the edges. Then nothing.

Another memory but not of me living. The memory was a different death, possibly my first, the one Luka claims brought me to him.

"Skye, can you hear me?" Luka's voice erupts through the screams sounding through my mind. *"Skye, listen to my voice."* I had no idea I was still screaming.

"What's happening? Where am I? This is your fault!" My fear turns to anger. I can't help it. I know this isn't truly Luka's fault, but I can't stop myself from blaming him for forcing me back here.

"I know you're scared—"

"I can't move or see or hear."

"It's because you're hurt. You've damaged your body, and they put you in the healing box. You shouldn't be awake, though."

I'm being punished. Of course I'm being punished. I tried to kill Caretaker Sienna, but I'd think her killing me would've been punishment enough.

"I hate you, you know," I say. I hate the world. I hate everything.

"Skye, I'm sorry. I didn't know you were injured or I would've warned you. She rarely ever damages our bodies."

"It doesn't matter. Just get out of my head." I don't want Luka in my mind. Whatever the reason he thinks he knows what's best for me doesn't mean crap to me. I just—I'm confused and feel like I'm out of my mind and in some twisted nightmare I'll wake up from if he'd let me stay in the galaxy.

"You're freaking out. Please, just listen to my voice."
"No!"

Luka doesn't listen to me. Instead, he hums. First it's soft, a deep whisper, but his voice grows louder and louder, pushing my own thoughts away until I can't think about anything apart from the familiar tune he hums. The song hangs out of my reach, like I've heard it a dozen times but the lyrics evade me.

I sink into another memory. Hot wind whips through the open window of a car. I'm riding shotgun, my elbow propped on the doorframe. In the side mirror, a dark storm looms behind us, but we head into the clear blue sky of a desert landscape on a straight stretch of road. Balmy air dances through my hair, cooling the sweat on my neck, and I reach my hand out and flick on the radio.

Another hand darts out, pushing my fingers away, and turns the dial to raise the volume. I catch sight of Luka in my peripheral vision, but I don't look at him directly. I listen to him, though. His voice projects over the music as he sings at the top of his lungs. It's the same song he hums now but an upbeat version. It's enough to calm my racing heart.

"I know that song," I say, pulling myself from the memory.

I wish I could lose myself in it and see what else happens, but it only loops over and over again in my mind. The storm behind us, the tepid air, our fingers meeting to fight over the radio dial. I don't know exactly what Luka meant to me, but he obviously meant something.

"You hated it," he says with a small laugh in my mind. I can picture him lying on his back now with his head tilted to look

at me. I bet that's what he'd be doing if we were next to each other. I'd probably turn away from his intensity.

"It's not so bad," I say. *"Keep humming?"*

He starts again, and I lose myself to the sound of his voice and the slow lull of the song. He never sings the words but keeps humming the melody, stopping every few minutes to whisper words of encouragement and how he thinks I'll be out soon.

I drift in and out of sleep, but Luka never stops humming. And when I dream, he's there. He's sitting next to me, his legs stretched out in front of him, his blond hair cut shorter than it is now. He just smiles and stares, and I do the same back.

But the world shifts, startling me from my dream. Icy air steals my warmth away, and rough hands rip the cover from my eyes, finally restoring my hearing and vision—the lemon-scented air disappears, too. Now, I can smell something chemical. Harsh. It stings my nose.

The hum of vents sound louder than my heart beating, but I still can't see anything except a row of fluorescent lights overhead. Spots dance across my aching eyes, and a figure leans over me. I catch my startled expression in Caretaker Sienna's protective glasses.

She glares. "I'm going to unbind your limbs. If you try to pull anything stupid again, you won't be returning to your room. Understand, subject four?"

I consider asking her where she'd take me if it weren't there but bite my tongue and nod my head. I can't see her just killing me for good. I'd probably end up somewhere that makes my dank room seem luxurious. I didn't think life could be worse but obviously it can.

"Good." She starts by unfastening my feet first. I remain utterly still, feeling her fingers brush my skin. She shifts to my arms, releases my left hand first before waiting a good minute to free my right. "Wait for my command before you get up."

We're alone in a small medical office, but instead of a wall of supplies, I glimpse a wall of monitors. All but the one with a view of the others is off. She purposely shut them off so I couldn't see anything.

Her tennis shoes squeak across the floor as she moves across the room. I lean up slightly to take a better look around and force myself to stay in place when her back faces me. But she's probably prepared for the worst in me now. I no longer have the element of surprise.

I study Caretaker Sienna, narrowing my eyes on her back like I can somehow see into her head, hear her thoughts, figure out what's going on in her mind. But I can't. It's strange. She never shares thoughts with me either, not like with the others who unintentionally force their way into my mind.

Caretaker Sienna shifts from her place looking over a folder on a table near the wall, and I lie back down and stare at the lights some more.

"You may sit up, subject four," she says.

I meet her gaze from across the room. A dull ache grips my stomach, and I glance down and realize I'm only wearing a blood-stained sheet. I wish she'd stop looking at me so I could inspect my body, but she doesn't. I'm too stubborn to show her

I care what happens to me. It's bad enough my left arm throbs with deep bruises from hitting the stairs, and I'm pretty sure I have a giant knot on the back of my head that I'll touch the moment I'm away from her.

"You will heal completely in a few days," she says, like she can read my mind. I don't think she can, though. If she could, she'd know Luka and I supposedly know each other—well, at least know that Luka knows me.

"Whatever," I say. "It doesn't matter."

"It does. It's important for you to stay in optimal health," she says.

My brows knit together at her admittance, though it does nothing to ease my lingering fear. "Optimal health? You—"

"*Skye, stop.*" It's Luka. "*She's baiting you. She wants you to give her a response.*"

I clench my aching fingers. "Never mind. It doesn't matter."

"You can say what's on your mind, subject four," she says.

Luka's right. One second she was scowling at me, and now she inches forward, curiosity peaking her brows on her forehead.

"I think you're a monster," I finally say.

She straightens her shoulders. "Come on, subject four. Stand up. Let me take you back to your room."

I smirk at the hint of disappointment in her voice, though she does try to disguise it with a stern gaze. She holds up her metallic canister when I close the distance and then instructs me where to go, not even giving me anything to change into. I drag my sheet along with me, my bare feet slapping on the shiny concrete floor. Voices sound from the end of the corridor, but they silence the second Caretaker Sienna's shoes squeak. I don't even have to know my way around to know I'll be coming up to my room soon enough.

I train my gaze toward the floor before we enter. I don't want to meet Gemma's stare, or anyone's for that matter. I feel like an utter failure. I wasted my chance.

Caretaker Sienna opens my door for me, and I enter without a word, shuffle to my mat exactly where I left it, and ease down, ignoring the screaming pain burning through me. I won't give Caretaker Sienna the satisfaction of seeing how I regret trying to escape in the first place.

She leaves the room without a word, and I curl my knees to my chest despite every ache that begs for my attention.

"You okay, Skye?" Gemma asks, rattling the chain-link. Her soft voice surprises me, considering how much snark lined her every word the last time I saw her, which feels like years ago.

I sniffle, wishing she didn't ask. It's easy to pretend to be okay when no one corners you to ask about your feelings. "Yeah." My voice sounds hoarse as it comes out, and I clear my throat a few times.

"God, hopefully the monster hasn't come up with new methods." Gemma's voice sounds through my mind. She's thinking about herself, but I don't blame her.

"As good as I'm going to be after being stabbed with a pencil and thrown down concrete stairs," I add.

"Oh, God. Poor Skye." Avery's voice sneaks into my mind

next.

Luka sucks in a small breath behind me, but he doesn't say anything.

"Ouch," Gemma says. "You must've really pissed the monster off."

Both girls are curious as to what I've done to garner such treatment from Caretaker Sienna, and I force their thoughts from my mind. I imagine building a giant wall to keep them out. They won't have to worry about that sort of thing. I doubt either of them would try to kill the caretaker.

"I don't want to talk about it," I say after a moment.

"Okay," Gemma says.

I peek from my sheet and watch her lie on her mat.

Without having to look, I know both girls are disappointed I don't want to get into things. This is probably the most excitement they've had that didn't involve them. But I'm not sure if I should engage. They might be my roommates, but I don't know them. Obviously, Gemma comes first to herself. Just like I come first to me. I'm sure Avery thinks the same. We're all selfish—except Luka.

A soft hand touches my shoulder through the fence, and I cringe as I slowly roll over to face Luka for the first time. His dark eyes meet mine, his face half hidden under the curtain, but even without seeing his face, the look he gives me speaks volumes. He stretches his arm through the barrier as far as he can and grazes the tips of his fingers across my forehead, brushing strands of my blond hair from my face. I'm pretty sure if we weren't separated he'd try to hug me. I might even let him.

"How bad do I look?" I finally ask, only to him, holding his glassy stare.

With his free hand, he shifts the curtain on his face and rubs his chin. *"I can only see your black eye."*

Slowly, I pull the sheet from my face.

He trails his finger across my bottom lip, and it stings under his touch.

"I think you hit your chin on a stair."

I slide my tongue over my teeth before I bare them at him.

"Your smile's still perfect," he says.

I continue to ease the sheet lower, showing off my shoulders because it hurts my head to try to look at them.

"God, Skye." His voice is barely a whisper. *"How much pain are you in?"*

"It's not bad," I think to him.

He frowns, clearly knowing I'm lying. *"Why don't you take a hot shower? The nozzle on your sink extends. I'm sure Gemma won't complain."*

The thought of leaving myself vulnerable like that freaks me out.

"Come on, Skye. I'll hang up my curtain. You have clean gowns on your shelf. There's even shampoo and body wash."

As much as the idea of showering with these strangers around freaks me out, the idea of sitting under a stream of hot water sounds amazing. After a moment of thinking about it, I finally relent to the idea.

"Do we get to take showers?" I ask out loud to no one in particular. I only do it because it would be strange if I knew that

I could shower at my sink when no one's taken one in front of me yet, and I'm sure Caretaker Sienna is watching or listening, being the creep she is.

"Your sink nozzle extends," Avery says.

"We usually take showers at the same time because everything gets wet, but I don't mind if Luka doesn't," Gemma says. "Everything you need is on your bookshelf."

"Can you please hang your curtain back up?" I ask Luka, even though I know he was moments from getting to his feet to do it. I don't know how much the other girls know, but Luka isn't jumping to tell them about our connection, so I won't either.

"Sure," Luka says, getting to his feet. He hangs his curtain back up and extends it all the way out.

I cross an arm over my chest, holding the bloody sheet to me and don't move for a minute, just gazing around my room. Even with my curtain and Luka's, it still feels so open. Swallowing my shyness, I grab a few things from my bookcase and set them on the counter near my sink. I turn on the water to warm up, and then decide to tie the bloody sheet to the chain-link for more privacy.

I groan the second I lift my arm over my head to spray a steady stream over me. It's the worst and best shower ever. The water tints pink as it washes the dried blood from my torso and legs. The wound where I took a pencil in my stomach seems to be glued shut or something. I don't care if it could open. Caretaker Sienna didn't even tell me what to do. But what does it matter if it does? I'm already hurting. At least I don't have to be disgusting.

I can't stop the groan from escaping my mouth every time I try to lift my arms. It's more embarrassing than knowing I'm blocked by only thin fabric. But I really want to wash my hair.

"Luka, this sucks. I can't even raise my arms." I don't know why I complain to him, but it makes me feel better and that confuses me. He pisses me off and comforts me all at once.

"I can hold the sprayer up through the fence. I won't look." The chain-link rattles as he sticks his hand through the fence at the open spot right next to the wall. He has to be standing over his toilet to be able to reach through there. At least my sink is close enough that he can do it because I'm not sure Gemma would if I were to ask.

"Thanks." I let the hot water run down my face, washing away all the blood and grime from me.

"Better?" Luka asks.

His voice stirs another memory within me. My blurry reflection smiles at me from a foggy mirror in an unfamiliar bathroom. I wipe my fingers across and spot the silhouette of a body behind an opaque shower curtain behind me. Luka peeks his head out, smiling at me, and then the water shuts off.

I'm pulled from my memory when the water stops pouring down my face. The faucet is still turned on, but nothing comes out from the nozzle.

"Looks like you're done," Luka says into my mind. *"Caretaker Sienna shuts off the water when she thinks we're using too much."*

I sigh, grab the towel from my counter, and dry off. I

would've stayed under forever if I could've. The squeak of shoes on the polished floor sounds through the air, and I rush to get into my undergarments and gown as quickly as possible, though I can't even stretch my arms back to tie it.

"Please remove the sheet, subject four," Caretaker Sienna says from the other side of my door.

I frown but do as she says. I ball up the sheet and hold it to my chest, standing just out of view from both Luka and Gemma.

Caretaker Sienna stands in front of Gemma's door, holding a tray of food. Instead of opening the door, she slides it through a slot. She comes to my door next and does the same thing. At least she doesn't ask for the sheet. I don't care if it's covered in my blood, I don't want to give it back. I'll wash it in the sink the next time the water is turned back on so I can use it without taking down my curtain.

After dishing out all the food trays, Caretaker Sienna leaves, surprising me. I thought for sure she'd hang around or try to do something to one of us. But thankfully, she didn't. I watch the dark corridor for a long moment before I step away from my sink.

"What's your tattoo of?" Gemma asks from her spot on the floor. She holds her tray of food on her lap.

It takes me a minute to realize she's asking me. I didn't even know I had one.

She points her fork at me. "On your back."

I blink a few times. Of course she can see my back since I couldn't tie the damn strings closed on my gown. Heat rushes into my face when I realize I turned toward Gemma, giving both Luka and Avery a view of me as well. At least I'm wearing underwear. Too bad they're hideous.

"Hearts," Luka says into my mind.

"Hearts?" I frown. Why would I get a heart tattooed on my back? *"Really? Ugh. Are they at least cool?"*

He chuckles out loud and plays it off with a cough, though it was obvious he was laughing.

I swivel and glare at him. "Something funny?"

He shrugs. "Just had a thought."

He doesn't elaborate, and his eyes dare me to say something. I hold his smiling gaze and watch him take a sip of some sort of soup from his tray. He wags his eyebrows at me, and I can feel Gemma watching us since I never answered her question, but Luka has a presence I can't ignore.

He takes another mouthful and then waves the spoon at me. "If you think I'm going to tell you, then guess again."

I roll my eyes. "Whatever. I bet it was lame anyway."

He laughs, but his laughter is cut off when he suddenly coughs. His face turns bright red, and he knocks his tray of food off his lap and grabs at his throat. The soup spills into my room, flowing over my mat, and I look from it to Luka. He falls to his side and starts convulsing, sending panic straight to my heart.

"What the hell?" I ask, trying to keep my voice even since neither Gemma nor Avery even move from their spots.

"Probably poison," Avery says, shrugging. She says it like it's something that's happened before.

"What?" I ask.

"Don't look so surprised. You can't always see death com-ing," Gemma says. "At least it's better than the freezer. You can only hope for something so quick."

I reach through the barrier and lock my hand around Lu-ka's fingers. I can't help it. I hate seeing him like this. No mat-ter how many times I've seen death or experienced it in the last few days, it doesn't get any easier. I think it actually gets worse.

Caretaker Sienna really is a monster.

And it's unfair Luka's the one to die this time. I never thought I'd be slightly jealous, because with death it means he gets to go to the stars.

My elbow sloshes through his soup that spilled across my mat. Closing my eyes, I press my lips to it and slurp in as much as I can. I know I shouldn't. I know there will probably be con-sequences. But I don't let it stop me.

My chest seizes a moment later, my throat swelling, steal-ing my air.

Five.

I grip my throat.

Four.

Caretaker Sienna strolls into the room.

Three.

My eyes roll back into my head.

Two.

My heart stops.

"Time of death: Seven twenty P.M."

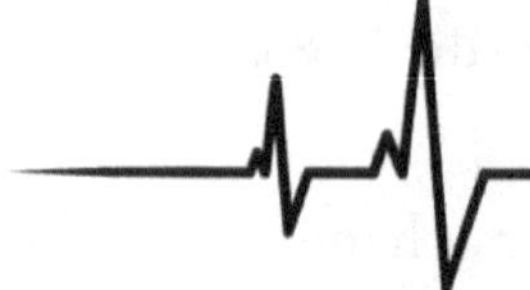

CHAPTER 6

HEARTBEATS

"DAMN IT, SKYE," Luka says from somewhere nearby. "You shouldn't be here."

I flip onto my stomach and stare at the glittering stars below me. Craning my neck, I turn to glance at Luka only inches away. He could reach out and wrap his arms around me if he wanted to. He doesn't, though.

I dangle my hands below me, reaching for nothing in particular. Here, I don't feel the throbbing pain swelling through my body. Here, among my stars, is only the feeling of peace.

"I don't care if I shouldn't be here," I say. "I'm here and it is what it is."

"You were always so stubborn," he mutters. "You'll attract too much of Monster Sienna's curiosity, you know."

"Maybe that's what I want," I say. "Because I can't sit around locked away all day, wondering what's going on. Wondering who I am. Who you are. What you mean to me. It's torture. I keep getting these visions—memories—but they never give me enough."

He flips to his stomach as well and reaches out to grab my arm. "What do you remember?"

"Just snapshots." I turn my gaze to stare down at the vast, endless stars beneath us. "A man and woman. A pool. I think I drowned."

"Drowned? What else?"

"Memories of you." I can't get my voice to rise above a whisper.

"We spent a lot of time together," he says.

"So, you mean you actually ran away with me when I showed up at your door?" I ask, remembering he told me that I'm the one who found him after we met in the stars. That's kind of insane. Actually, all of this is kind of insane. It has me questioning my entire existence, almost like I need to if I'm ever going to make sense of things. If I'm ever going to learn what the purpose of this all is, if I even have a purpose anymore.

"Not right away," he says.

"I guess I can cross irresistible off my list of things I used to be then, huh?" I smirk at him, watching the stars reflect in his eyes. "'Cause if I was, you'd have come right away."

He chuckles. "Wouldn't you like to know?"

I would. I really, really would, especially with how his smile pulls up on one side and tiny crinkles form in the corners of his eyes as he looks at me. I can't deny how hot he is and how I'm starting to enjoy all of these private conversations.

His smile widens, and I wonder if I projected the thought to him, but then he winces. The smile leaves his face, and he closes his eyes.

"What's wrong?" I ask.

"You don't feel it?"

I grip his fingers tighter. "No."

"I can't stay here," he says.

Frowning, I say, "But I don't want to go. I don't even feel anything."

He sucks in a breath. "Please, Skye. Let me take you back."

"You don't think I can find my own way?" I ask, knowing that's not the reason. He doesn't trust that I won't stay. I don't even trust that I won't stay. Because I'm pretty sure I would, especially if he wasn't here to plead with me.

"Skye..." His voice trails off, and heat crawls from his fingers to mine.

I huff out a breath. "Fine. I'll come with you, but I'm not going to let you die without me. Ever. You want me to live with you, then you have to be okay with me dying with you, too."

Something lights his eyes, but I can't decipher the emotion. After a second, he says, "Why am I surprised? It's what I'd do for you."

I realize he speaks the truth. Every time Caretaker Sienna has killed me, Luka's been waiting for me. Always here to make sure I go back. That kind of gives a new meaning to dying for someone. I don't mention it, though. Luka doesn't like to go there, and I'm glad he doesn't.

"Okay, show me the way then," I say instead of what's on my mind.

Luka tugs my arm, pulling me close to him. He slides his arms around me, sending warmth from where his fingers touch my stomach to the top of my head and to my toes. He pushes us through the galaxy and heads toward the darkest spot. It's a small blip among our galaxy where no light touches. I push away the sudden dread washing over me.

"Get ready," Luka says.

A door appears, and I can't tell if it's my imagination creating it. The galaxy feels so utterly real, but the sudden appearance of a door in the middle of the universe screams wrong. But why?

Five.

I don't have time to think before the door swings open, and Luka drags us into the void beyond.

Four.

My heart starts beating.

Three.

Pain explodes through my body.

Two.

I gasp.

"Time of life: Seven thirty-two P.M." Caretaker Sienna nudges my side with her shoe, and I can't stop myself from bolting upright. "Both subject one and subject four seem to have revived simultaneously once again." She's not talking to either of us.

The pain in my stomach forces me to bend forward and press my palms to the cold floor.

"Subject four." Caretaker Sienna softly kicks me with her dirty tennis shoe again. "Did you purposely swallow some of subject one's dinner?"

I meet her hard gaze. "No. He spilled it where I was laying." It's a flat out lie, and I'm sure she would be able to see that if she records us, but I'd still deny it even with the evidence in front of me.

"I see," she says.

"Maybe you shouldn't poison people's dinners, and we wouldn't have this problem," I say.

A groan sounds from behind me, and I twist to look despite my better judgment. I'm surprised to see how slowly Luka comes to his senses. It was like I was in the galaxy one second and here the next without really any transition. I wonder if Caretaker Sienna noticed it before.

"Subject one, nice to have you with us," she says, focusing on Luka.

He doesn't respond.

I turn my attention back to her. Curiosity lingers on her raised brows. She looks like if I ask the right questions, she might actually tell me something useful. Maybe give me some insight I can hold onto to give me an advantage against her.

"How do you do it?" I ask.

"Do what?" she retorts.

I glare. "Revive us."

"With you, nothing," she says. "Which is why I find it so fascinating you've been reviving yourself at the same time as subject one."

"Shit, Skye." Luka's voice cuts through my mind.

"Maybe I don't really die." I keep my voice even. "Maybe I'm immortal. Do you believe in that?"

Caretaker Sienna doesn't give a reaction.

"Maybe I'm an alien. Maybe none of this is real," I continue. A strange fear creeps through me as I throw out a bunch of made-up theories. They don't even seem that farfetched. "Because people don't die and come back over and over again," I say.

"Skye, calm down," Luka says into my mind.

I turn to him, my eyes wild. *"Are you even real? Is this real?"*

Caretaker Sienna pulls out her cell phone from her pocket. "Subject four currently shows signs of duress and paranoia after death count six."

I get to my feet. "Why are you recording this? What is the purpose?"

Caretaker Sienna reaches into her other pocket and tugs out the metallic canister of poison. I just came back from death not even minutes ago, and she's ready to send me back.

"Go ahead," I say. "Kill me. You know you want to."

"Calm down, subject four. This is just part of the realignment. I'm doing what's necessary. You'll understand soon enough."

"Use my name!" I scream.

"Skye, I said calm down. You'll adjust. Things will even out. You're all over the place, but you're strong. You just have to prove it. He's waiting."

Her words trickle through me. None of them make sense. "Who? What are you talking about?"

"You're lost, Skye, but we found you. You're one of us. You'll remember." Her eyes widen, and she tenses. I don't think she intended to say any of that out loud. Jerking her hand up, she aims the canister. *Just move slowly, Sienna. You let her in. Just walk to the door. Show her you're not a threat. Get out. Get out. Get out.*

For the first time, I can hear into the caretaker's mind. I grin at her nervous thoughts. She's afraid of me and for once for reasons I'm not sure but so desperately want to find out about. Because I can use them against her.

I swivel to look at Luka. "What is she talking about?" When I turn back to Caretaker Sienna, she's already near the door. I missed my opportunity to scare her into revealing her thoughts. I try to pry into her head, but I'm locked out. Nothing. Not even a blip of fear.

Luka closes the space between us and slides his hand into mine, pulling me to him. "Stop," he whispers. "She's trying to get to you."

He embraces me right in front of Caretaker Sienna, and I wish I knew if it was because he really wanted to hug me or if he's trying to stop me from doing something that'll have consequences neither of us wants to face. The one thing I do know is that he does it for me and not for the monster.

I hear a lock slide into place and slowly pull away from Luka. Shaking my head back, I cause my hair to slap against my cheeks. The movement is enough to send pain into my head, and that pain stops the sudden panic from rattling in my chest.

"This isn't real. This is all so crazy." I shake my head back and forth. "This isn't real. This isn't happening."

"I'm real," he whispers into my ear instead of my mind. "You're real. Unfortunately, so is everything else."

Squeezing my eyes shut, I press my face into his chest. "I wish it wasn't."

"I know."

"I wish I'd just remember, but now I'm afraid. I'm here for a reason."

He hugs me tighter. "I know. We all are."

"What? Tell me," I say.

"I can't, Skye. They're always listening."

His response is as annoying as Caretaker Sienna's but something in his dark eyes begs me not to argue or persist.

Taking a deep breath, I pull myself together and move away from him. He reluctantly lets me go, but touching him like this, outside of our galaxy world, doesn't feel the same. There, it's so full of warmth and everything that's good. Here, we're both cold and awkward. My gown is still untied in the back, and I'm self-conscious of the state I'm in.

It doesn't help I'm afraid Caretaker Sienna will come back any second to either kill us or subdue me. I don't think she'll do it to Luka. She can't carry him unprepared.

Running my fingers through my hair, I brush it from my

face and take a good look around the room we're in. It isn't like the medical room from earlier, but it looks like it gets used with the well worn furnishings and a camera set up on a tripod meant to film what goes on in here. Whatever that may be. It's similar to a living room. Almost comfortable.

I shuffle away from Luka and stroll to the door. Peeking through the window cutout, I try to get a view of what's in the hallway. All I see is familiar concrete. I'm pretty sure this room is near the one with what Luka called the healing box.

"What do you think will happen next?" My gown falls down my shoulder, and I pull it up, annoyed at the screaming pain coursing through me when I fail once again to tie the stupid thing closed. What I wouldn't give for a T-shirt.

"Let me help you with the ties," Luka says without answering my question. I sense him behind me, but I don't turn from the window. His fingers brush my skin as he helps me stay covered.

"I think I scared the caretaker." I hold as still as possible, trying not to think about Luka behind me. *I know I scared her,* I add silently.

"Doubt it." Luka hovers so close I can feel his breath on my shoulder. *She was shaking,* he thinks to me, contradicting the response he gave for show. A coldness forms behind me, the warmth he created gone now that he's moved away. "And there. All done."

I spin around to face him, smiling. "Thanks. I just hate showing off that lame tattoo of mine."

"I like it." His eyebrows knit together. *You'd like it if you saw it,"* he thinks. *"You used to stand in front of the bathroom mirror holding up your compact to stare at it."*

I ignore his mental comment. It's hard not to lose myself in our internal conversation. If Caretaker Sienna is watching us, I don't want her getting suspicious. She's curious enough as it is. "You have a tattoo, too. I saw part of it."

"Want to see it?" he asks.

He spins around without waiting for my response and tugs the top strings on his hospital gown, shifting it off one of his shoulders. I can't see all of it, so I step closer and open it enough to see two lines stacked on top of each other. They each follow a jagged pattern, like an EKG reading of the same heartbeat, though they flatline in the middle of his back before starting up again. Reaching up, I glide my finger across his skin, tracing the lines of the tattoo.

A memory pops into my mind, stealing the room away, and I suddenly feel like I'm experiencing déjà vu. Luka stands in front of me with his back facing me. I stare at the same tattoo, though his shirt is off completely and dark jeans hang on his hips. He turns his head and smiles from over his shoulder, and I trace my finger along the entire tattoo, memorizing it with my finger like I'm making a map of his body in my mind.

"I still think you should've gotten the hearts," I say to the boy in my memory. But it's not me actually saying it. It's like I'm watching a movie from within my own mind, experiencing the moment all over again, but without control. Because memories don't change. I can't control them.

He laughs, turning to face me. "You got the hearts, I get

the beats."

I reach out and press my palms to his bare chest, feeling the thrum of his heart against my fingers. "And no one can take these from us."

Luka's smile disappears, and I blink, realizing that no matter how hard I try to steal back that moment, it's long in the past. I push the memory away and shiver, staring at Luka's back. "It's cool." My voice barely comes out as a whisper, my heart still racing, and I release a small breath. I can't hear Luka breathing at all.

"You drew it," he thinks to me. *"It's when we realized our hearts beat the same."*

"You should've gotten the hearts, too," I think, playing the memory over.

Luka straightens his shoulders. *"You remember."*

I think back. I thought I might have picked the tattoos out because of the feeling from the memory, but I had no idea I actually designed them for us. *"But I'm glad you didn't get the hearts. I like the heartbeats. I like that it goes with mine."* Who knew I was the type to get a couple's tattoo.

He reaches back to touch my side. *"Good, 'cause we went through a lot of trouble to get them."*

"So, we are *a couple?"*

That small bit of information is another clue to the life I had before. Another piece to the puzzle I'm slowly putting together. But none of these pieces show me the bigger picture. None of them show me why I'm here, what I did before. Luka's been here for close to a year. Where have I been all that time? I feel like if I could just think of a single moment, everything would fall into place, but the only thing falling into place is that Luka was important.

"Yeah," he thinks. *"At least before you forgot what an amazing guy I am."* I wish he'd turn around to look at me again, but he just hides his tattoo before moving across the room to sit down on one of the two folding chairs at a glass table.

I don't join him. I don't want to get comfortable. I want to be on alert for when Caretaker Sienna comes back. And she will come back. I think leaving me alone with Luka is all a part of some test, and if I let my guard down, I won't pass. We might've failed already.

"Should we make small talk?" I ask in my mind. *"You've done this before. Tell me what to do."*

Groaning, Luka draws my attention to him. He rubs his hands up his face and into his hair, pushing it back. "You should sit," he says. "She's probably not coming back for a while."

"I don't want to," I say. I jiggle the door handle even though I heard Caretaker Sienna lock it. "I'm too antsy."

"You never could sit still," he thinks to me. "You want to exercise or something?"

I grimace. "No. It hurts to even lift my arm. I'd rather gossip. Tell me everything about this place. Tell me about Gemma and Avery, too."

Luka kicks the chair across from him from the table and points to it, motioning for me to sit. I've been focusing too much on trying to figure him out that I haven't really thought more about the others. About anything really.

I take a seat and stare at my dirty nails instead of looking at him.

"Avery came in about a month after me and Gemma maybe three. It's hard to remember and keep track of days," he says. "Avery was a runaway with her boyfriend. They got into a car accident and ended up in a lake. She said she woke up here. I'm pretty sure her boyfriend didn't survive. Gemma's first death happened when she was a kid. She strangled herself on a cord, but the paramedics revived her. Apparently Monster Sienna tricked her, bringing her in after her dad died of an overdose or something. Don't know, really. She doesn't talk about it much."

Both of the girls' stories sound tragic, and it makes me angry that after everything they've been through, they've ended up here.

"And you?" I ask, because it's something I'd ask if I didn't know the truth. "What's your story, Luka?"

He raises an eyebrow. "You first."

I press my lips into a thin line. He knows I can't remember the time before, and even when I did, apparently I never shared my first death with him. But that one doesn't matter. It took me to Luka, not here. And the one that brought me here is the only death I remember outside of the last five here in this hellhole.

Flicking my gaze to meet his, I say, "Someone attacked me and left me for dead. In the snowy woods, I think. I remember the cold. The trees sparkled, and I could see the night sky." I lean on my elbows. *"Caretaker Sienna was there when I took my last breath, but I don't think she was the one who killed me,"* I add to him through my thoughts.

He reaches out his hand but realizes what he's doing and opens and closes his fist like he's stretching. *"You stayed. You shouldn't have stayed."* Wrinkles form on his forehead, his brows lowering over his dark eyes. "I was shot," he says out loud, answering my question about his death. It takes me a moment to process his words, especially with the two conversations—one out loud and one mentally—we're having.

My mouth drops open when I realize it's not the death—him being suffocated by his mom's boyfriend—that I know of. "What?" I try not to say everything going on in my mind out loud. *"I stayed where? And what do you mean you were shot?"*

Too many questions swarm through my mind at both his statements. It triggers another memory. A bullet hole in the trunk of a sugar pine tree. I can see it clearly in my mind. But I'm alone in the memory, standing near the frost-covered window of a shabby cabin. Blankets clutter the couch, and I know it's where I slept. In front of it, takeout containers pile on the dirty glass coffee table. Loneliness, and something rawer, sinks into me looking at the bullet hole. My vision blurs. I'm crying. And then the tree disappears when I turn away.

"Skye?" Luka questions, pulling me from the terrible memory, one I wish would've stayed forgotten.

I blink my eyes a few times, realizing that my tears splash the table in front of me. Swiping my hand over the surface, I wipe them away. "Talking about death is depressing. Not like we stay dead." I compose myself and stand from the table to pace.

"You're right," he says.

"Is that why we're here? Because we don't stay dead?" I'm afraid another horrible memory will light up the darkness hiding my past.

"Not exactly. We're what some call the acquired." That's what he meant when he warned me not to reveal what I've acquired from death the first moment I realized I was a telepath. "Monster Sienna thinks death jumpstarts parts of our brains we've never used before and gives us cognitive abilities."

I tilt my head back and laugh. It's the fakest sound ever and makes me end up laughing a real, genuine laugh.

"Funny, right?" Luka says, though his eyes hold a seriousness to them. We both know Caretaker Sienna is onto something. Telepathy isn't normal, and we can both do it.

"That's crazy. Even if we somehow acquire these cognitive abilities, what does she expect from us?"

"Power? Who knows? She's not working alone." He shrugs. *"This is all a lie. I'm here because…well, because of you. I'm not sure about the others. But Caretaker Sienna is a pawn. Her job is to break me. To use death to open my mind up."*

I hum softly. "Well, if I suddenly acquire cool powers, I'll definitely use them against her." My voice shakes at the words I say out loud. *"You're here because of me? What did I do?"*

He twists his lips to the side, fake amusement crossing his face. "You could try." He leans forward. *"It's what you didn't do."*

I wish Luka would just be straight forward with me. But the way he tiptoes around my past makes me feel like he's trying to protect me from it, from who I was, and what I was involved with.

"I'll explain as much as I can, but Caretaker Sienna is here now," Luka says, thinking to me. Our fake conversation out loud must've made the caretaker nervous.

I turn and glance at the door in time to watch it swing open. Jumping to my feet, I move around the table until I'm behind Luka. I don't know why I do it, but it's just where my legs took me.

Caretaker Sienna stands in the doorway, hidden behind all her protective wear. She clutches the canister of poison in her hand, aiming it at us, but she doesn't spray it. She doesn't step into the room, either. Having us together makes her nervous. I can tell by how she shifts on her tennis shoes.

"Subject one, please come to me," she says. "I'll escort you back to your room."

I frown. "What about me?" Before Luka can stand up, I move forward and place my hands on his shoulders. "Are you leaving me here?"

Her eyes narrow. "Release subject one, Skye. You'll be escorted back to your room soon enough."

She called me by my name. I don't know who's more shocked, me or Luka. Luka, definitely Luka. He peers at me from over his shoulder and gives me a small nod. I step away from him and cross my arms over my chest, wincing at the sudden movement. It takes everything in me to remain where I'm standing while Luka shuffles to the door and exits into the hallway with Caretaker Sienna.

She shuts and locks the door without another word.

Luka meets my gaze once through the glass. *"Please, don't get yourself killed, Skye. I need a break from dying. There are other ways to meet in the stars."*

I press my lips together. *"I'll try my best."* I wish he didn't leave with that sort of information. What does he mean that there are other ways for us to meet in the stars?

"Concentrate, Skye." The voice comes from behind me, and I turn around. "Do you see it?"

"No," I say, answering the woman with the toffee eyes from my memory. She's not really sitting in front of me, but the memory feels so utterly real. It's like I'm sitting on the floor of a quaint living room with the woman I know I love like I would my own mother.

"Don't give me that bullshit. You're not even trying. I know you're really thinking about some boy. Who is he? From school?" She smirks at me, the corners of her eyes crinkling.

I twine my fingers together on my lap. I wish I knew what she was talking about, but I don't remember what was on my mind in that moment. It's like I'm watching a movie from my own perspective without any narrative commentary.

"Not from school. I don't know who he is," I say.

She releases a breath. "Thank the stars. I don't want to have to pull you from school early. The last thing I need is for some distraction to come along and turn you off course of our journey."

I frown.

She laughs. "What? It's just until your birthday ceremony. After that, have at it. There are plenty of nice boys at the Knezha—"

The lock on the door clicks, pulling me from the memory. I expected to be left in this room for hours. I expected to spend the night alone in here, forced to sleep on the tile floor or propped between the chairs. But I guess Caretaker Sienna wouldn't give me that kind of luxury. If only I could remember the woman's name from my memory and what she meant to me maybe I could remember something helpful. The only comfort I have now is that there's someone still out in the world who loves me and who knows I'm meant for a life that isn't this one.

Caretaker Sienna opens the door, nearly panting, like she rushed back here after walking Luka to his room to ruin any chance of me reliving one of my memories. And it's one memory I want to cling onto more than anything. The woman said what I thought was my last name. My real last name. Not the one on my door that says, Stone. Skye Stone sounds like someone boring. Skye Knezha on the other hand? Dangerous.

I blink, wondering why I just thought my name sounded dangerous.

Caretaker Sienna steps into the room, leaving the door open for an easy escape. I gaze at the canister gripped in her hand before meeting her hazel eyes through her protective glasses.

I sneer. Her eyes are nothing like the woman's from my memory. Where the caretaker's are cold and calculated, untrusting, sadistic even, the woman's shined with adoration and warmth. They reminded me of the feeling I get from seeing Luka among the stars.

Caretaker Sienna struts forward, straightening her shoulders. *"Get yourself together. You have a job to do,"* she thinks to herself. *"She's too unpredictable. I must either gain her trust so she cooperates or break her so she does. He's been waiting long enough. He just wants her home."*

I want to ask her who she's talking about and what hellhole type of home I'm wanted at. Instead, I ask, "Is this where you make me plead for my life or something?"

I can't tell her reaction under her medical mask. "You've always been tougher than the others."

The others? I shrug. "Death doesn't scare me."

She balls her free hand into a fist. "Why's that?"

I shrug again. "Just doesn't."

"Now you're lying."

I glare at her. "No, actually I'm not. You know why?"

She doesn't respond.

"Because look around. Living is scarier."

CHAPTER 7

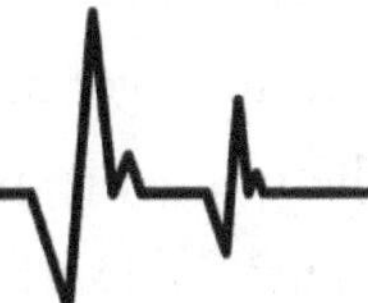

THE KNEZHA FAMILY

CARETAKER SIENNA SITS across from me, her phone set out on the table between us, recording what I say. "Favorite food?"

"Don't know."

"Last person you saw before you woke up here?"

"You."

"So, you know who I am?"

I nod. "A monster."

"Do you know subject one, two, or three?"

I keep my face expressionless. "Should I?"

Ignoring me, she asks, "Special talents?"

I press my lips together. "Obviously not murder."

She sighs. "What happens when you die?"

"You tell me." My back aches, and I lean on my elbows. I've been sitting across from Caretaker Sienna for hours as she asks question after question without giving me any answers.

"Why is she being so difficult? She's going to jeopardize me." Her thoughts ring clear in my mind.

"Maybe because you keep killing me," I snap. My eyes widen and I cover my mouth with my hand.

She grins, picking up her phone to hit a button. "Did you catch that? Subject four exhibits telepathic abilities."

I blink, frowning. She wasn't recording me. Someone was listening through the line. "Who is that?"

Without looking up, she jots down some notes on the pad of paper in front of her. "You're right. This is a good sign. She's as tough as ever, but I know she'll open up. I think she did what she did as a form of rebellion. Testing her place on our journey."

Our journey. The words sneak up on me, reminding me of the woman from the apartment, the one who said my last name.

"Who is that?" I ask again. "What are you talking about? Why won't you tell me anything?" Lunging across the table, I grab for Caretaker Sienna's phone. She yells out as I snatch it from her fingers.

I press the phone to my ear and listen. "...afraid she'll stray too far. What she's done could ruin everything. And all for—"

Caretaker Sienna raises her hand and hits the button on the nozzle of her metallic canister. I suck in some sort of sweet smelling gas into my lungs, sending shadows through my vision. I wobble in my seat, the room spinning. I know I'll fall from my chair and die at any second. I can't help thinking about Luka. Something about knowing he'll try to meet me in the galaxy—committing suicide to do so—leaves me unnerved. As much as I don't want to be alone, I also don't want him dying on my account. Such a pact could not have been something I'd have agreed to despite my yearning to forget about this world. There's just something about the stars—like I know there is something out there for me—that tries to get me to stay.

"Luka." I think his name, and I can see him clearly in my mind. Not the boy from the cage next to me but the Luka I imagine from my past.

But I'm not standing with him. I'm watching him from a distance. A familiar presence hovers out of my view. If only I could turn my head to look, I could see who it is. But in my memory, I'm engrossed with everything about Luka. The way the light catches the gold in his hair, how his shirt pulls over his shoulders, how he rubs his hand on the back of his neck to wipe away the sweat from working outside.

"He's perfect." The familiar masculine voice crawls under my skin, and I can't believe who I'm hearing. It's the voice from the phone, the one who talked about me. And it's not the man talking to me that gets to me. It's his words. He's referring to Luka.

"I know," I say. "But he has no idea about anything. I'm afraid I'll scare him off."

"I doubt that's possible, my beautiful girl. If he's who you say he is, then he'll come around willingly eventually. He'll make a great addition to our family. He'll see the way. You'll shift his journey."

I still don't meet the gaze of the man talking to me, and I wish old me from the memory I'm reliving had. I cannot summon his face for anything, like I'm purposely blocking him out. But it's because I'm so engrossed with the boy in front of me. Luka pushes a lawnmower through the weedy grass in front of a small craftsman bungalow. An old Dodge sits in the driveway, the truck's paint fading along the roof from the sun. Sweat spots pepper his shirt along his back, and he stops pushing the mower to take it off before wiping it across his forehead.

"Give me a few more weeks," I say.

"You have until the weekend," the man says.

Pain slithers around my chest, squeezing my lungs. It's enough to pull me from my memories. I stare up at Caretaker Sienna's silhouette in the harsh lighting from above. I must've fallen out of my chair without realizing it.

My chest heaves, the poison stealing my life away, stopping me from imagining the man from my memory, the man she was talking to on the phone. The one who said I was part of his family. But if that's the case, and I was part of his family, why am I here? Why am I being tortured and killed. Why did he want Luka? Why don't the others know?

My questions fade as a voice counts down.

Five.

I think about Luka again.

Four.

I can't die. Not now. If I die, he'll follow.

Three.

My vision fails, fear sneaking through me.

Two.

"We control death, my dear. It cannot control you. You're the key." It's the man's voice, the one from my memory, but this isn't a memory. It's like he heard my screams, like he's breaking into my thoughts. And words never felt truer, but I don't know how to stop my demise.

One.

My heart stops.

"Time of death: Two fifteen A.M."

I glimpse the stars. I can't be here. Not now.

Five.

I'm alone in a world that I didn't think I'd ever want to leave. But a deep-seated need to return to life grips onto me.

Four.

I peer around for the blip of darkness. The void. But it's not a void. It's a door. It's the way out.

Three.

I thrust myself into it, thinking about Luka and the man and woman from my memories. About a life I yearn to remember. One I can't do so if I choose to stay in the galaxy.

Two.

My heart beats, the quick thuds ringing in my ears.

One.

I snap my eyes open.

Caretaker Sienna stumbles away from me, holding the canister up again, but she doesn't spray. I missed a few heartbeats, but I've managed to bring myself back to life. I didn't want to stay in the stars. I wanted to be here.

"Subject four pulled herself from death," Caretaker Sienna says into her phone.

"Walk slowly to the door, Sienna. Skye's unpredictable. You must better prepare yourself from now on if she starts to remember, but this is what we want." The man's thoughts come to me louder than my own as he thinks them as he says them to Caretaker Sienna.

I press my hands to the floor and rise to my feet. Without her dumb death spray, I might be able to fight her to get out of here. I thought I had lost my one opportunity, but I haven't. I charge toward Sienna in an attempt to tackle her. Unfortunately, with the pain in my shoulder and now a new pain in my hip, she's faster.

She slides the lock closed, locking me in the room. A scream rips from my throat, and I bang my hands on the door over and over again like I can somehow break it down. Now, I'm stuck in a room with no idea what to expect next. She'll figure out some other way to kill me, and I don't know if coming back will be so easy the next time. I don't know what coming back so quickly has done to me. I feel strange. Disconnected. Almost like I'm watching myself hit the door from behind me.

"Skye? What's happening?" Luka's voice comes into my mind fast and hard, and it leaves me breathless. I bend over and grip my knees, trying my best to get the world to stabilize.

"You've been blocking me for hours. I can hear your screams."

"She killed me, but I came back right away like you showed me, and it freaked her out. She left me. I'm afraid it's going to be worse," I think to him.

"You what? Shit, Skye."

A weird hissing noise sounds through the air, stopping me from pounding on the door. Smoke drifts in through the vents, and I spin around, looking for anything I can use to cover my face. Not even my hospital gown stops the fumes from getting into my lungs.

"She's killing me again!" My voice shouts in my mind.

"Calm down, Skye. She's not. That knocks us out. It's coming in here, too."

I sit on the ground, the air so thick it hurts to breathe.

"Luka," I whisper through my mind.

He doesn't respond.

Darkness claims me.

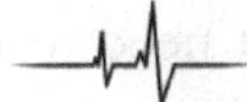

"Are you avoiding me?" A familiar voice sounds through the darkness, pulling me from the recesses of my mind.

I snap my eyes open. Bright sunshine glitters on the snowy steps I stand on, staring at the forest in front of a familiar cabin. But something is different. The memory doesn't hold anything horrible within it. No loneliness. No bullet holes. The scent of burning wood swirls through the air, and I turn and glance inside through the front window.

"Why would I be avoiding you?" I ask. I hold a phone to my ear and peer back at the snowy forest. The feeling that comes along with the familiar voice contradicts the panic that gripped at me when I heard the man talking to Caretaker Sienna. It's like some moments, I trust the mysterious man, care for him even, but when I heard him on the phone in that room, all those fond emotions disappeared. "You're my family."

Family? Again with the family. What the hell kind of family locks you in a basement?

"I'm starting to think you've forgotten your journey in this life, Skye. You know how much you mean to the rest of our family. They're counting on you to return. You're the key to bringing prosperity to our eternity."

A door slams, and I turn back to look inside the cabin. Luka strolls into the living room and stands in front of the glowing fireplace. He raises his hands, warming them on the orange flames. I don't take my eyes off him. I couldn't if I tried. I have no control over what's happened in the past as I remember these fractured moments. "Our eternity is the most important. I won't disappoint you. I just need to make sure Luka's ready for his own destiny by our side. He's meant to be a guardian—my guardian. You see he—"

"Skye, it's freezing out here." Luka's voice stops my conversation with the man on the other line. I'd been too focused to realize he'd come to the door. "You should come in."

I hold my hand up. "Hey, I gotta go. I'll call soon."

"Don't make me come visit."

I hang up without responding and turn to Luka. He smiles at me, his dark eyes shining. I shuffle forward and fall into his open arms. Pushing him back, I guide us inside the cabin and kick the door closed with my foot. My arms travel up to his neck, and I gaze into his eyes.

"God, I love when you're so protective," Luka says. He just stands and looks down at me like I'm the best thing he's ever looked upon. I could stay frozen in this memory forever with how he holds me in his intensity.

I smile, though something dark stirs within me. "Luka, I don't know how long we can run for. The life I had with—" I snap my mouth closed. "The path I was put on isn't one I want to journey anymore. I thought it was how things were supposed to be. I thought I was fated to be the girl who opened the door for our family, but I'm not so sure that's what I'm supposed to do."

"If it makes you feel any better, I think N—"

My eyes widen, and I press my finger to his lips. "Don't say his name. Never say his name. You have no idea what he's capable of—what I've had to do for him."

"You know you can talk to me."

"I'm afraid of how you'll see me if I tell you everything, Luka. I ju—I thought I was doing the right thing. But after—" I wish I had just spilled my heart out to Luka in that moment so I could learn everything I need to know. I hate how even my memories keep my secrets locked tightly away, like if they're ever released, something terrible will come. There has to be a reason for this, and I'm starting to think it's because of the man whose name I didn't want Luka mentioning out loud.

"You don't have to say anything. I trust you, Skye. I trust only you," he says.

"Maybe you shouldn't," I say.

He laughs.

I don't.

"It's going to be okay, you know. Who can stop us when we have the stars? When we can open the door?"

"No one can stop us," I say. "I won't let them. I promise."

"Skye? What do you promise?" Cool fingers brush along my forehead, pushing hair from my face.

Bolting upright, I swing my arm out, knocking someone back. I scream as I get to my feet and manage to trip and fall into the chain-link barrier. I peer around, confusion fogging my head. I'm not sure if I was experiencing a memory or just dreaming. It felt so real, but now that I stand in this humid room, surrounded by chain-link barriers, I can't be sure if my conversation with Luka in the cabin was a figment of my imagination.

Luka groans. "Calm down. It's me. You're okay. You don't have to fight."

"You scared me!" I yell, sucking in breath after breath to calm my racing heart. Confusion rattles my memory, and I want nothing more than to believe it. It takes me peering around the room for a few minutes to realize I'm not in my assigned room. I'm in Luka's.

"I'm sorry," Luka says. *"I had to wake you up, Skye. You were whispering things about us. I was afraid someone would hear,"* he finishes silently.

"I don't think it was a dream. Who were we running from Luka?" I think to him, groaning while I rattle the barrier with

my hands, so many questions tumbling through my mind.

"Shut up already. Some of us are trying to sleep," Gemma says from her room, cutting into our conversation. She doesn't get up from her mat but lies there on her back.

I shift my gaze to Avery's room. She remains asleep on her folded mat with her knees curled to her chest. Luka stands in the corner of the room, giving me as much space as humanly possible. He grips the curtain in his hands, wringing it while we study each other.

"Why am I in here with you?" I whisper. My thoughts are all over the place, and I can't sort them out enough to talk to Luka telepathically anymore.

He motions for me to come closer, and I hesitate for a second before shuffling to the mat on the floor. I sit on it, keeping my legs straight so that my gown covers my thighs. Luka moves and sits on the cold ground next to me without invading my space.

"I don't know," he whispers. "You were in here when I woke up. Monster Sienna is playing some sort of game. What happened between you two?"

I lean closer, trying to mute my voice. "She interrogated me for hours until she called a man. Luka, I knew him. And then I—who was he? He's who we were running from."

Luka rubs his hand over his forehead, and I know he wants to have a silent conversation, but my head throbs and exhaustion threatens to send me crashing to my side. The last twenty-four hours have felt like forty, and it's felt like the longest day in existence.

"You told me never to say his name, but he's not who we're running from—it was all of them," he whispers, shifting to move even closer. Our legs press together, and I stiffen, extremely aware of his bare skin touching mine.

I rest my head on his shoulder. I don't know why I do it, but I can't help myself, not with how the memory of us in the cabin reminded me of another moment with Luka, a moment that makes my heart flutter just thinking about it. He feels different now than from who he was in the memory, but he's still the same, too. "Them? Is that why we're here."

"The Knezha Family, Skye," he says. "It's why I'm here. But you? No. You'd have never ended up here because of them. You're here because of you. I can't think of another explanation."

He thinks I'm here because of me? I was attacked in a forest, one I'm starting to believe was the same forest as the cabin. Am I here because I messed up? Is that why I can't remember any of this? "I don't understand. Why would I run from my family? I'm a Knezha," I say. "That's my last name. I know it."

Luka doesn't answer me right away. After a quiet moment, he whispers, "You're not a Knezha. And N—that man? He was someone you'll be glad you forgot. I wish I could. Gemma and Avery have."

"They know him?"

"Knew him, I think. I don't know much. All I know is he's looking for something. They all are. That's why we don't show them our power."

I grimace, wishing he'd tell me more than that, wishing

he'd tell me the man's name. But he doesn't, and I'm too exhausted to beg him. "They know I'm a telepath."

He sighs. "How do you think you ended up that way? But, Skye, I don't want to talk about this anymore. There's nothing we can do right now. I don't want to—your mind isn't—I'm afraid you don't have memories for a reason, and I don't know if that's good or bad for us."

I slouch, anger sneaking up on me, but what's the point of getting mad? He knows things I don't, and I obviously trusted him in my past—another life. "Okay, whatever. I'm too tired to deal with all this anyway."

He offers out the curtain to me. "Don't be upset at me for protecting you."

"I'm not upset."

He raises an eyebrow "It's your biggest pet peeve, Skye," he whispers. He shakes the curtain, still holding it up to me, because I'm not quick to take it from him. "And you can sleep on the mat if you want. I don't mind."

The mat is measly, barely an inch thick, but it's still better than the floor. I'd feel guilty for making Luka suffer after his help keeping me calm. After all our quiet conversations. After the glimpses of memories. And a part of me doesn't want to be away from him. I like the way he feels sitting next to me, like the emotions he ignites in me might help me remember things, even if they're things I might have wanted to forget before.

"It's big enough for the both of us if we sleep on our sides," I say quietly, shifting to lie down.

"You sure?" His voice lowers as he asks the question almost

breathlessly—maybe a little nervously.

I nod. "Yeah, come on. Not like we haven't seen each other naked."

A smile crosses his lips.

I blush. I can't help it. I wish I didn't even mention it, because the little glimpse of the memory of him in the shower felt intrusive almost, despite knowing I was there. "Unless you don't want to."

"I want to," he whispers.

Turning over, I face my back to him and link my fingers into the chain-link barrier so he can sleep on the outside. He adjusts the curtain over me and settles down onto the mat. I expect to feel his back press into mine, but his arm slides under my head like a makeshift pillow and his heartbeat thuds against my back. His warm breath tickles my blond hair, and I don't move, letting the heat of his body warm my cool skin.

His presence lingering so close pushes my whirlwind thoughts away, silencing everything within my mind until it's just our breathing and the hum of the vents. I can't even hear Gemma or Avery.

"Is this okay?" Luka asks into my mind.

"Yeah," I respond. *"Thanks. I mean, for everything."*

"I'd do anything for you."

His soft voice in my mind, the words he speaks, awakens something within me. If I close my eyes, I can imagine the stars around us. I can feel the peacefulness of our galaxy. I can feel the connection. It reminds me of a time before I woke up here.

Another memory comes hot and fast. Luka lies on a queen

bed in a darkened room. Moonlight shines in through the window, sending a silver streak across his white, cotton T-shirt. I move closer, padding across the carpet of the bedroom, and he shifts to look at me with dark, intense eyes.

"It's not safe." The words hang heavy in the air. They came from me.

A frown pinches Luka's forehead. His mouth moves, but I can't hear what he's saying over the sound of my panicking heartbeat.

My hands fly out in front of me. I remember the anger. I wasn't mad at him, though. I was mad at something else. Someone else.

"I'd do anything for you, you know." The words make him smile, and they feel so true. They are true. At least if I'm remembering things correctly. The memory loops over and over again. The same words, *It's not safe* and *I'd do anything for you, you know,* playing in my mind. I wonder what it was about and if it had anything to do with the man on the phone. I wonder why it feels so important to me now.

Luka's hand drapes over my side, settling above my bellybutton. It stops me from telling him about having another memory of him—one of us in a bedroom in the dark no less.

My heart remembers what my mind can't, and it's waging a war inside of me. How can someone feel so familiar yet like a stranger? Nothing about the memories of Luka are awkward, not like being with him now, how things feel so new, like this is the first time we've touched. Like this is the first time we've ever been close enough to feel the warmth of each other's breaths, though I know it isn't. My attraction to him runs far deeper than noticing how handsome he is even wearing a hospital gown with messy hair and dark circles under his eyes.

Shifting, I turn to face Luka. His eyes meet mine, the curtain covering both our heads so no one can see us from the outside. We're lying so close together that our noses almost touch. He laces his fingers with mine, holding our hands between us. A million silent thoughts cross his mind, but he doesn't share any with me. I wish he would.

It's like getting tiny glimpses of him in my memory isn't enough. I want to know everything. Feel everything. It's frustrating that I can't. It's even worse that he won't tell me. What if he's hiding something? What if something happened between us? There was a reason he was here before me and that we weren't together. From the glimpses of memories, I know I'd have fought to keep him safe. I'd have never let him out of my sight. I guess something changed.

"Skye." He thinks my name so softly, with such intensity, that I find myself closing the space between us.

Meeting my lips to his, I kiss him. At first he doesn't react, just freezes, and a thousand thoughts consume me thinking maybe my heart is messing with me. That maybe I've missed something despite knowing that he cares enough about me to die for me, to meet me in the stars. But then he kisses me back. He brushes his lips against mine, ever so lightly, just testing me. I lean in closer, wishing with everything in me that his kiss could somehow unlock everything in me. That his kiss could reveal what my life was like, what our lives together meant.

But it's not the key. It doesn't unravel the blanket covering my past to keep it from my present.

And the kiss ends too soon.

With a soft breath, almost like a whispered plea, he pulls away to glance into my eyes. We stare at each other for a long moment, and he lets go of my hand to run his fingers from the skin below my ear to my lips.

"I'm sorry," I think to him. *"I shouldn't have done that. This whole situation is so messed up, and if Caretaker Sienna finds out, who knows what she'll d—"*

He interrupts my thoughts with another kiss. *"You know, I've told you this at least a dozen times before, but you over-think things."*

"What else have you told me?" I ask, a smile playing on my lips because he's opening up more to me.

"That you're infuriating and brave and sometimes a little scary when you're angry."

"I am?"

He chuckles softly. *"You scare Monster Sienna. You scare the Knezha Family…"*

"I do, don't I?"

"It's why I think you came here willingly," he says. *"You'd have never gotten taken otherwise. I know it. I know you. You have a plan somewhere in that unbreakable mind of yours."*

My brows knit together. I can't say for sure, but he might be right. My instincts say his words are true. He's filling in the pieces I can't.

But why? Why would I willingly put myself in this position? For Luka? Maybe. But I think there's more to it. I think this place might contain the answers to the questions I've forgotten about.

I need to figure it all out and remember.

If I don't, then this will probably be the last place I ever see.

CHAPTER 8

SUFFER

"WHAT THE HELL is going on?" Gemma's voice rips me from sleep.

I scramble to sit up without success. Luka's heavy arm drapes over my side, holding me to him so I can't move more than an inch. He doesn't stir at the sound of her voice, but he releases a warm breath on my neck. I know he's awake and doesn't want to move.

"Are you guys crazy?" The lights overhead flicker through the thin sheet. "How did you even get in there, Skye?"

I nudge Luka's hand from my stomach and groan as I sit up. Everything hurts. My head, my shoulders, my back, my stomach. I'm not only sore, but I'm stiff like I've been in the same position for weeks instead of hours.

"Chill out," Luka says for me, sitting up when I do. "The monster put her in here."

I wobble, trying to remain sitting straight, and Luka slides his hand behind me so I can lean against his arm. It's not an obvious gesture, just looks like he's leaning on his hand, but I know he's doing it for me.

"So you slept together?" Gemma asks.

Any sort of response stays locked in my throat. Blush slithers up my chest and into my cheeks. She's technically right. We did *sleep* together. Just not the way she makes it sound.

"Oh, shut up, Gemma," Avery says. "I'm sure you'd curl right up with Luka if given the opportunity."

Her comment makes it worse. It even leaves Luka speechless.

"Fuck off, Avery."

"Oh, sure. Say that when you're way over there."

The lights flicker more, and then the chain-link barrier starts rattling. The whole room shakes around us, sending fear up my stiff back and into my throbbing head. The plant on the bookcase in my room falls onto the floor, potting soil cascading all over the polished concrete.

"God, she's going to make it worse for all of us." Avery's thoughts sneak into my mind, and I automatically shake my head.

"Gemma, Avery, stop!" I yell. "Stop. Why are you even fighting?"

Gemma smacks her hand on the barrier. "Stay out of it."

Linking my fingers to the chain-link, I pull myself to my feet. Luka rises behind me, but then crosses the room to lean against his sink without getting involved. It's not the first time he's kept himself out of the animosity between Gemma and Avery, but this is ridiculous.

"No. You're giving Caretaker Sienna what she wants. You're giving her an excuse to come in here and kill us all again," I say.

The lights return to normal and the room settles. Luka and I aren't the only ones who have acquired something from death. I think both Gemma and Avery have gained some sort of telekinetic ability.

Gemma plops down on her mat. "You know, she'll come here and kill us anyway, even without an excuse."

"So, why have her come sooner?" I ask.

Gemma doesn't respond. I turn my head to glance at Avery, who offers the tiniest smile. Luka doesn't react at all. He remains standing with his arms folded across his chest. I can't tell if he's mad I put a stop to Gemma and Avery's bickering, but he does look slightly disappointed. Maybe because it would've been them the caretaker would've come after, leaving us alone. But I doubt it. I have a feeling it'll be me again regardless.

"Why do you even care about that? It's Avery's turn anyway," Gemma asks after a moment. "We have a schedule."

"Maybe because she's not a selfish bitch," Avery snaps.

"You don't even know her."

"I already know she's better than—"

A memory flashes into my mind, pulling me away from the screaming match. The screams melt to laughter, and I smile at the picture displaying on my phone. A hand slides over my shoulder and tendrils of red hair cascade forward.

"The newbies don't stand a chance against us." A familiar voice rings in my ears. It's Gemma.

I watch myself swipe through a few more photos on the phone, and I can't believe my eyes. All the pictures I scroll through are of me, Gemma, and Avery together.

A finger touches my screen. "This one. Print it. Take it. Don't you dare forget us on your mission," Avery says.

I tilt my head, catching sight of her. Her tight curls bounce with her excited smile. "I won't."

"She should. Mission Luka should totally keep her occupied for as long as possible. Plus, I definitely don't want her to think of me when she—"

We all laugh.

"Shut up!" Luka yells, ripping me right from a memory of the girls in the rooms on both sides of us. I can't even believe it. How? How are they here and don't know me? They were my friends. At least, I think they were my friends. And they knew Luka. They knew whatever was happening that put me in his path on a supposed mission for the mysterious man.

Luka clenches his hands at his sides, and a muscle twitches in his cheek. "You guys have no idea what's going on. Just leave Skye out of your crap. She hasn't done anything to deserve being dragged in the middle of you two."

Or maybe I have.

Gemma raises an eyebrow, looking past me to Avery. "Told you. Sleeping together."

My mouth drops open, and I scowl, the warm and fuzzy feeling created from that blip of a memory with these two girls now fizzled out. "What is your problem? One second you're nice and the next it's like you're some other person."

"Well, we can't all be Miss Sunshine after being repeatedly killed, now can we?"

"And to think I actually tried to escape with plans to help you," I retort.

She rolls her eyes. "Whatever."

"Skye, it's pointless. It'll take another death to snap her out of her attitude," Luka thinks to me.

"Guess I'll have to kill her then."

He chuckles out loud, drawing everyone's attention to him, but he ignores Gemma's glares and Avery's curiosity. Silence falls between everyone, and I ease myself back to the floor even though all I really want is to take another hot shower and try to remember everything I've forgotten. No way I'm doing that now.

Luka follows my lead and sits down across from me, studying me as I shift my position four times, never finding one I like that leaves me comfortable.

"You still in pain?" he asks out loud, and I'm glad he does, because the silence claws under my skin.

I nod. "Yeah, I feel worse today." Glancing down, I take in the bruises traveling up my legs and then notice a bloody spot on the front of my gown. "And I'm pretty sure that's not supposed to happen."

Luka sucks in a breath. "Let me look at it."

I crinkle my nose. "What?" Letting him look at it would require me to lift my gown.

He realizes my hesitation before I even say anything and reaches over to grab the discarded curtain from the mat. I lay it across my lap, covering my legs and waist, and then slowly tug the hem of my hospital gown up.

"Ew, Skye. That's infected," Avery says before Luka can make his unprofessional diagnosis.

"She's right," Luka says.

"I guess it's back to the healing box for you," Gemma chimes in.

Her words send icy fear straight through me. The last time I was in the healing box was torture being unable to move, hear, or see. I'd rather not go through that again. Ridiculous to say this, but I'd rather die.

Narrowing his eyes, Luka burns Gemma a look. "Shut up. You're not helping." His eyes soften when he brings them back to me. "It's not that bad. Monster Sienna has access to antibiotics. I doubt she'd really waste more time on something that could be fixed with medication."

I don't know who to believe. Either way, I'll find out soon. The familiar squeak of tennis shoes draws my attention away from my inflamed stomach and to the dark corridor. I automatically drop my gown down and scoot away from the door and back to the mat. Luka remains in place, nearly blocking me.

Caretaker Sienna would have to get through Luka to get to me if we decided to put up a fight.

"Mornin'," Caretaker Sienna says, wheeling in a cart with food trays on them. How the others even accept them to eat baffles me. I want nothing to do with food that could possibly poison me again. That was an awful way to die, though all of my deaths have been pretty bad. "How's everyone doing to-day?"

The caretaker's chipper mood leaves me on edge. It makes her scarier than when she's on guard, waiting for me to threaten her to give her an excuse to hurt me. This is the first time she's gone out of her way to speak to us like human beings and not prisoners or science experiments.

No one responds to her question, and I meet Avery's wide eyes through the barrier. I guess this is definitely not normal, and I'm not the only one suddenly afraid.

"First one to respond to me will get a pass," she says, standing in front of Gemma's door.

"I'm just *great*. How are you?" Gemma asks first. Her words are sharp and full of sarcasm, but Caretaker Sienna isn't fazed by them.

Caretaker Sienna slides a tray of food through the door. "Looks like subject three gets to skip her next turn."

Gemma pumps her fist while crossing the room to grab her food. I roll my eyes at her brilliant smile. You'd think she was offered a ticket out of here.

Wheeling the cart past my empty room, Caretaker Sienna stops in front of Luka's door. Her eyes smile, the corners crinkling, and I'm pretty sure if she wasn't wearing her mask, I would be able to see all her teeth.

"And how are you, Skye?" she asks, using my name. It doesn't go unnoticed because both Gemma and Avery glance at each other from across the room. "I hope you don't mind the sudden shift in living arrangements."

I grimace, showing my bottom teeth, but don't respond to her. This can't be good. It means whatever I heard the man on the phone say yesterday has changed things. If the man knew about Luka before, he might be using him to get to me now.

Because from the short phone conversation where he mentioned my memory, I'm wondering if my losing it was an accident. He said they wanted my memory to come back. Caretaker Sienna assumed it has something to do with the blunt force trauma of the supposed first death on my sheet, the one that brought me here, though I know it wasn't my first and so does Luka. This whole situation is starting to feel like some sort of game, but I don't know the rules.

"Why is she with me?" Luka asks from in front of me, surprising me.

"You two seem to have an interesting connection I'd like to explore," she says, tilting her head. "You bring something out in Skye that we—I have to take advantage of. Plus, I'd thought you'd like her company. You like it, right?"

Luka tenses in front of me. She's baiting him, playing with us. "Can you at least provide us with another mat and curtain?" He doesn't even humor her with a response.

Caretaker Sienna slides two trays in through the slot, one

right after the other. "I suppose that can be arranged." Her gaze shifts to me. "Now, back to my original question. How are you doing, Skye?"

"Fine," I mutter.

"Don't lie," Gemma says from her room. If I could break through the chain-link barrier to smack her, I would. "The wound on her stomach is infected."

"Lift up your gown, Skye," Caretaker Sienna says.

I hold myself protectively. "No."

She narrows her eyes. "Would you like to die of an infection? It's a terrible way to go."

"Yeah, whatever," I say.

"Subject four." Her sharp tone makes me wince, though I still don't comply. If she wants to inspect the wound she caused, she can open up the door and come in here to check for herself.

She touches the chain on the door, and I expect her to do just that, but then she drops her arms to her sides. "I'll take subject three's word for it and bring you an antibiotic," she adds.

I hold my expression even, despite feeling like screaming out in frustration. My attempt to irritate her and make her lose composure failed. I know the more emotional she gets, the more mistakes she makes, the more she lets me into her head. She's trying to break me, but if I can break her first... I'm counting on her making a mistake. I'm counting on her to give me a second chance to best her.

She moves on from Luka's—now our—room and stands in front of Avery's. Messing with the chain, she unlocks the door. It's then that I realize there are no more food trays on the cart.

Gemma was right. It is Avery's turn.

"Subject three, stand up and come to me," Caretaker Sienna says.

Without a fight, Avery gets to her feet and shuffles across the room. She glances once over her shoulder at me, and I pout my bottom lip. Unlike Gemma, she doesn't resist at all. It's sad that she's come to a point where she's accepted this is how her life is now. That there's nothing she can do.

That has to change.

But how?

Before I have a chance to get up the nerve to say something, Luka twists around to look at me. His serious gaze locks onto mine, stopping me from instigating Caretaker Sienna to take me instead. I didn't realize I wanted all her attention until now. Because if I have it, I'd have a better chance of figuring things out. I could stop her.

"You need to take a break, Skye. You can't come back from death if your body is damaged beyond repair," he thinks to me.

Narrowing my eyes, I lean closer to him and think, *"I can handle it, and who cares if I can't. I'm getting out of here one way or another."*

"If you guys start making out, I'm going to throw up," Gemma says from her room, drawing my attention away from Luka.

"Ignore her," he thinks to me.

I smirk at Luka. "Wanna make out?"

Luka cracks up, a smile lighting his face brighter than the harsh fluorescent lighting above us. I'm sure that was the last thing he expected me to say, but I can't help myself. Gemma annoys the crap out of me, and I can't help wondering about the tiny memory I have of her. The moment we were friends. Because now? I want to kiss Luka just to spite her, though the idea of kissing Luka again is more appealing by the second when I trail my gaze from his dark eyes to his full bottom lip.

My suddenly serious gaze wipes the smile off his face, and I'm pretty sure he's thinking about last night, too.

Gemma heaves a sigh and slaps her hands against the chain-links. "I swear to God if you even consider it, I'm going to sc—"

"Subject four," Caretaker Sienna says from the hallway, stealing away the lightheartedness of the moment. I hadn't even heard her coming. "I have your antibiotics. Take one every twelve hours. I'll leave the bottle in case I can't make it back here tonight."

"You're leaving?" I ask.

She opens the slot in the door and drops the bottle of pills through. Next, she shoves in a rolled up mat and a white sheet instead of a curtain. "I'll be back tomorrow at the latest. You have enough food on your trays to last you until then just in case."

I get to my feet and limp past Luka to stare at Caretaker Sienna through the door. "What about Avery?"

"What about her?" she asks.

"You can't just—"

"Subject four, that's enough."

"But—"

"Skye, stop. Don't worry about Avery," Luka says into my mind.

Caretaker Sienna straightens her shoulders. "Last warning, subject four."

"You can't just leave!" I scream, ignoring both Luka and the caretaker. The fierce need to look out for the girl I barely know now but suddenly feel protective over pushes away my good senses. I slam my hands against the door, shaking it on its frame. It barely moves. I hurt myself more than anything, but I don't let it stop me.

Pounding my fists over and over again, I release all the pent up rage I've been carrying around since Caretaker Sienna stabbed me and threw me down the stairs. I can't help it. She can't just leave us locked up with a promise to return. It'd take nothing short of a miracle to break out if she didn't come back. And Avery? Where is she? What if she leaves her in the freezer or something? How horrible. The Knezhas are monsters. Does that mean I was a monster?

Strong hands reach around my waist, pulling me away from the door. The pressure of Luka's fingers sends fire bursting in my torso as he accidentally touches my infected wound. He releases me when my angry yells turn into a high-pitched screech, but I push past the pain and rush forward.

Caretaker Sienna has the door already open, and I charge at her even with the black canister she aims at me. It's new, different from the metallic one, but I don't even care.

"Skye!" Luka yells from behind me, but I don't listen.

His hands lace around my arms this time, pulling me back.

It doesn't stop Caretaker Sienna from pressing her thumb on the nozzle. A stream of liquid hits me directly in the face, and my eyes burn while the rest of my skin stings like I press my face into the snow without it numbing from cold. Luka coughs from behind me, pulling us both back into his room.

The edges of my vision blur, and I bow forward and dry heave. I heave so hard that it feels like my insides are ripping free to come out, but something stops them. And then, suddenly, I'm blind as my eyes swell shut.

"I warned you, subject four," Caretaker Sienna says from somewhere behind me. "I didn't want to have to do this, but you need to learn your place. And look what you've done to poor subject one. He has to suffer with you." She clicks her tongue.

I turn in the direction of Luka and see his blurry form sitting on the ground in front of me. Kneeling, I reach out and touch his shoulder and move my hands down his arm until I reach his fingers. Whatever new crap she carries is more unpleasant than anything she's done to us so far. I guess since I pulled myself so easily from death the last time she made sure she had something new this time. Something I won't want to experience ever again. And she was right.

I cough. My throat tightens, and I'm unable to breathe. Luka squeezes my hand, my head pounding, my whole body shuddering.

Five.

I fall over.

Four.

I drop Luka's hand.

Three.

I lose feeling in my body.

Two.

My heart stops.

"Time of death: Eight twenty-three A.M."

CHAPTER 9

REMEMBER

"**L**OOK WHAT ARRIVED today." The familiar woman, with her long hair twisted into a bun and her toffee eyes lined with black eyeliner and heavy shadow, drapes a gown against her chest. "It was designed for your ceremony. You'll be stunning."

Stepping forward, I close the distance and run my fingers over the soft, gray-blue material the same color of my eyes. "I never thought that the last thing I might ever wear would be something like this. You sure I can't wear jeans and a T-shirt. It's *my* birthday celebration."

The woman scowls at me. "Don't talk like that. Your journey will not end with you in a party dress. And it's not your birthday celebration, Skye. It is your Acquiring Ceremony and your time to step through the door and shine like all those stars in our eternity."

"If I am who you think I am," I mutter.

"You are. My visions don't deceive me. It's you who'll grow our family and help us thrive among this life and the next. Our journeys didn't collide for no reason. You have to believe that. Now, I want you to open the door for me just like we've practiced."

I close my eyes, the world turning dark around me. It's in this moment I realize that the woman isn't real, and I'm lost in another memory brought on by my death. Snapping my eyes open, I stare around me at the galaxy world, all images of the familiar woman now gone.

"No," I whisper. "Please, let me remember. Please."

"Skye?" Luka's soft voice tugs at me, and I blink tears from my eyes. "Are you okay?"

Something about the memory of the woman stabs right into my heart, leaving me depressed and lonely even with Luka hovering right next to me.

I sniffle. "Yeah, it was just another memory."

"Of me?"

I shake my head. "A woman. I don't know her name, but she was taking care of me. Do you know her?"

Luka's brows pinch together. "You never talked about your mother. All I know is she died when you were little."

"It wasn't my mother. She was like us. She mentioned

some sort of ceremony that was supposed to happen."

"You never mentioned her. When you came to my door, you were alone and had run away from—" He snaps his mouth closed like he doesn't want to tell me everything he knows.

I roll over to face him. The stars glitter all around us, reflecting sparks of light in Luka's dark eyes. "Stop that," I say.

"What?"

"Stop keeping things from me, Luka. Please, I have to know. Maybe it'll help me," I say.

He sighs. "It might also hurt you."

Anger rushes through me. Luka has no right to keep my past from me even if it's what the mysterious man and Caretaker Sienna want. And I'm not the only one feeling this way. A wave of negative energy swirls over me from Luka, and I want nothing to do with them. I've already been through enough. This world was meant to strip the awfulness of life away not allow it to cling onto me. It feels like my life and death colliding with me in the middle of the destruction.

"Well, *you* are hurting me, Luka," I snap. I know it's unfair, but I can't help it. "You know, I get these tiny fragments of my time with you before, and these little memories make me feel like we belong together. But then the second it's over, and I'm back here, I can't help but wonder if it's all in my head. If I'm making up some past with you because I'm losing my mind or something."

He reaches out and grabs my hand. "You're not losing your mind, Skye, and I'd give anything for you to remember every-thing we were together, but I can't just tell you about your life for you. I refuse to put you through that kind of pain when your mind decided it was time for you to finally escape it."

"You make it sound like I had some horrible life before, but it can't be any worse than the life I'm living right now. Look what Caretaker Sienna did to us. She was going to leave us locked away, and Avery—"

"Is fine, Skye." He glances at me in his peripheral vision. "If you would've listened to me, I could have told you that. We could still be together, finally getting a damn break from the monster, but you—"

"So this is my fault? You have no idea whether or not Avery would be fine. I know I don't know her well, but I did once. I can't sit back and accept what Caretaker Sienna does without a fight."

"But you have to pick your fights, Skye. And let me help you. If you would've listened to me, I could've told you she was taking Avery with her. Something you would've known had you not acted so impulsively. Now, who knows what's going to happen to us. She could leave us in the freezer," he says, he doesn't ask me about knowing Avery, and I wonder how much he knew. I know Avery and Gemma don't. I think if they did, they'd have said something. We couldn't all have been together. But Caretaker Sienna did something to them to make me stand alone...yet they gave me Luka.

I huff a breath, his words swirling through my mind. "Well, I'm sorry, Luka. I never imagined Caretaker Sienna would take any of us out of here. What about you? Have you gotten to leave? Do you think Avery will try to get help?"

"Avery's been broken. She won't help us," he says.

I groan. "This is all too much. I can't do this. I'm staying here in the stars. You can't make me go back."

"You're seriously doing this? Giving up? And what about me?"

A memory flashes through my mind, pulling me into myself and away from Luka's hurt expression. The memory feels so real that I can smell the pine trees reaching for the azure sky outside our opened cabin door.

I glare at Luka, who hovers in the doorway, blocking my path to exit. He presses his hands against the frame, taking up the whole space with his broad shoulders. I close the distance between us, nearly pressing into him to get into his face. His jaw clenches, his eyes slits, and he shakes his head at me.

"What about me?" His low voice hums through the air.

"I'm doing this for you," I say. "Why can't you see that?" Doing what? I wish I knew. I wish so desperately that the memory would spell it all out for me. That I ask him what I was doing for him. Figure out why we were arguing.

The room shifts as I lean up. I close my eyes and kiss Luka, but I can't feel the sensation. I'm trapped in the girl I was before without any control. The familiar gesture pulls at my very soul, causing my heart to race.

I want nothing more than to stay stuck in this memory. It's better than the memory of the woman and the dress. Because every time I remember the woman, it not only stirs happiness within me, it also awakens something darker. Sorrow. Deep down, I know something happened to her, and since I never mentioned her to Luka, I'm sure that the something that had happened to her was terrible.

But with Luka, the memories only unchain desire—more than that maybe. It's an intense need. A need to replay every second over and over. A need to forget the present and stay locked in the past, because I want to relive the past, experience everything I've forgotten. I yearn for the memory to loop over and over again in my mind. But it fades away, and I'm left staring at Luka's questioning eyes.

"Skye?" he whispers. "Where'd you go?"

I blink a few times. "Nowhere."

"You were with me but weren't."

I extend my hand out and brush my fingers along the side of his face. "I had another memory. We were in a cabin, and I think we were arguing. I wanted to leave. You wanted me to stay. You asked me the same question...what about you?" My voice trails off as I play the new memory again in my mind, skipping over the bad stuff to think about the kiss. My heart beating. The desire it stirred within me.

"Always circles with you, Skye," he says, a new lightness to his voice. "Yet, you still manage to surprise me."

"So, did I stay?" I move my hand from his face to lace my fingers with his. In this galaxy world among the stars, I'm closer to Luka than ever, like our very souls touch here.

He brings both our hands back to his face, pressing the back of mine into his cheek, needing to feel me close to him. I let him. "I wish you did."

I pout my bottom lip. I'm starting to really dislike the old me. "Why?"

He doesn't respond, but the answer plasters across his face in the form of a frown.

"Please, you have to tell me what happened. Give me something. Anything." I squeeze my eyes shut, begging the locked memories to break free. I've never wanted something so much, not even to stay here.

"If you had stayed, I wouldn't have followed you," he finally says.

"You mean..." I sigh. "Was this all my fault, Luka?" I don't even know why I ask.

"No, it was mine." He might not blame me, but something shifts in his dark eyes, and I just know it was my fault. I know it is. I know he's here because of me, because of something I did. I'm afraid I'm the reason for Avery and Gemma, too.

"Luka," I say.

"It doesn't matter."

"It does to me."

He tugs me closer by my arm. "Then remember."

"I can't," I whisper.

"And I can't stay here." His words awaken something within me. The same intense desire I got from the memory. Every molecule on my body buzzes—grabs hold of me, making it impossible to consider staying here without Luka. If he goes, I must follow. I have to. I can't leave everything as it is. I need to remember. But I can't do that on my own.

"Neither can I," I say after a moment. "Not without you."

He smiles. All the stars in our galaxy take on the light from within him and reflect it out through our universe, lighting everything brighter than ever before. It leaves the void where the door to life awaits a cold, foreboding contrast. I let Luka pull me toward it anyway.

Five.

The galaxy disappears.

Four.

I hear the sound of running water.

Three.

Pain settles through my body.

Two.

My heart starts beating.

"Time of life: Ten fifty-five A.M. You hear me, Skye? Ten fifty-five. You better remember that for your log."

I gasp, bolting upright. Freezing water sprays my face, and I accidentally inhale. Coughing, I lean forward and clutch my knees, trying to orient myself. We must have stayed in the galaxy world for longer than I thought. There, it felt like minutes. But hours have passed.

I rub my hands over my eyes, flicking water away. "Luka?" My voice sounds through the open room, and it takes me a minute to realize I'm exactly where Caretaker Sienna left me.

"Welcome back, Skye," Gemma says from her room two over.

It's then that I realize that Caretaker Sienna isn't here. It wasn't she who announced my arrival back into life but Gemma.

"I can't believe Caretaker Sienna was right," she says, locking her fingers to the chain-link barrier. "She said you guys would come back without her help."

I grimace, ignoring her. Luka lies on his stomach, his cheek pressed to the shiny concrete floor right over the drain so the water just flows out of our room. Slowly getting to my feet, I cross the room and shut off the faucet.

Whatever chemical Caretaker Sienna sprayed on us rinsed off with the water. Luka's face is tinted pink and one of his eyes looks a little swollen, but there doesn't seem to be any other lasting effects.

I kneel down next to him and shake his shoulders. "Luka, come on. Wake up."

A few minutes pass, my heart pounding in my head the entire time. Luka finally groans, and I pull his head into my lap, brushing the sopping strands of his blond hair from his face. He reaches up and rubs his swollen eye for a second and then he blinks.

"You're okay. You're with me," I whisper, tracing my fingers along his cheek.

Blood seeps from the front of his shirt, startling me, stealing my breath away. Panic rises in my stomach. I press my hands against his chest, trying to staunch the wound. Tears seep from my eyes and drip onto his forehead. He's losing color fast. And I can't stop the bleeding. It's turning the melting snow crimson. Snow? *This isn't real. It's a memory. Everything's okay.*

I can't push the memory away. I can't do anything except watch Luka bleed out in my arms. He's as cold as I am, and no matter how hard I press my hands against the bloody hole in his

T-shirt, the bleeding doesn't stop. He's dying without me, and I can't mend his body.

"Luka!" I scream, my voice echoing through the quiet forest. "You promised me! Never alone." A string of curse words shortly follow. I beg and plead for him to hold on. I beg and plead for the universe not to take him away from me.

He convulses under me, and I run my bloody hands to his face, pulling him closer like I can somehow make it all stop if I hold onto him tight enough. But nothing I do, nothing I say, stops Luka from dying.

"Why did you follow me?" I ask, anger lacing my words. "You shouldn't have followed me."

His mouth opens and shuts, his dark eyes wide and afraid. And then, he takes his last breath, tearing my whole universe apart. Everything within me crumbles piece by piece. A sob wracks my chest, and I shake him a few dozen times more.

"Please, you have to remember the way. Remember, Luka," I say.

A branch snaps in the forest behind me, and I spin to look through the trees. Something has me on my feet, but I can't remember what it was. The memory of the emotions—grief and heartache, fear and full blown panic consume me. This is not a memory I want. *Make it stop!*

I twist, searching the ground for something. Whatever it is I'm looking for is important enough for me to abandon Luka's body.

I spot something black in the snow. A gun. *My* gun. I shot Luka. I know I did.

Yet I still pick it up and aim it at the forest, the sound of my heart beating the only thing I can now hear in the memory.

I glance down at Luka, his glassy eyes staring past me, and then I aim the gun in the direction my senses tell me our cabin is located and pull the trigger. Turning on my feet to run, I leave Luka dead in the snow. I don't have a choice. Someone is coming through the forest.

I don't look back, and I don't stop until I end up on a desolate road.

Then I scream.

"Skye? Skye! Please, what's wrong? You have to tell me what's wrong." Luka's voice rings in my ears, ripping me from the memory. My own voice echoes through the room with my screams. I didn't even realize I was doing it.

My breath comes fast and ragged. I can't gasp deep enough to calm my nerves. Gemma stands silently with her mouth agape, just watching me from her room exactly where I last saw her. The memory of Luka's oncoming death before he ended up here was so intense it felt real. I was reliving it all over again, and it ripped me open to pour me out all over the water-drenched concrete.

"Skye," Luka says again.

I can't find my words so I just fling my arms around him, half crawling into his lap to bury my face against his chest. He holds me without a word, petting my soaked hair from my face with one hand while drawing small circles on my back with the other.

I cover my face with my hands. "I shot you," I whisper so

softly that even Luka might not hear. "Why did I shoot you?"

"It wasn't your fault," he thinks to me instead of saying the words out loud.

"You're here because of me," I think back. *"If I hadn't have shot you, we'd have never ended up here."*

"Caretaker Sienna would've gotten me regardless, Skye. It was only a matter of time before they came looking." He squeezes me tighter. *"If it weren't for you, she'd have found me even sooner."*

"What about me?" I ask.

He subtly shakes his head. *"You were always good about covering your tracks and keeping your mind closed to people like us. But I slipped up."*

"Who was I, Luka? I didn't even know I could shoot a gun."

"You can throw a mean punch, too. Knocked me on my ass a dozen times." He smiles at whatever memories of us together he has and I don't. I wish I could look deeper into his mind so I can sort through them myself.

"What the hell are both of your malfunctions?" Gemma asks, pulling us away from our telepathic conversation with each other. "Death really mess you up this time?"

I release a long, shuddering breath. "Something like that. I'm okay now."

"You don't look okay. You look like hell," she quips.

"Not like I need to impress anyone," I retort, darting my gaze to Luka.

I suddenly feel self-conscious, especially with how close our bodies are with only the thin, drenched hospital gowns separating our skin. Luka's muscles tighten, and without having to read his thoughts, I know he's as aware as I am. He doesn't move to let me go. He actually shifts to turn us away from Gemma's judgmental gaze.

"I swear, if you guys even think about—"

"Shut up, Gemma," Luka says. "I don't want to hear it."

I don't either, but I don't say it. I refuse to even look in her direction. And I won't, not unless she goes through another death-induced attitude adjustment.

"Whatever," she says.

Luka holds me tighter against him, like I'll somehow wash from his arms and down the drain if he were to accidentally let me go. And I allow him, feeling his heart beat on my shoulder and the warmth of his body smothering the chill from my bones.

We don't move or say anything for a few minutes, just being together, feeling each other near. It helps extinguish the turmoil rolling through me that came with the memory of what I had done to him—how I shot him in the middle of a forest and then left him there. How could I do such a thing? Especially if we were together. I don't even love—at least I don't remember if I love—Luka now, and I don't think I'd be heartless enough to leave him. The old Skye, the me I now wish I would stop remembering, felt something for Luka. I ran away with him and then lived with him. But I abandoned him. And I don't even know why. Who was I?

Warm breath tickles my ear, and Luka finally shifts to put me on the mat beside him. I wish he didn't, though. I wish I could remain in his embrace until my heart stops beating...again. Because now that I sit on the cold, damp mat, I'm forced to meet his dark eyes. And he uses them against me, locking me in his brooding stare like he can read every single thought rushing through my mind in this very moment.

He doesn't say anything if he does. Instead, he pushes to his feet and picks up the dripping curtain from the floor to hang it back up. He pulls it across the chain-link divider until I can no longer feel Gemma's glare burning into the back of my head. Luka then takes the sheet Caretaker Sienna gave us and ties it in front of us, blocking the door, surrounding us in dripping fabric. And because Avery kept her curtain up, we're completely blocked from the camera on the wall.

It's almost as if we're alone.

Without a word, Luka takes his place beside me, leaning his back against the curtain and chain-link barrier, making it rattle under his weight. I turn my gaze to the now sheer fabric of my hospital gown as it clings to my thighs, but I don't pull it to cover my knees.

"Do you want to talk about it?" Luka's voice slides into my mind, and I release a heavy sigh at his words. Should I? Do I even want to go there?

"Yes." The thought was intended for me, but I accidentally project it to Luka.

"You have to know I don't blame you. I shouldn't have been following you. I knew better. But I was afraid," he thinks to me.

Scrunching my brows, I crane my neck to peek at him. *"For good reason, apparently. Why did I have a gun? What was I doing? Why didn't I—"* I suck in a deep breath, gathering the thoughts I want to share with him but am too afraid to even think.

"Why didn't you stay?" he asks for me.

I nod.

"Because there was nothing you could do for me."

"But I should've stayed. You wouldn't be in here if I just stayed," I think.

He doesn't respond right away because he knows I'm right. It's not like he could know what I was thinking either. I bet he's been asking himself the same question ever since he ended up here. I can't imagine what he's been thinking about. I don't even know why he's even sitting next to me, close enough to touch, but still giving me the space he thinks I need.

"Don't beat yourself up over it, Skye. You always had good reasons for doing stuff, and I know you would have stayed if you could've."

"How do you not hate me?"

His mouth presses into a thin line, and he turns his gaze away from me. *"I just don't."*

"You should. I shot you. I left you."

"But you came back for me," he says.

I grimace. *"How do you even know? What if I ended up here like you? What if I had just moved on?"*

"I know you, Skye. You found me after my first death, and I knew you'd find me again."

"But do you really know me? I never even told you about my first death. And look how long it's taken for me to get here? That is, if I even came here for you."

"You did come for me." He sounds so certain.

"You don't know that!"

He rubs his eyes. *"Neither do you."*

Nothing I can say will ever make Luka doubt me even for a second. Even after everything. And it pisses me off. He sees something in me that I can't. Not from my memories. Not now in this room. Something that has him trying to comfort me, assure me. But what if I don't deserve any of it? After the last memory, I'm certain I don't.

"Luka, I don't want to think about this anymore. Seeing you—remembering what I did—it hurts. Even though I know you're alive and sitting next to me, I still feel the grief I felt that day. It's just that this is so hard. Every time I try to remember more, I hit a wall. And then I think that maybe it's better if I don't remember anything from before."

"Even us?"

"Yes, even us. Because I'm not who you remember. I don't know if I ever was this person you remember or if I can ever be her."

He doesn't respond, and I can feel his intense gaze boring into the side of my face. I can't bear to look at him. This is all too confusing. The memories, how easy Luka is to forgive me for something so horrible. How I'm locked away only God knows where with death hanging over my head all the time. Death I keep escaping. Death that keeps unlocking the memories that have been stolen from me.

Wrapping my arms around my legs, I rest my chin on my cool knees. My stomach still throbs, my back and shoulder still aching. I'm pretty sure my head is going to explode at any second to scatter what's left of me onto the concrete floor, and even then, I still won't be able to see who I was—who I am.

"Skye…"

I stay frozen, just letting the cold soak into my bones.

"Skye, please. Talk to me."

I shake my head. *"No. I can't. I can't do this."*

The mat squeaks as Luka's damp body shifts on it. *"Can I just hold you then? You're shivering."*

All I can do is nod.

His arms slide around my back. He pulls me close until he cradles me on his lap, and I can rest my head against his chest. Rubbing his hand up and down my arm, he smoothes out the goosebumps from my cold skin and doesn't stop until my teeth stop chattering.

Luka hums softly in my ear, and I close my eyes.

"It's going to be okay," Luka thinks into my mind.

I don't respond to him. No matter how much I want to believe him, I'm not sure I can believe in anything in this moment except that death is coming again. And it'll keep coming unless I figure out who I was before. Because I think only she has the answers.

CHAPTER 10

SOUL MATE

"**Y**OU CAME," I say, sitting on a park bench under the bright, white-hot sun.

Sweat gleams on Luka's forehead. His chest heaves as he bends forward to grip his legs for a moment. He's been running. I know all too well what that looks like, because I've been running for a while.

"I told you I would," Luka says, straightening his back. His tall figure blocks out the sun from behind him, casting a shadow over me, but it does nothing to cool the humid air on this record-high temperatures summer day.

I shrug. "Wasn't sure you'd believe me."

"Still not sure if I do," he says.

I laugh. "Good. You should never be too trusting. It'll only get you into trouble."

"I have a feeling you'll do that to me whether or not I trust you." A smile plays on his full lips, and I lean back, taking in the rest of him—his broad shoulders, his messy blond hair, his dark eyes, his worn tennis shoes, and the small cluster of holes on the hem of his plain green T-shirt. Even though his clothes have seen better days—so have mine for that matter—he's still as cute as he was when I rang his doorbell to ask him to meet me here.

"Possibly."

Something's different about this memory. It's like seeing Luka standing before me unlocks information within me that I haven't known until this very moment. Without reliving our first memory, I can still see his face after I rang his doorbell. He looked like he saw a ghost, or maybe like he thought he was losing his mind, because really, how else is someone supposed to react when a girl he's only met between life and death shows up to ask him to run away with her.

"So what now?" Luka asks, pulling me from my thoughts.

"We get out of this town and never look back," I say, getting to my feet.

"And you'll tell me everything? You'll teach me more about being an acquired?"

I nod. "Yes. I'll teach you just as I was taught." *Because you're my soul mate.* It's the first time I've heard a memory of what I was thinking. Luka doesn't react, so I know I didn't think it to him in this moment, but the words hold such an importance that I'd do anything to convince him to run with me.

"By who?"

Angelica. "It's not important."

"Why not?"

I don't respond to him. I can't. Grief pulls at my heart thinking about Angelica. Without even having to put a name to the face, I know Angelica was my guardian and the woman from my memory. She knew I was special and was partly responsible for turning me into an acquired. She showed me the door into the galaxy world even before I needed it, because she died and came back to life long before me. She sought me out to join her family, though I can't remember much more.

"Did something happen?" Luka asks, filling the silence.

I nod. "I don't like to talk about it."

"I get it. We just met. Maybe some other time," he says. I guess that other time never did come.

I hold out my hand to Luka, and he takes it, helping me to my feet. Sweat drips from my hairline and onto my forehead, the sun feeling like it's getting hotter by the second. "Thanks for understanding. I know all this has to be hard. I just hope you can trust me."

"Would it be weird if I told you I already do? I just—" He doesn't finish his sentence, but I somehow know he was going to say that he felt connected to me—because I feel it. I've felt it from the moment we met in the stars. Even now.

"It's not weird," I say, squeezing his hand.

"Skye! Skye, wake up!"

Luka's voice rings in my mind. I bolt upright, disoriented and confused. The curtains surrounding us have dried along with the concrete floor and our gowns. But something's wrong. I'm still cold. I shiver, groaning, and rub my hands into my eyes.

"You're burning up, Skye," Luka says. It takes me a minute to realize he's standing over me.

My neck aches when I look up at him. "I'm freezing."

"Damn it!" His voice rises through the quiet air. He rips the sheet from where he hung it, frantically peering around our small room, searching for something. He knocks everything off the top of his bookshelf onto the floor. The new wildness in his eyes frightens me.

"Stop it, Luka." I reach out to pull the sheet from the floor to drape over me. My stomach screams with the movement, and I release a loud cry.

Luka rushes to my side. I don't even have time to protest when he yanks up my gown to inspect my stomach. Shadows edge my vision. Pus oozes from the glued wound on my stomach, the skin around it puffy and red.

"That's disgusting," Gemma says from her room.

I can't even look at it again. I'll either pass out or throw up if I do. And now that I did get a good look at it, it hurts like hell. Even more so than it did.

"Where did you put the antibiotics, Skye?" Luka asks, carefully lowering my gown again. A huge stain covers the front of me.

I close my eyes, trying to think, but I can't remember. "I

don't know."

Luka tears the room apart, shifting the curtain, moving the mats, checking the counter. He even dumps out the potted plant, piling the soil near the door. But the pill bottle is gone. Caretaker Sienna could've just taken it away to spite me, to make me suffer for standing up against her. Now, I'm pretty sure I'll die. And horribly.

"Where are they, Gemma? Did the monster take them back?" Luka asks, drawing his attention away from me.

"I don't think so," she says, a new softness to her voice that wasn't there when I fell asleep.

Luka laces his fingers behind his head and peers around again. I groan, shifting to my side, resting my head on my arm. I stare into Avery's empty room and see the orange pill bottle on its side against the concrete wall.

"I found them," I say from the mat.

Luka releases a breath, turning to me. "Thank God. Let me get you some water."

I rub my dry lips together. "I don't have them."

"What?" he asks.

I tilt my chin to Avery's room. "Over there."

A string of swear words escapes Luka's mouth. He links his fingers through the metal barrier and shakes it a few dozen times, like if he rattles it hard enough, he could break through. I almost think he can, but after a few minutes, he stops. Blood drips onto the floor from his fingers, and he wipes his hands on the hem of his hospital gown.

"Gemma, you can get them," Luka says glancing from me

to her.

"I don't know what you're talking about," she says. I'm in too much pain to look at her. Her mat squeaks, and I think she might've turned away from him.

"Gemma, please," he says. "She's going to die."

"We all die, Luka," Gemma says. "*God, he knows if Monster Sienna finds out that I can control my telekinesis, I'll never get left alone.*"

"Luka, it's fine," I say, grinding my teeth as I roll onto my back. Black starbursts dance across my vision.

"It's not fine." His voice rises through the air. "She can help you, but she's nothing but a coward."

"Shut up, Luka," Gemma says. "I don't even know why you care so much. You met Skye, like what, a few days ago? Now you're acting like you're in love with her."

"Fuck off," he says, slamming his hands on the barrier. "You just wait. When you need help, we're going to sit back and do nothing."

"What—"

Everything goes black, cutting off what Gemma was saying. All I can hear is the pounding in my head.

"*Skye. Skye, wake up.*" Luka's voice tugs at my consciousness.

I open my eyes just enough to peek at him through my lashes.

"I need to cool you down, Skye," he says out loud. "This is going to be uncomfortable."

Luka covers me in a wet sheet, one he must've soaked in

the sink, and I thrash on my mat. My teeth chatter, making it incredibly hard to even form words or thoughts. Tears drip onto my cheeks. All I do is stare at Luka kneeling next to me.

"Hold on, Skye. Please, just don't die before Monster Sienna gets back. This might be a test. She might be trying to see how far death can take you and if you're strong enough to come back. I can't lose you again."

"I can't lose you." The memory comes hard and fast, Luka's words resonating within me, but they're now in my voice.

Luka sits across from me in a booth, a plate with a cheeseburger and fries between us. He cuts the burger with a steak knife and hands half over to me, though I just set it back on the plate without taking my eyes from him. I won't eat it. Luka must've realized fast that I was a vegetarian.

The whole restaurant bustles with life, but I can't hear anyone talking. Most of the faces are just blurs. Nameless, faceless, meaningless bystanders out for a meal like me and Luka. Except I notice a man. His face is clear as day, and he sits alone in a booth across the room near the door. My gaze doesn't stay on his for long, just a quick glance. But he stirs something within me—something dark, something indescribable unlike the grief brought on from the memory of Angelica, even from the memory of shooting Luka.

"You're not going to lose me," Luka says before taking a bite of the cheeseburger. "You couldn't even if you tried. You know I'll follow you anywhere. Chase you if I have to."

Like the memories before, this one feels utterly real, like I'm living in the moment. If it weren't for my inability to control anything, I'd think I'd magically transported myself here. I can smell the scent of the pickles Luka tosses onto the plate for me, hear the ice clanking in his glass of water as he brings it to his lips, feel the warmth of his fingers when he reaches out to touch me.

His words bring a smile to my lips. "You'll never have to chase me."

"Good, because you're a helluva fast runner."

I grin again and shift my gaze around the room, catching sight of the only man in focus. He stares at me intently, his blue eyes stopping me from turning back to Luka who now links his fingers with mine.

"Skye?" he asks. "What's wrong?"

"We need to leave," I say. "Get up and walk to the kitchen. There will be an exit out the back. I'll meet you at the car." Reaching down, I dig into my bag, feeling the cool metal of an object. A gun. The weight feels familiar in my hand, like I've held it a dozen times. In this memory, it doesn't freak me out, not like in the memory in the snowy forest. It feels safe and not horribly dangerous. Safe because I sense that it's protected me countless times.

"I can help you," Luka says.

The world blurs as I shake my head. "No, if you try, I will lose you. I know it. What you need to do is get to the car. If I'm not there in five, I want you to leave."

"What about you?"

"I'll find you. I promise."

"Skye."

"I *will* find you. Please, go now."

We stand at the same time and cross paths, him strolling toward the kitchen behind me and me in the direction of the front door where the man now stands. The man's outside before I make it across the room, and I break out into a sprint. Whoever the man is, the need to catch up to him is the only thing I can remember. It's all that's important in this specific moment. But who is he? His familiarity claws at my mind, but I can't get his name to stick out for me to recall.

The second I'm out the door, a figure pops up in my peripheral vision. I raise the gun without caring who sees me. The man, with his ridiculously blue eyes, holds his hands up in the air while pressing his lips into a thin line.

"Put the gun down. I just want to talk, Skye," the man says, his voice familiar. He knows me. And I know him. It's the man that's been haunting my memory, the one who's been interested in Luka. Just staring at him in this memory makes me uneasy.

"You shouldn't be here. Luka's not ready." The words come from my mouth, but I can't remember the context behind them. The memory of the diner, of Luka leaving out the back, of this strangely familiar man, starts breaking up.

"I'm here to warn you," he says. "The only safe place for you and Luka is with me. There has been trouble—"

"Don't. I can handle myself. Angelica made sure of it. So did you. Did you forget already?"

"*Skye,*" Luka's voice cuts through my memory.

I wish I could stay in the memory with the man. I know he

has some of the answers I'm dying to figure out. Along with Luka and Angelica, he's obviously a part of my past, and an important part at that.

"*Skye,*" Luka repeats.

The man's voice whirls over Luka's. "I'd never forget, my beautiful girl. Just be careful. You're so important to me. Your journey is with me and the Knezha Family."

"*Skye? Can you hear me?*" Luka asks.

"My journey is with the Knezha Family," I murmur.

A hot hand covers my mouth. "*Don't talk out loud, Skye.*"

"My journey is with the Knezha Family," I mumble again, my lips brushing against Luka's hand.

I can't get the thought from my mind. I should be worried about the people I keep calling family. I'm certain I carried a gun because of them. But I can't piece anything else together. The man, he felt like he was my friend but also my foe. And Luka? What wasn't he ready for?

The memory leaves me in complete confusion.

"Luka," I whisper into his hand. Now that I'm back in reality, I realize just how hard it is for me to speak. How I can't even focus on Luka's figure over me. "Luka."

"*Skye, please. Don't say anything more out loud. Can you do that? Can you just think things to me?*"

I squeeze my eyes shut. "*I know where we are.*" I think to him.

"*You had another memory?*" he asks.

It's like my fever is pulling all my memories from the recesses of my mind. Caretaker Sienna—she is looking for something specific. But I can't remember what. A door? A key? It's something to do with the galaxy. Something she can't access. Something the man can't access without me.

"Think, Skye. Think," I say to myself instead of answering his question. His question isn't important. What's important is that I remember. *"Come on. Think. The Knezha Family. The man. The diner. Angelica? What happened to her? What does Sienna want? Luka? Luka wasn't ready. Have to keep running. Have to stay alive. Don't die. No more dying. Think. Think."*

My mind races with a dozen thoughts, tiny pieces from a life I don't remember. One I need to remember.

"Skye, calm down." Luka's soft voice barely reaches my crowded thoughts.

Still, I ignore him.

"The snow. The blood. So much blood. The car. Driving. Blue eyes. The bullet hole. Trees. The scent of pine. Alone. So alone. Stars. Pain. Luka, stay. Luka, I'll find you. I'll always find you. Don't die. Soul mates. The key. The door. The Knezha Family. Think. Think. Think!"

"Skye!" Luka's voice rips through the air, pulling me from my disoriented thoughts. His warm hands slide under me, and he lifts me from the ground and onto his lap. I blink a few times, the room shadowing over until I close my eyes again and keep them closed.

I jerk uncontrollably in Luka's arms, a shudder gripping my chest. A weird noise sounds through the air, and I realize it's coming from my mouth, but my lips are numb. My feet lose feeling next.

"Skye, stay with me," he pleads.

I don't respond. I can't.

My head fogs.

Five.

The world silences.

Four.

My body turns numb.

Three.

I gasp one last breath.

Two.

My heart stops.

"Time of death: Eleven thirteen A.M."

CHAPTER 11

FATE

THE GALAXY WORLD is as beautiful as ever. But lonely. Oh, so lonely.

I peer around the flickering stars, letting them light up my skin in their ethereal glow. I look around for the void, the door back to the living, but all I see is an endless array of stars. It's in this moment I realize that maybe there's no going back for me.

But Luka.

Luka will live on without you...

"I can't live on if something were to happen to you." The memory hits me like a cool current, dragging me away from the beautiful stars I've grown familiar with and back to the cabin in the woods that feels like home. Feels like Luka and life and everything I know I love, even if it's all still foggy pieces waiting for me to snap together as best as I can.

"You're being dramatic," Luka says from the couch next to me. My legs drape over his, and he rests his hands on my knees. His voice circles me, hugging me in an emotion that seems to be attached to every memory involving him, but it's hard to place. I enjoy it and despise it at once. The feeling leaves my heart racing and the rest of me a ball of nerves—good ones.

I turn and look at him, the room fuzzy around us as I search his dark eyes. "And you're not being serious. If you can't find the way in, you'll never find the way out without me. Now concentrate."

He smirks, his pouty lips just begging for my attention. If I could reach out and graze my finger across them, I would. "That look you're giving me is making it incredibly difficult."

Sighing, I cover my eyes with my hands. I listen to the sound of Luka's quiet breathing without looking at him. I really, really want to look at him, but I can't. The memory won't allow it.

"Give me your hand," I say after a long moment of listening to Luka.

His fingers lace through mine, the recollection feeling utterly real. But I'm not in control. I can't change the past. I can only watch through my eyes like a spy of sorts.

Bringing his hand up, I press his palm to my chest.

"Now you're making it impossible," he says. I can hear the

smile in his voice, which makes my heart beat faster.

"If you keep messing around, I'll go without you," I say.

"You wouldn't."

"Wait for it. Wait for the pause between heart beats."

"Your heart's racing."

"I can still get in. Now let's go."

"Skye? Skye, where are you?" The sound of Luka's voice in my mind pulls me from the memory, leaving me yearning to be back in the cabin, on the couch, in a moment that felt important.

"Skye, I feel you. Answer me."

"I'm right here," I say, my voice sounding through the vast galaxy. "Where are you?"

"Please, don't leave me, okay. Just hold on."

"How are you talking to me? I don't see you. Are you...?"

"I'm alive, and I can't stay long. They'll know. They've been waiting."

"I don't understand."

"I'll explain later. Just please. Don't go anywhere. I can't live without you."

"Luka," I say.

"Promise me."

"Okay, I promise. Now stop being dramatic."

He chuckles softly, his voice fading a moment later, leaving me hovering in the galaxy alone. And being here alone, I realize it was never the galaxy I loved. It was never what brought me peace. It was Luka.

It's always been Luka.

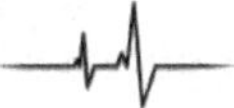

"I've changed my mind, Angelica," I say, hugging myself. "I can't do it."

"We've talked about this already," she says, resting her hands on my shoulders. Having a name to go along with the familiar woman makes her more alive than ever. Her toffee brown eyes hold mine for a long moment. It's the same look she's given me every time I've argued with her about becoming like her—an acquired. I don't know how I know, but I do. "You've already opened the door. Don't be afraid to go through."

But I am afraid. Because beyond the door lies an unfamiliar place no one should come back from unless you're special. Unless your soul figures out a way. And I'll supposedly know it when I see it, at least, that's what Angelica's been telling me for months. There's no definitive proof that I'm meant to join her true family except for a dream she had of me opening a door to the world of stars.

"I'm not afraid. I'm just not sure if I'm ready yet. I'm not sure I'll be successful." I blow strands of blond hair from my face. "I don't want to die a disappointment."

She ties her curly brown hair into a ponytail. "You can't start lacking faith in our eternity now, and we can't waste another year. The family needs you to grow, Skye. You're ready. I promise."

For what? I'll find out soon enough. "That's easy for you to say. Your death was unexpected." The conversation sparks another light on the mystery of the woman who I know had taken care of me before meeting Luka. I know she drowned as a child and was resuscitated and that death opened the door for her. But it's not the case for everyone.

Angelica tugs me forward. "And yours will be a celebration. I will be with you the whole time. Now, come on. We have to go. Nikolai is waiting for us in the car." *Nikolai?* The name pulls free an image of a man with the brightest blue eyes I've ever seen. It's the same man who's been showing up in my memories of Luka. Without a doubt, I know he's my guardian of sorts. He looked out for me when Angelica couldn't. But I ran. I couldn't stay with him. I only wish I knew why. And this memory, Nikolai, the man who has summoned fear and dread in me now ignites emotions to combat the harsh feeling. Hearing Angelica use his name makes him more man than hidden monster.

I release a puff of air, peering around the small, empty apartment once more. Movers came for our stuff yesterday, and by tonight, we'll move into The Knezha Estate. I should be happy for once. I should be thankful I'm wanted. That Angelica took me in and has treated me like her daughter since the moment she found me stealing change from the fountain in the Tanglewood Plaza Shopping Center after the landlord came in and changed the locks when my dad never came back from what was supposed to be a weekend getaway with his girlfriend.

Angelica said it was fate.

The moment I saw the spare room in her apartment, I had to agree.

"What if Nikolai hates me?" I ask, stopping just before our

door. I've only seen the pictures Angelica had of him on the wall.

"He won't."

The memory suddenly shifts, stealing me away from Angelica and the apartment. Now, I stand in front of a full-length mirror in a lavish room of whites and grays. Sheer curtains drape over the windows, and through them, I spot a full moon hovering in a black sky.

Running my fingers over the soft material of my gray-blue gown, I study myself in the mirror. I barely recognize the girl who stands before me. While I feel like me, something's different. My eyes shine with a softness I don't remember ever having, innocence lost to death. To the brutality my life threw at me.

"May I come in, my girl?" The familiar man's voice—Nikolai's voice—drifts into my mind. I can't see him, but I sense him on the other side of the door.

"Yes, come in," I say.

The door swings open. I don't turn from the mirror but instead glance at Nikolai's reflection strolling up behind me. His suit screams of the wealth the rest of his estate holds, and my hands shake at my sides.

He stops behind me and meets my gaze in the mirror. "You're nervous."

I swallow, my throat tightening. "Yes, sir."

He rests his manicured hand on my shoulder. "You're family, Skye. Call me Nik."

"Okay, Nik," I say. "Is it time? Where's Angelica?"

"She's waiting with the others in the ballroom. We have a few minutes to spare, so I thought I'd escort you. I hope you find everything to your liking." He motions around the room. "I also thought I could take you shopping this week. Or if you'd prefer to go with some friends, I can arrange that, too. I just want you to be happy. Your happiness is important to me."

I press my lips into a thin line. I've never met Nikolai before, but he's treating me better than my own father ever treated me. I thought Angelica might have been embellishing the idea of my new family, but Nikolai feels so genuine. I can't help but nod.

"Why?" The question startles me as it flies from my mouth. I cringe at my crassness.

Nikolai only laughs. "Everyone who joins my family is just that—family. We take care of each other. We protect each other. I'll always be here for you as long as you're here for me in return. The same goes for everyone. I know it'll take some time for you to adjust and trust me, but I promise your sacrifice will be worth it."

Sacrifice. I'm sacrificing my life as it is in this moment for a chance to be something greater. To create something greater. And the problem? I'm not so sure I want to or if I can no matter how encouraging Angelica's been or how nice Nikolai is now.

He spins me around to face him. "Don't be scared, my girl. The pain is a fleeting moment you'll forget once you open the door. And when you return, we can prepare for our great eternity as a family."

I force myself to smile. "That sounds amazing."

He checks the time on his platinum and onyx wristwatch. "Are you ready? It's ten to midnight and imperative that your end and beginning collide."

I suppose it's fitting that the whole world will be counting the seconds until my last heartbeat seeing as I was born when the clock struck twelve on New Year's Day. According to Angelica, it makes me special. The fact that I can open the door to the place between life and death already without having acquired whatever the universe will bestow on me proves Angelica's theory that I'm the key. That with me, I can guarantee access to the galaxy to those deserving of our family. How they're chosen, I have no idea.

I straighten my shoulders. "I'm ready."

Nikolai guides me down the hallway to the ballroom of the estate. My bare feet don't make a sound on the cool marble floor. The room, only lit by candlelight, allows a clear view of the glittering sky through the glass ceiling. It's too dark to see the faces of my new family, but the whisper of voices swirls around me, some out loud and some into my mind.

Angelica steps from the perimeter, holding a simple white candle between her hands. She stops in front of me and smiles, the firelight dancing in her glassy eyes. "I'm so proud of you, Skye."

"Thank you, Angelica. For everything. And if I don't return just know—"

She reaches out, cutting off my words. "This is not a moment for final words."

I nod. "I love you."

"And I love you."

Angelica blows out her candle, returning to the perimeter of the room where I can no longer see her. Nikolai slides his hand from my elbow to link his fingers around mine. He squeezes my fingers, stopping them from trembling and tugs me forward. The glowing moon reflects across the rippling floor in front of us, and I stare at a rectangular glass pool on a platform.

Nikolai climbs the small step to the platform, pulling me with him. He hands me a candle to hold to shine light on my face. I take a deep breath, settling my nerves.

"We have gathered here tonight to welcome the newest addition to our eternal family. Skye's path in this life led her right into our arms where we as a family promise to teach her, protect her, guide her, and love her. May the stars shine upon her and hold the door open for her return to our family. Until we meet again."

"Until we meet again." The chorus of soft voices wraps around me, filling me with the bravery I need to step into the warm water.

Bringing the candle to my mouth, I blow it out. Nikolai takes it from my hands. I step deeper into the pool, the water soaking my gown. As the water reaches my waist, I hesitate, standing frozen in the pool. I never imagined my life would end like this, but I also never imagined it would begin like this, either.

"Five minutes, my girl," Nikolai says.

He steps into the water next to me, nudging me to lower

myself down until it reaches my neck. I suck in a long breath, filling my lungs, and then relax enough to float on my back. Water fills my ears, muting the soft murmurs of anticipation. Nikolai stands over me, placing his hands on my shoulders.

"Four minutes, Skye." Nikolai's voice slithers into my mind.

A bright light flashes from across the room, drawing my attention away from the stars speckling the winter sky through the glass ceiling. Sitting up, I peer at the door to the grand hallway. Light from outside the room silhouettes a figure—a man—and Nikolai stiffens.

"You lunatics!" the man yells from his place in the doorway. "Stop this, now."

I try to sit up more, but Nikolai shoves me back down, blocking my view of the man. A boom rips through the air, startling me. The glass ceiling fissures and people scream. Another resonating pop pierces my ears, and I realize the man's firing a gun.

A light shines in my eyes, blinding me. "Get away from the girl, you monster. I won't let you murder her in the name of your fucking beliefs." He fires another shot at the ceiling. "The next one will be in you, Knezha. I won't let what happened to Anita happen to this girl."

Nikolai doesn't move. "Three minutes, Skye."

The man's arm shakes as he offers his free hand to me. He's close enough that I can see his wild eyes shine. "Come with me. I'll make sure this man and these people never hurt you. And they will hurt you just like they hurt my daughter."

My heart bangs against my ribcage, panic grabbing hold of

me. I shake my head. "Leave me alone."

He doesn't.

Bolting forward, he punches Nikolai in the face, knocking him off the platform. He locks his fingers to my wrist. I scream, slipping in the pool, but I can't get away. He drags me out by my sopping wet hair.

I scream again, jerking away. "Stop it! You're going to ruin my eternity!"

"Oh, God." He grabs me again. "Honey, they're going to kill you. You know that, right?"

"It's how you open the door," I say. "It's my choice to join Nikolai's family. My life. My decision."

"So brainwashed," he mutters. "This ain't no family. It's a damn cult."

"One minute, Skye." I don't see Nikolai anywhere, though I can hear him. *"You're running out of time."*

The ground begins to shake beneath us, and suddenly, the ceiling shatters. Glass rains down on me, slicing my skin. Pain washes over me in waves. The man swears, shoving away a dark figure that tries to get to me. All the candles snuff out, leaving the room almost pitch black except for the light coming from the hallway.

A gunshot rings through the air, and a familiar scream soon follows. My head pounds, my ears ringing with the noise. The man tries to yank me again. This time, I reach out for his arm and to snatch his gun.

Another pop.

Pain explodes through me, fire burning from my torso to

my chest. I gasp and sputter, my eyes filling with tears that trickle in hot paths down my cheeks.

"Twenty seconds." Where is Nikolai?

The lights flick on, and I stare wide-eyed at the man. He releases a sob, dropping his gun on the floor. I fall to my knees, blood seeping from the bullet hole in my stomach, ruining my beautiful dress.

He closes the foot of distance and tries to press his hands against my wound. The world spins around, ice traveling from my toes to my head. I shiver through my sobs, unable to do anything except pray that the pain ends soon.

"I'm so sorry," the man says.

A figure towers behind him.

"I'm not," Nikolai says.

He holds up the gun to the back of the man's head and pulls the trigger.

Blood splatters across my face, and I release a cry. The man slumps onto me, knocking me back, and we tumble into the pool together. I can't stop myself from inhaling water as I gasp through the pain.

The world goes silent.

Five.

I lose feeling in my body.

Four.

The pain stops.

Three.

My heart slows.

Two.

I see the door.

One.

The stars swallow me whole.

CHAPTER 12

WHEN SOULS COLLIDE

"*S**KYE? SKYE? I'M coming for you.*"

"Nikolai?" I ask, staring around the galaxy.

"*No, Skye. It's me.*"

Luka.

His voice pulls me from my memory—one that felt so real I didn't even realize I was in the galaxy world all along. I have no idea how long I've been here, but I'm sure if Luka didn't pull me from my own mind, I might've stayed lost in it forever. Because what I was remembering was my first death. It was the death that brought me to Luka. It was the death that showed me Angelica was right all along. That I had opened the door

Nikolai was eager to access. But what no one—especially not me—expected was I wouldn't come back alone. That I'd bring Luka with me when our souls collided.

But things are still foggy, and I can only glimpse fragments of what happened.

"Skye," Luka says from next to me.

Tears sheen my eyes when I meet his intense gaze. "You're here."

"I had to make sure you'd come back," he says.

"Angelica and Nikolai were wrong. They said I opened the door, but I couldn't find it," I say.

He frowns. "What are you talking about? Who's Angelica? You've mentioned that name twice now."

I squeeze my eyes shut. "I think she was my guardian. She was like us, but something happened. And Nikolai—"

"I know Nikolai, Skye," he says.

"He's the man from the phone," I say.

"What do you remember about him? You used to warn me about saying his name, because that could let him into our minds when we were hiding."

It's why the memories of Luka never mentioned Nikolai's name. But if he's the reason I'm here, there's no point in not saying it. "So much for that thought, huh? He was there during my—I remember my first death, Luka, and I think I know why I never told you about it. It was..." I let my words trail off. How on earth am I to tell him my life before him led to a man who wasn't afraid to kill people? A man who I was willing to sacrifice my life for. A man who stirs something both dark and light in me that it makes me hate that I want to make up excuses as to why I'm not freaking out that Nikolai would've drowned me if I wasn't shot by some man claiming my family was a—I don't even want to repeat the words. It wasn't like that. I just know it.

Luka pulls my floating body closer so there isn't space between us. "You don't have to tell me, Skye. Your past has always been a touchy subject. Especially anything involving Nikolai Knezha."

"I don't think I was a good person," I say.

He looks away from me. "He made you that way. I hate him, Skye. He made you hate yourself so much, and there was never anything I could do to make you see—he's probably why you don't remember. This is my punishment for turning you against him."

"It's so hard for me to wrap my mind around. He felt like my family. I felt safe with him. What happened?"

"I happened, Skye. Being an acquired—and not accidental ones like Gemma and Avery, or basically most acquired people you'd meet—comes with power people crave. You have access to the galaxy anytime you want—and it's what Nikolai wants."

"There's nothing even here but you and me."

He shrugs. "That's all they need."

"Because I'm the key. I can open the door for anyone," I say. I don't know how I know it, but something that Angelica said in my memory—about growing our family—sticks with me. And Nikolai talking about my path leading me to my eternal family...this is more than acquiring some special ability from touching death. I can cheat death and help others. I'm immortal.

"It's going to be okay, my girl." A sudden memory pulls me away from the galaxy world and Luka. It's like now that I shattered the glass wall to my memories, Nikolai keeps seeping out, filling my head.

Tears blur my vision. "How? She promised me we'd never be apart. *You* promised me our family would be together forever."

A warm hand slides into mine and tugs my arm up. Nikolai kisses the back of my hand. "I know you're grieving, Skye. I know this isn't how your life with our family was supposed to start, but you should know that even if Angelica isn't in this life, it doesn't mean she's not waiting for us elsewhere. I know this life isn't our only one, and I have faith that you'll bring the worlds together for us and make a better existence for us now. Because this world we're in, it's awful. You saw that. You felt it. But we're here and Angelica would want you to stay on your journey."

I sniffle. "I know. I just—"

"Don't start setting blame on yourself. I wasn't going to tell you this, but Angelica knew this is where her journey would end. She knew the sacrifice she'd have to make to see you thrive with us."

I swivel and yank my hand away. "She knew? She could've told me. Prepared me."

He doesn't let me get far before he pulls me into a hug and kisses my head. "Please, my girl. You have to understand. What Angelica did was *for* you. She foresaw what would happen if she had not interfered. You'd have missed your countdown and the door back to us would've sealed with you in it. You're our key. Our everything."

I take a deep breath. "I'm sorry, Nik. I shouldn't complain. This family has given me so much." *But not everything.*

"But something feels missing," he says. It takes me a moment to realize he's acknowledging a thought of mine out loud.

"Not something." My voice barely comes out a whisper.

His blond brows furrow over his ice-blue eyes. "The boy from your dreams?"

I blink the surprise from my expression. "Angelica told you?"

"We don't keep secrets around here, Skye. Honesty is fundamental to our family." His eyes narrow for a split second like he's trying to get into my head. He might be. I'm not sure. "Now tell me about this dream boy." His tight mouth curves into a smile.

I relax under his scrutiny. "He's not a dream. He's real. I met him."

Nikolai tilts his head to the side. "He's part of our family?"

I glance at the floor. "No, not at all. I didn't meet him in life, Nik. The door led me to him. He was waiting for me in the stars."

"And you showed him the door?"

"I did."

His smile widens. "What an unexpected surprise. We must find him. He should be here with us."

"I don't even know if I can."

"Of course you can, my girl. I will help you. You should be with your soul mate, and he should be with us."

"Skye, snap out of it," Luka says, pulling me from my thoughts.

It's getting harder and harder to stay in the present when my past beckons me to unravel the secrets my own mind wants to keep with me.

"I'm sorry. I'm having a hard time focusing." I blink the image of Nikolai from my mind.

He releases a low noise, almost like a growl. "He's getting to you."

"He just felt so safe, Luka. I don't understand why I would want to run away with you from him. He wanted you to join our family." I meet his serious eyes.

"As long as you were his perfect little girl and didn't question him or go against him, Skye. He was using you. He's still trying. Look at where we are."

"Maybe I need to give in to fix this," I say.

"Don't talk like that. You would never—"

There's so much missing from my memory. I can't process what any of it means. Angelica took me off the streets, she gave me a home. Nikolai supposedly gave me a life—a family. He gave me Luka. Somehow, it got messed up along the way and forced us to end up here.

I glare at him. He doesn't have the memories I have. "Stop saying that like you know me."

"Skye, I—"

"He protected me. Took care of me."

"Not without a price."

I frown. "What does that even mean?"

He doesn't answer right away, like he's trying to figure out how to tell me something he really doesn't want to. A ball of nerves twists through my very being, the drawn out anticipation ruining what's good about the stars around us.

I reach out and brush my fingers over his ethereal hand. "Please, Luka. You have to tell me. I can't take it not knowing."

He shakes his head. "I don't want to."

"Luka." A spike of anger flares through me. "Tell me."

Slowly bringing his hand up to my face, he traces my jawline. "If there is one thing I know about you it's that you wanted nothing more than to forget about that part of your life. Nikolai was charming as hell. He could tell people the sky was purple and rain was the fountain of youth and they'd believe him. But underneath it all, he was an awful man with a god complex. If he wasn't your purpose for living, there was no purpose. And you saw that."

"How could you know all this? I never let him get near you," I say.

"You told me."

I twist my lips to the side. "And you believed me?"

He releases a deep, smooth laugh I wish I could listen to forever despite it being condescending. "You're asking me like I shouldn't have."

I can't stop the smile crossing my face. "Maybe you shouldn't have. I could've been Nikolai's evil minion using my irresistible charm to sneak into your life to use you."

His smile falters, speaking a million unsaid words.

My mouth falls agape. "Are you kidding me?"

"Relax. It's not what you think. You really didn't want anything to do with Nikolai when you showed up at my door. You fought hard to keep us both away from him."

"But I didn't. I saw him after we ran away. I had a memory of it."

Again more silence.

The conversation about my time with Nikolai triggers a darkness in Luka. He shuts me out, closing me off from the emotions I could feel flowing between us. His gaze bores into me, his dark eyes locking me in their intensity. The information Luka holds slips through my fingers like all the fleeting good memories I wish to live over and over again.

It's in this moment I realize that all these memories of Nikolai are trying to wedge themselves between me and Luka, and it takes everything in me to separate each piece to keep my good senses about them. My memory exploded into a million fragments, and whatever is happening here, whatever I'm feeling is the pieces being shoved together improperly and out of place.

"You know what? I'm not doing this," I say. Because I can't. I can't open myself up like this, even to Luka.

His jaw tightens, and he shifts his gaze away. "Doing what?"

I push away from him, suddenly needing space. "Whatever *this* is between us. You're obviously too afraid to be honest with me—not like you're obligated or whatever. I get it. I messed up your life. I *shot* you." I suck in a deep breath, running my hands into my hair. There's a reason I forgot Luka, and it wasn't Nikolai's doing. Maybe he's my trigger to my past.

And despite its vastness, the galaxy feels awfully small with Luka's presence.

Tingles blossom from my fingertips and up my arm. Turning back to Luka, I meet his serious eyes though his lips pull up in the corners. He laces our fingers together. "Feel better now?"

I glare. "Seriously?" He's not going to let me distance myself so easily. How can I resist him?

His smile widens. "Yeah, seriously. You think this is the first time you've tried to push me away when you've felt lost? Or tried to mess with my ego to get to me?"

I sigh. "Luka, please."

He laughs, which makes my heart jump toward him from my chest. "You forget, Skye. I know you, and I know what a pain you are. You want answers? Then remember. I'm not doing it for you. I don't want to open that door. I deserve the chance to try to protect you. Old Skye would hug me and tell me she lov—" He snaps his mouth closed, cutting off his sentence.

"Well, sorry, but old Skye is dead and gone and a jerk for leaving us in this position. I'd slap old Skye if I could."

"She slaps back," Luka says.

I roll my eyes. "She sounds charming."

He grins. "And just as beautiful as you are. You'd probably get along. Kick ass together. Take out every threat like a damn assassin. Gang up on me for being a slob. Hell, you'd probably ditch me for not keeping up."

"I'd—she'd never," I say.

The look he gives me—his intense eyes softening, the corners crinkling—makes me wish he'd never look at me any other way. "Damn right you wouldn't. Not even if you could. We're soul mates."

Soul mates. I knew that. It happened when our souls collided. But hearing him say it, hearing him confirm the pieces of my memory that have come back to me, makes me a jumbled mess of emotions I can't even understand. They're familiar and good yet they feel so utterly new and scary and overwhelming. And as natural and necessary as breathing. Like if the feelings disappear, so will I.

"I—"

"Don't say anything, Skye. I know you don't really remember what I meant to you, and you're still processing everything. I didn't want you to hear it from me, because I didn't want to influence you or try to sway you or change everything we had, but it's important you know what you mean to me, and what our life means to us. This is why I can't tell you everything. About Nikolai. About your past. I just can't do that to you."

I stay silent, his words sinking in. Everything is so confusing and upsetting. It's not that Luka upsets me—it's myself. It's this memory loss. It's everything. I want to feel what he feels and to be able to just close my eyes and know everything. But I can't. I've tried.

"So, will you try to get through all this with me in the here and now?" he whispers. "Let me earn your trust and get to know this new version of you?"

My lip quivers. "What if you end up hating this version?"

"I could never."

"You don't know that."

"I do."

Luka pulls me into his arms again, and I allow him to wrap me in everything that he is. His soul against mine doesn't feel foreign or new. It feels like me. It feels like his soul fills up a part of me that goes missing when he's not this close. When we're not together.

"We should go back," he whispers.

I nod, suddenly terrified of losing myself among the stars. "You're right. If I stay here any longer, I just might—"

Five.

My thought cuts off and the galaxy fades.

Four.

My ears ring.

Three.

I curl my fingers.

Two.

My heart beats.

"Time of life: Four fifty-one P.M."

Snapping my eyes open, I stare into my startled reflection glaring at me from Caretaker Sienna's protective glasses. I bite my tongue to stop myself from screaming out Luka's name, but it would be pointless. He's not here in this room. It's just the monster and me.

"It's nice to see you again, subject four," Caretaker Sienna says, straightening her shoulders before stepping back.

I don't respond to her.

I don't do anything but continue to stare at my reflection in her glasses.

"You've been out for a while. You had me worried that you might've passed on for good."

If it weren't for Luka, I probably would have. I'd have stayed lost in my mind forever with Nikolai and the Knezha Family—watching strange men die and dying myself. It's probably what Caretaker Sienna wants.

Her words get under my skin. "Guess I'll try harder next time. You know, lock the door for good."

"What did you say?"

Slowly opening my eyes, I look at her. "You heard me. I'll try harder next time. Who knows, maybe I won't come back."

CHAPTER 13

NIKOLAI

"OPEN THE DOOR," Caretaker Sienna says, holding the black canister up like she'll spray it in my face if I don't. The only thing stopping me from launching at her in this close proximity is that I don't want to die by that burning poison again. I might be able to pull myself from death, but the pain leaves me wanting to cling to life.

Straightening my aching shoulders, I stroll to the door and put my fingers on the handle.

"Not that door."

I spin around and wince at the canister an inch from my

face. "I don't know what you're talking about."

"*You do,*" she thinks to me. "*You were so close to fooling me, but I caught you, Skye. You were never one to hold your tongue.*"

I don't respond. I stand in the same spot, unmoving, and stare at the ground like I didn't hear her voice in my mind. Caretaker Sienna shifts on her tennis shoes, adding more space between us.

"What is it that you want?" I ask out loud. "Maybe if you just told me why I'm in this basement, why you keep killing us over and over, then maybe I can give you whatever it is you're looking for. Please."

"Admit what you know so he can get in," she says.

"Who?"

"Sienna, a word." The familiar, smooth voice comes from her pocket, and I realize Nikolai's been listening in all along. I've known that he's behind things, that I'm here because I ran away and now he's punishing me, but I know it's more.

Sienna holds the canister up to me, extending her index finger at me like I have the choice of not giving her a moment to talk on the phone. She presses it to her ear with her free hand, and listens.

"She's lying," she says. "Haven't you seen her with subject one? Strangers don't treat each other like that."

I wish I could hear the entire conversation. I wish I could run over there and take the phone again to listen to more answers. But that damn canister of burning poison. I don't think I could be fast enough.

"Yes, I understand that, but I just—" More listening. "I'll

get her to do it. I know how important the key is, but I need leverage. Let me—" She glances at me. *"Let me complete the others' journeys. Don't you think that's what they're here for?"*

My heart races, hearing her thoughts in my mind. The only time I've heard any reference to a journey's end was with Angelica. And Angelica is dead.

Without thinking, I charge forward toward the caretaker, hands outstretched to tackle her. I brace myself for the poison to hit my face, but Caretaker Sienna only moves out of the way to bolt to the door.

She slams it shut, peering at me through the window.

A hissing noise sounds through the vent. "Let me out!" I scream, banging on the glass.

Holding her hand up, she touches her fingers to the window. *"The door might be locked, Skye, but I will find the key."*

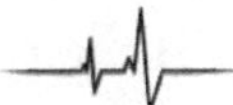

Bright sunlight sparkles overhead, and I stretch my legs out into the soft grass in front of me. A warm breeze swirls my blond hair from my shoulders and into my face, veiling the world from my view until a gentle hand moves the loose strands behind my ear.

"You're distracted again," I say, drawing my hand up to my face to lock my fingers around Luka's before he can guide my chin to face him. I don't look at him, but his presence is so all encompassing that I don't need to see him to know he's beside me.

"Can you blame me?" His warm breath tickles my hand, and I shiver at the feather lightness of lips brushing against my knuckles.

The world darkens as I close my eyes. I wish with everything in me that I had control of the memory. I wish I'd turn my head and open my eyes. I wish I could take my other hand to reach out to Luka so it didn't run over the grass at my side instead.

"You know I blame you," I say.

My eyes finally open, and blue stars swirl in my vision as it adjusts to the brightness again. I shift to peer at Luka. He smiles the most easy-going smile, his eyes crinkling, his lips pulling up in the corners but somehow still managing to be all pouty.

He reaches out his other hand, just holding it in front of me expectantly. Slowly lifting my hand from the grass, I allow him to take it. "Well, I blame you, too."

"You can't do that," I quip, a smile crossing my lips.

"I just did," he says, his smile turning into a full-blown, irresistible grin that has me shifting on the grass until I find myself wrapped in his arms. "How do you expect me to concentrate when you're not?"

"I am concentrating," I say.

"On me, not on opening the door."

"Because the door is already open, Luka," I say. "Close your eyes and look. I've already given you the key."

"The key. Where's the key? I need to find the key. I must've misplaced it. If I can't find it, then Caretaker Sienna might. Nikolai will get it." The thoughts come hot and fast, stealing away a memory I never want to leave, one I could survive in for the rest of time—time I might have an endless supply of.

Gentle hands touch my shoulders, shaking me just slightly. *"Skye? Skye, open your eyes."*

Blinking in the harsh lighting, I stare at Luka hovering over me. The fluorescent lighting haloes him in a blue-white glow, making him look older—almost sickly—compared to the boy I remember from my memory of sitting in the grass outside our cabin.

"Luka?" My hoarse voice barely sounds through the chilly air. "God, Luka." My shoulders ache as I lift my arms, but I can't stop myself.

Luka stiffens in my embrace without hugging me back. "Whoa, Skye. You're disoriented."

I bury my face in the crook of his neck. "No, I'm not. Now stop acting like I carry the plague and hug me, because I really need it."

Ever so slowly, he laces his hands around my back. He only half hugs me for a second before he pulls me closer until I'm on his lap, cradled against his warm body. He inhales a long, shuddering breath, and even though I feel the presence of an audience staring at my back, I don't let go.

What's the point of hiding the fact that I remember Luka? Caretaker Sienna said she suspected that I was lying about whatever it is she thinks I'm lying about—my memory loss? My ability? My trickling knowledge about Nikolai Knezha and whatever it is he wants from me. To open a door—whatever that truly means.

"Luka, I know why we're here. Why Nikolai is punishing us," I think to him. *"It's not because I ran away to be with you or to*

keep you away. He's upset about losing access to the galaxy world, I think. I'm the key."

"And you won't give it to him."

"I'm afraid they'll use you against me. That's why Nik—that's why he wanted you to join the Knezha Family."

He cups my face, looking into my eyes. *"They've tried. They took me from you. They know they can't."*

"But I'm here."

"You didn't remember me."

"But I'm starting to. I remember enough—" I cut off my thought, my heart pounding, my mind sorting the memories of my past into two piles—the ones of Luka and the ones of Nikolai and the Knezha Family—but there's still a hugely important pile missing: the memories of me. The memories about me and who I was. I'm afraid that maybe I'll never know, that my life as I know it was defined by who Luka made me or who Nikolai made me.

"Skye, you won't let him break you. You won't. I hate admitting this, but I started to doubt the universe because it stole what we had from you, but maybe it was protecting you."

"The universe?"

"The stars. Our world. That's our place, Skye. That's the only thing I'm certain about in this life is you, me, and the stars."

"I'd say get a room—"

Luka jerks his head up, the sudden intrusion of Gemma's voice interrupting our private conversation. "Really, Gemma? Can't you ever keep your mouth shut?"

Something about the protectiveness in his voice digs into

me. He shouldn't be showing such feeling toward me. It's obvious Caretaker Sienna knows about our connection, but I don't want to confirm it. I don't want Luka to give it away. He's been strong enough to protect himself for almost a year, and I don't want to be the reason for his undoing.

"Let me complete the others' journeys." Caretaker Sienna's words float through my mind.

I try to pull away from Luka. "Stop, Luka," I whisper.

"Not when it looks like she's about to pull that gown right off you," Gemma says without hearing his words.

I grimace, turning my head away from Luka, who holds me tighter.

"You only say that because it's what you want to do," Avery says.

She's back. Caretaker Sienna brought her back like Luka said she would. I peek in her direction.

"Whatever, Avery," Gemma says.

"Shut up!" I yell, getting to my feet. "Everyone, just shut up. This is what they want. They're trying to divide us."

"You don't even know what these monsters want. They—"

"We'll meet in a few weeks. I promise." My voice rings through the air, and I blink to stare at Avery leaning against a black car. The memory comes so fast, stealing me away from the basement. "I wish you didn't have to go," she says, adjusting her blouse. The dress shirt looks strange, like it's something she doesn't usually wear, but I can't be sure.

"I don't have a choice, but our journeys will cross again," I say. It's such a weird thing to say, and I wish I knew more about what it meant. I'm an outsider looking at everything from eyes I don't remember.

"I hope so," she says.

"They will."

"Skye?" The soft voice pulls me from my memory. "Are you okay?" I shift my gaze to meet Avery's dark eyes. Looking into them, seeing the concern on her face, draws an emotion from deep within me. It's not the same type of connection I have with Luka, but a bond all the same.

"Death broke her," Gemma says, speaking up. "Three days is the longest for any of us to be gone."

"Three days?" I ask, my voice going shrill. "I've been gone for three days?" I turn to Avery. "What about you?"

"Not just gone. Dead," Gemma says, inserting herself into the conversation I'm trying to have with Avery, like her words will somehow make it better. "I thought you figured out how to escape unlike the rest of us."

"I was—I—I don't know," Avery says.

"Avery never remembers after leaving with the monster," Gemma says.

"You don't remember?" I ask Avery.

"I—"

"You don't think we were together?" I ask.

I can't wrap my head around the passage of time. It felt like only moments had passed from when I died and met Luka in the stars to the moment I woke up to be interrogated by Caretaker Sienna. How could they have stripped days away from me? It's as bad as my missing memory.

"I don't know," Avery answers.

I lock my fingers to the chain-link. "Try to remember." If she can remember even a moment, maybe I can fill in more missing pieces to use to beat Caretaker Sienna at her game.

"I can't."

"Remember!" I yell, rattling the barrier. "Come on, remember, Avery!"

Luka reaches out for me, yanking me closer when the lights flicker. He hugs me against him like he won't ever let me go. His breath tickles my ear, and I tune out Gemma trying to talk over the sudden clanking of metal.

"What are you doing?" Luka whispers into my ear instead of my mind.

I dig my fingers into his hospital gown. "I need answers."

He shifts me on his lap, reaching behind him to grab the discarded curtain. He wraps it around us, like the flimsy fabric will somehow protect us if Avery can't see us.

"Not like this," he says.

"Then how?" I ask.

"Avery," Luka says. "Please, you need to calm down before you hurt one of us."

"That's exactly what I want!" Avery screams.

Everything happens so fast that neither Luka nor I have a chance to react. One moment, I'm hugging Luka, and then in the next, the chain-link barrier hits my back as I crash into it. The lights flicker overhead before turning off completely. The barrier shakes against me, but I can't move. Books fly from Luka's bookcase and hit me in the chest and stomach—one barely missing my head.

I hang imprisoned by an invisible weight that threatens to crush me, sitting so heavy on my chest I can barely manage a breath. Avery stands feet away at the divider between our rooms, holding her open palms to me.

Luka's on his feet, covering me the best he can from Avery's view, but she flicks out her hand, sending Luka crashing into our plexiglass door. Water bubbles from the faucet in our sink, and then a steady stream of icy water splashes me in the face.

I thrash, still trapped against the chain-link barrier, while this girl I thought I was friends with attacks me on a level I can't even fight against. Panic rises into my throat. I can't breathe with the water shooting into my face. Avery will kill me if no one can stop her, but I don't think Gemma will try, and Luka, he's trapped by Avery as well.

"I'm going to drown," I think to Luka.

"Hold on, Skye."

But I can't. My vision hazes with shadows, and my mouth automatically opens, sucking water into my lungs.

Five.

My body slackens.

Four.

My vision darkens.

Three.

My head spins.

Two.

My heart slows.

One.

I see an open door and slam it shut.

Five.

My ears ring.

Four.

My body falls to the ground.

Three.

My heart beats.

Two.

I project my thoughts to Avery. *"Stop it! Stop it now!"*

One.

The room falls utterly silent apart from the sound of water seeping into the drain in the center of my room. Coughing, I spit out water, my breath heaving. I manage to lean on my elbows and sit up. Avery stands in the middle of her room, her hands clenched at her sides. A look of pure hatred furrows her brows and narrows her lips as she gazes at me. But she doesn't do anything else. She doesn't look like she could if she tried.

"What the hell was that about?" I stumble to my feet, crossing the room like I can somehow break through the chain-link to attack Avery. Luka cuts in front of me, standing protectively in my way like he's even a match against Avery who seems to have lost her mind.

I shake dripping water from my face. "What happened, Avery?"

"I remember, Skye," she says.

I stand on my tiptoes to peer at her from over Luka's shoulder. "Oh, God. What have they done to you the last few days?"

"They didn't do anything. This is your fault," she says.

"What? What did I do? I've been dead."

The chain-link barrier shakes again. "It's not what you did here."

"What?" I ask.

"I'm never going to forgive you."

My chest tightens, and it feels like I'm drowning all over again even with the constant humid air entering my lungs with every breath. "Avery."

"You're why I'm here!" she screams. "You're the one who killed me. You ruined everything!"

CHAPTER 14

KILLER

"WHAT DO YOU mean I killed you?" I ask.

No one moves, and I'm pretty sure everyone, including me, holds their breaths in anticipation, waiting for the drama to unfold. I can't believe how much my memory of Avery has failed me. How could I have been so wrong about where I stood with her?

And of course this is my fault. I knew it was my fault. But I had no idea to what extent. It makes me question everything.

As for Avery's accusation? Who the hell was I? I thought there was a darkness in me that my memory was suppressing but being a killer? Taking the life of a girl my memory tells me I was friends with? This is crazy. Maybe that's why I barely remember my past and not much outside of Luka. My brain might've been trying to rewire me to stop me from being a psycho murderer. I'd be lying to myself if I said I wasn't capable of being one.

Avery doesn't respond but continues to glare, the chain-link clanking and shaking. *"She's playing stupid. She knows what she did for Nikolai,"* she thinks, her anger seeping into me.

"Avery, chill out," Gemma says. "You're going to bring the monster in here."

"Now everything is ruined. And of course everyone will take Skye's side because she's a master manipulator. Nikolai was right. She was trying to change my journey."

Whoa. I don't even know how to react to her unpleasant thoughts and her agreeing with something Nikolai supposedly said about me. Luka stiffens in front of me, clearly hearing everything Avery thinks, which means she must not know how to block me out of her head. And if I'm the reason why she's here, maybe that's why she couldn't remember me until I pulled the hot hatred from her. I wish I could get her mind to shut off, because now she's basically projecting everything to me—and who knows who else—through a megaphone in her head.

"I'm sure this is all a misunderstanding," I say even though I know she's probably right about whatever happened in my past. She knows Nikolai, and I know I would've done anything for him when he took me in. And in this moment, it sounds like he has gotten to Avery. She's been turned against me and whatever memory I had of her only shows what I've lost. It helps dull the confusing emotions I have toward Nikolai. How dare he do this.

"Whatever, Skye," she says. *If she thinks she can play games, she's an idiot. I can't believe she thought she could get away with messing with my head.* With one more glare, she looks away and plops back onto her mat to stare off into space again.

Luka turns his attention to me, fear widening his eyes as Avery continues to think about all the ways she's going to get her revenge on me for killing her and messing with her head, something I didn't even think I was capable of, something I forget how to even do. Maybe she's right and I do deserve this, but I'm not going to sit back and allow her to turn my already nightmarish life into an unbearable hell.

I continue to stare at Avery, though she doesn't look at me. "You might have forgotten, but we were friends, and anything I did was bec—"

"Careful, Skye," Luka thinks to me.

"I'm sorry if I did whatever it is you said I did," I add when she doesn't look at me.

"You killed me." Her voice lowers in pitch, digging under my skin. "You're a fucking monster."

"Watch it," Luka says from next to me.

I brush my fingers to his. "It's okay, Luka. She's probably right."

"I don't care if you murdered her. I'm not going to let her talk to you this way," he thinks to me.

Luka's words trigger a memory, pulling me away from Avery and into my own mind.

"I don't care, Skye." We're back in our cabin, the only light in the room coming from the silvery moonlight cutting across the coffee table in front of us, bouncing off the glass top.

"But you should care. I've done some unthinkable things," I say.

Luka's brows lower on his forehead, pinching a line between them. "It can't be that bad."

"It's worse."

His stare bores into me, and I think at any second he'll get up and leave, though I know he doesn't. He won't. Not according to the few memories I have of him. But how he can sit there, holding my hands, waiting for me to bare my soul and not care enough to run away makes me question why.

"You've killed people," he says, his jaw twitching.

My eyes blur with tears, distorting the memory. "Yes." It takes me a second, but I realize he read my thoughts to discover the secrets I carry. Thoughts I can't hear anymore, because all I'm aware of in this memory is Luka and how he remains composed knowing that I'm a killer, and how important he is to me.

"This is why you asked me to run away with you," he says.

I shrug. "It's one of the reasons, but I wasn't lying when I told you N—*he* wanted me to bring you to him, and I couldn't do it." The information sparks something dark within me.

"Because you killed people for him. Did he want you to kill me?" It's another thought he listened in on in my mind.

"I didn't just kill people for him, Luka. I dragged them through the door and pulled them right back out before handing them over to Nik to be a part of our supposed family. But he lied. He's gone against everything he promised. He's not building a family to guide us down our eternal path to transcend this life. He's building a following to control like puppets, destroying those who refuse to fall in line."

Luka leans forward. "Have you told anyone? We have to stop him."

"I can't Luka. He's different than us. He can get into people's heads and make them do things. It's especially easy if they've touched death and opened their minds. Once he gets to them, they're his. They'd rather die than be away from their guide to an eternity he's using me to create."

"What about you?"

Yeah, what about me? I'm glad Luka asks, because the mind of old Skye is as locked as my mind is now.

My gaze flicks from Luka to stare at the streak of light on the coffee table. "I've locked him out, which locked him out from your mind, too."

"Because we're connected?"

"Soul mates. But it's not so easy with anyone else. I can't help them alone, but I—"

Luka slides his hand around my waist, pulling me closer to him, cutting off words I wish he would've let me finish, like they hold answers of how to rise against a man who controls my entire existence. "You know, I won't ever let him get to you again, right? If I ever see him, I'll—"

I cut him off with a kiss before he can finish his sentence. Slowly pulling away, I hold his dark gaze. "I'm the one who's supposed to protect you, got it?"

"Skye! Snap out of it." Luka's voice rings in my head.

"I'm the one who's supposed to protect you..." I can't stop the memory from replaying again and again.

"We protect each other," Luka thinks to me. *"Now cover your nose."*

I blink, pulling myself from the memory. The sound of silence is almost deafening, and it takes me a moment to realize Luka's standing in front of me, holding the sheet over my mouth and nose while trying to cover his own. A strange fog swirls through the air, hazing the room in nauseating gas. Gemma lies on the floor, knocked out. I swivel to glance behind me and catch sight of Avery curled on her side.

This is exactly like when Caretaker Sienna knocked out Luka when both Gemma and Avery were dead. My heart pounds in my ears the longer I hold my breath. Luka wobbles on his feet, and I step forward to pull him down to the floor with me. The last thing I want is for him to fall and hurt himself.

"I'm going to breathe in," Luka thinks to me.

I shake my head. *"No, just hold on."*

"It has to be me or you, and I'm not letting it be you."

I link my fingers with his. *"I don't think this is like the other times, Luka. Things are changing. We're breaking."*

His face reddens the longer he covers his mouth to stop the gas from getting into his lungs the best he can. I do the same, pinching my nose while covering my mouth through the sheet. My chest burns, and the edges of my vision redden. I'll black out on my own if I have to hold my breath much longer.

"It has to be the both of us," I think to him. *"I know it."*

"God, Skye."

I reach out and grab his hand. *"I'm going to figure this out. I didn't come here to just fail."*

"I know," Luka says. *"I won't let you."*

Unable to hold my breath a moment longer, I think, *"I'm going to breathe in now."*

I drop the sheet from my face and purposely suck in a breath of the gag-inducing, toxic chemicals pouring in from the vents. My lungs burn and my eyes blur with tears, but I don't fall unconscious immediately. I fight through the nausea rolling through me.

A cool hand slides under my back, and Luka pulls me to him. Resting my head against his chest, I listen to the sound of his heartbeat, thudding slower and slower the longer I press my ear to him.

He slumps back, yanking me with him. The chemicals shut off from the vent, and I tense. I was wrong, and Luka breathed in before me. He made sure I'd be the last one awake just in case, and it's what he meant about not letting me fail.

"Damn it, Luka," I think to him. *"How can you still want to protect me after everything?"* It was supposed to be me. It should've been me. Because I'm not the innocent one in this situation. He is. His whole life is messed up because of me.

The squeak of tennis shoes draws my attention from Luka and to the dark corridor. "Last one standing again I see," Caretaker Sienna says. "Just as I suspected."

I push to my feet and close the distance to the door. Banging my fists on the unbreakable plastic, I shake all the chain-link barriers around me. If I thought I could rip the metal from the floor and ceiling, I'd beat on the door until the whole place came crashing down.

"I'm not letting you take Luka," I say. "You'll have to kill me first."

She ignores me and opens the door to Gemma's room. "Subject three suffered minor abrasions from a fall but will not need the healing box." She strolls into Gemma's section and drags Gemma the short distance to a gurney she's lowered to the floor. It takes her a few tries, but she eventually manages to get Gemma's front half to stay on.

"I could help you if you want," I say, watching her enter Avery's room next.

"Subject two has showed signs of aggression toward subject four on the video feed," Caretaker Sienna says. "Will monitor and determine if subject two's journey will be terminated."

"Wait, what? You're going to finalize her death because she acted out toward me?" I ask. "Gemma and Avery don't like each other either. Why haven't you threatened this before?"

She continues to act as if I'm not standing only feet away.

I knock my knuckles on the door. "Hello? It's rude to ig-nore me."

With a heavy sigh, Caretaker Sienna drops Avery's legs back to the cold polished concrete. She turns to me and places her hands on her hips. "Why does it concern you, Skye? Do you suddenly feel connected to subject two now?"

I grimace. "I—"

"Some people aren't meant for this. You should know that better than anyone."

"What does that even mean?" I shouldn't care so much about Avery, especially after how she acted toward me. How she aligned herself toward Nikolai, accusing me of being the one who is a master manipulator. But I can't help it. I still cling onto the few feelings from the blips of memories I have of her. I'm afraid I'll have to give up without a fight. It's what Caretaker Sienna wants. It's what Nikolai wants. If I can somehow make up for everything that has led to this moment, I have to try no matter the price.

She shrugs. "I guess you'll find out soon enough."

CHAPTER 15

EMPTY

TWO HOURS PASS before Luka stirs in my arms. He starts to thrash, but I hold him tighter and pet his hair until he opens his eyes. When our gazes lock, his wide eyes soften and he relaxes, letting me hold him against me.

"We're alone," I say. "Caretaker Sienna took the others."

He smirks. "Did you protect me?"

Warmth rushes through me. "According to one of my memories, I promised I always would." My voice is so soft I doubt Caretaker Sienna would be able to hear me over the whoosh of the fan.

"You know, I'm plenty capable of protecting you, too," he

whispers, shifting away so he can sit up.

"But that's no fun for me."

His whole face lights up with his smile. He tilts his head back and laughs, the sound of his voice cutting through the air and over the soft hum of the AC vents. His laugh is the best thing I've ever heard, deep and so pure and full of everything good I remember about the outside world all bottled up in this boy who cares about me more than himself—he doesn't even have to say anything for me to know.

"Too bad memory loss didn't steal away your stubbornness." He continues to smile while he says it. "Because I might be okay you forgot about me if it meant I could protect you for one damn second."

"I must've been terrible for your ego."

"The worst. Infuriating."

"But you never stayed mad long," I whisper, leaning toward him without even thinking about it, like I need to close the space between us.

He does it for me, shifting his body and sliding his arm around my lower back. "Oh, I try."

His fingers press into my side, curling around my waist. I rest my head on his shoulder and stare at our bare legs, wishing with everything in me that another memory of our lives before would break free.

"I'm sorry, Luka." I don't know why I say it, but it feels like I have to put the words out there, because I don't know what's going to happen. Nikolai broke through to Avery to turn her against me. I'm afraid everyone else will soon follow.

If I can't figure out a way to get through this, to give them what they want—and I hate to even think this—the others all might die permanently. I'm not letting anyone ruin my chance of escaping here with Luka even if it has to be under the thumb of Nikolai. I'm too tired. Too spent thinking about my past and the price of a future out of this mess.

The universe obviously doesn't want me to leave. Maybe this really is my journey to follow, but maybe I'm here so Luka doesn't have to be. Maybe it's why I can't remember. If I have nothing to remember, I have nothing to truly fight for. I'm the perfect empty shell to be filled.

"You don't have to apologize to me," Luka says, his breath tickling my forehead.

"I do. You know I do."

"No, Skye. You might get on my nerves sometimes, but I know I used to drive you crazy. I'm here because of me, not you. Avery? She's here because of something she did. Gemma, too. But mostly, we're here because of—" He presses his lips together, and I know he means Nikolai without him even saying or thinking his name. "You might not believe me, but you're not some horrible person. You did what you had to do. I know it. I saw it in your mind on more than one occasion. If you didn't care, you would've never given up a cozy life to run from Nikolai. You wouldn't have taught me everything you did so I could protect myself if I needed to. And you sure as hell wouldn't be in this room now if you were a monster like Avery accused. You're the smartest and bravest person I know."

I squeeze my eyes shut. "I just wish I could remember. I'm

sure I had a plan, but I can't think of it. I can't see much of anything after your death. Just one memory of grief. Maybe I came here as I did to—"

"The Skye I know wouldn't have come in here to give up."

He can't really know that, but I believe in his faith in me. "But that Skye is gone for now—maybe forever," I say, pouting my bottom lip.

Luka surprises me with a kiss. His warm lips brush against mine, kissing the frown right off my face. I lean into him, moving my hands from my lap to slide them over his neck and into his hair. He pulls me closer, and I shift until I'm in his lap with my legs curling around his waist. I shiver at the feeling of his fingers running up my back in a soft yet desperate motion. One that makes my whole body scream in a good way. One that makes me kiss Luka harder, caressing his tongue with mine, stealing his breath while he also leaves me breathless.

He leans back on the mat and scoops the curtain off the floor before draping it over us, shielding us from the rest of the world. His hands move from my back to rest on my thighs, now bare because my thin hospital gown hikes up toward my stomach. And I don't even feel embarrassed—the only blush rushing over me is caused by my own desire. Luka awakens a need within me I didn't know was there. He fills an emptiness I didn't recognize until this moment—I didn't even realize how starved for attention—his attention—I've been. I could drown in his familiarity and still be able to breathe.

"You have no idea how much I've missed you, Skye," Luka thinks to me.

"I think I do," I think back to him, smiling as he continues to kiss me.

"I swear we'll figure out how to get out of here. It was one thing for me to be here, but it kills me you're here with me now, you know."

Slowly, I break our kiss so I can pull back to stare into Luka's eyes. "I might have to be a monster to do so," I whisper.

"What do you mean?"

"Caretaker Sienna threatened me, said she was going to kill Avery for good for acting out against me."

His brows crinkle. "She's trying to scare you."

It worked. "Luka, I don't want to find out."

He swears.

"I might not remember how I got here or everything from our past, but I know I didn't come here to just be with you. I'll do what I need to do to get us out. I'm seeing that now. I can't wait any longer for Nikolai to break me. He got to Avery. He's going to get to Gemma. I'm terrified he'll get to you."

"Skye..."

I press my lips into a line. "I'm an awful human being. Maybe I deserve this for thinking this way. But if it came down to doing the right thing and you, I'll be the monster for Nikolai."

Luka leans his head back and drops his arms from my hips. "We can think of another way. We're in this together. We've always been. You can't seem to realize that—even now."

"I'm sorry. I need to protect you from ever being like me."

"Right, I'm some scared kid who can't handle himself."

Sarcasm drips in his voice. "You know, I've changed a lot this last year. You might think you know me, but you know the me I was before as well. We're different now."

I slide from his lap to sit next to him. I doubt he'd knock me off him or anything, but his annoyance makes me want to put space between us. "Maybe we are."

"So, what now? You're going to give up after everything?"

"I don't even remember everything, Luka. Don't you get it? I was worse off before. But now? I'm not putting myself before you. Not anymore. I shouldn't have run after I killed you in the forest. Whoever that girl was, she obviously knew she made a mistake and that's why she came back here. And who knows? Maybe I've been with Nikolai this entire time, and this is all a gift to me, reuniting me with you and reminding me what I did and teaching me a lesson."

He doesn't respond, which I'm grateful for. Nothing he says will change my mind. He can't see beyond these barriers, and if he can, he's blinded from seeing who I truly am— whoever that may be.

Covering my face with my hands, I close myself off from Luka and the world around us. It's hard to think about any-thing outside of his presence. I want so badly to see myself through his eyes, to reconsider, to remember what I should fight for, but I'm afraid of not standing up to how he remem-bers me. A lot changes in a year.

"Please, don't shut me out," he whispers, gently pulling my hands from my face to force me to meet his dark gaze. His brows pinch in the middle, lowering to the point that his dark eyelashes touch them. "You think it's Nikolai breaking me, but you're wrong. It's you."

I suck in a breath, my heart splintering at his words. "It's what I do best."

He leans his forehead to mine, closing his eyes, and doesn't do anything.

The silence hangs heavy between us. The intensity burns through me, searing my already aching heart as I fail to live up to Luka's expectations of the girl he thought he knew and fell in love with. The girl who was his soul mate but has turned into the monster she warned him about. Because I'll take comfort in knowing that it's me who breaks him as long as it's not Nikolai or the Knezha Family.

"Luka," I think to him. *"Say something."*

"Why? You keep shutting me out. Obviously nothing I say to you will make a difference. I'd rather sit here and just be with you for as long as I can."

"I'm sorry." Apologies seem to be the only response I can form, and I know it's not what he wants to hear.

"Just stop, Skye."

Tears burn the back of my eyelids. I can't help it. And it makes me feel stupid. Weak, even.

Luka's warm finger brushes along my cheek.

"God, I'm pathetic," I think when he doesn't say anything but continues to wipe my tears as they fall.

"You're not. But you're lost. I see it. You would never resort to what you want to do, and I would give anything to change your mind."

"*Then help me remember.*"

"*If I could, you damn well know I would. But all I have are my memories, and while they're of us, they're not yours.*"

"*There has to be a way to get them back. You've helped some of them return. Maybe you can help me unlock more. You said I taught you things before. Can't you try something?*"

"*I can't unlock something you've sealed off completely. Your memories aren't just behind some locked door. You've hid your mind behind moats and metal and bulletproof glass.*"

"*But I've let you in now,*" I think to him.

He shakes his head. "*You've only cracked the window open for me.*"

I frown. "*We're soul mates. I'd think I'd have given you special access.*"

He chuckles. "*To a lot of things, sure. But not your mind. You've always been a little bit of a mystery.*"

"*I sound like a terrible soul mate.*"

"*No, you definitely aren't. I like to think you were protecting me.*"

"*Or hiding some shady crap.*" I pat my chest. "*Hello? Psycho murderer, here.*"

"*No, you were always honest about all that.*"

I heave a breath. "*Then why? Why did I have to be so complicated?*"

He leans in closer. "*It always kept things interesting.*"

That's one way to put it. "*Oh, shut up.*"

Smiling, he leans in, kissing me again. It's sweet and familiar, and speeds up my heart rate. I don't let him pull back. "*I was right about you,"* I add. *"You really can't stay mad at me for long."*

Cupping his face, I kiss him deeper, sliding my tongue into his mouth, caressing it against his. He tugs me to the mat with him, letting me lie on top of him. My elbows frame his face, and he moans breathlessly as I press into him. The only thing separating our skin is flimsy cotton.

His hands tighten around me, trailing down my lower back, exploring my body through the thin fabric of my gown. He squeezes my hips, sending a burst of tingles through me, and I suck in a soft breath.

I could lose myself in everything he is and everything he awakens in me. I don't have to remember anything at all to feel our deep-seated connection—to know we have a past in some other life I'd rip a hole in the universe to find. I'd climb every fence, break through every wall, knock down every door if it meant I could get back everything stolen from me.

"Skye," Luka thinks to me. *"You opened a door."*

I freeze mid kiss, my heart nearly ramming through my ribcage to propel itself directly at Luka's. His thoughts weren't exactly what I was expecting him to say in this moment.

"You remembered how," he adds.

"What?" I say the words out loud, pulling away from Luka. "I don't understand."

I twist in his arms, yanking the sheet away, expecting to see the clear plastic door of our room wide open. But it's not. It's a different door completely, and the sight of it throws me off so much that I scramble from Luka's arms to get to my feet.

I glance at Luka, who's already standing, and back to the red door in front of us, blocking our view of the clear plastic one.

Taking a small step forward, I raise my hand and press my fingers against cool, solid wood. I whirl around and nearly knock Luka over as I collide into his chest. He steadies me on my feet and spins me back so we're both facing the mysterious door that appeared out of nowhere.

"What's happening? It feels real," I say.

"It is real." Luka steps forward. I follow his lead, locking my fingers around his hand, almost afraid that if I let him go, he'll abandon me through the door. "Let me show you." I knew I had it in me to access some magical door, but the last thing I expected was to manifest a door in the physical world. I knew I could access the galaxy world, and I knew I could take people in it, but I imagined something else altogether.

Fear drips down my back in an icy wave, making me shiver. Luka touches his fingers to the doorknob. I flinch, expecting the door to suddenly explode or disappear or even fall over like a movie prop, but all it does is swing open like a door should.

"Oh, crap," I say, blinking the surprise from my eyes. "Is that?"

He pulls me forward. "Yeah."

"This is what Nikolai wanted."

I can't believe I'm seeing the galaxy world behind a door that just appeared out of nowhere.

I'm not even sure how I did it, but now all I want to do is step through it—to see the space between this life and the next while I'm still firmly tethered to this life. I want to explore the stars. I want to see what else is out there. Find the answers that have been hidden from me.

I take another step closer, tugging Luka with me. "Come on. We have to go through. This might be our only chance."

He doesn't argue like I expect him to. I think he knows in this moment that all our choices are crappy, and he'd rather try to leave somewhere with me than risk me losing myself to the man who makes me a person I'm sure I despise.

As a wave of peace and excitement crashes over me, washing away all the anger and annoyance—all the sadness and uncertainty—I've been clinging to, the sound of rubber soles on polished concrete cuts through the air. I halt in place, gripping Luka tighter. The fear of Caretaker Sienna breaks my concentration on the door, and when I blink my eyes, the door vanishes.

"Where'd it go?" I ask Luka.

Before he can respond, Caretaker Sienna enters the room from the dark corridor. I'd scream if I knew it could bring the door back, and then I'd push Caretaker Sienna and her stupid masked face through it myself before slamming it shut and locking it forever.

But I don't scream.

I don't do anything but stand in front of the plexiglass door and gape at the woman.

"Skye," she says, stopping in front of the door. I'm surprised she doesn't call me subject four. "Please, step forward for sedation."

"Sedation? What for?" I ask.

She narrows her eyes. "Transportation."

I glance to Luka and back to the caretaker. "Fine, but I want Luka to come with me."

She shakes her head. "This isn't how it works."

I tense, glaring at her. "He's coming with me."

She doesn't respond for a long moment, considering my threat.

"If I try anything, you can kill me," Luka says.

Caretaker Sienna focuses on Luka. "Permanently."

My mouth falls agape. "What? No."

"Deal," Luka says, ignoring me.

I grab his hand. "Forget it."

"Deal," Caretaker Sienna responds, ignoring me, too.

"Are you crazy?" I think to Luka.

"You started this, Skye. And now I'm helping. You don't always get to save the day alone. Not anymore."

I glower at him. "Whatever. Fine. But know if you hurt him, Sienna, I will tear this place apart before I kill you. And there won't be any coming back for you."

"Raise your arm, Skye," she says, pretending like I didn't threaten her again. It might be beneficial that she doesn't believe I'm capable of it. Surprise is something I know I need on my side.

Slowly, I raise my arm up to the chain-link barrier, but I don't stop glowering. She pricks me with a needle, and shadows haze my vision.

"I mean it. I'll even lock the door," I say, my words slur-

ring as I try to fight the sedative.
    But it's no use.
    The world fades to black.

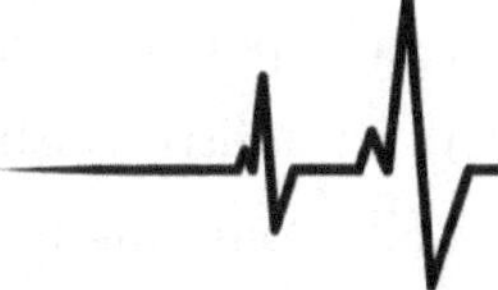

CHAPTER 16

BETRAYAL

*"S*KYE, WAKE UP.*"*

Snapping my eyes open to pitch blackness, I scramble from the icy floor and turn directly into a metal wall.

The freezer. I can't believe she shoved me in the freezer. I didn't even get a chance to negotiate anything. My fingers tremble and my teeth chatter, a mixture of fear and cold sinking deep into my bones. It takes everything in me not to scream out in panic.

"It's okay, Skye. I'm right outside the door. But I have to warn you. You're not alone. Avery's in there." Luka's voice wraps

around me like a familiar blanket, easing the fear enough so I get my bearings together to start pacing off the chill. I don't leave the wall, because the moment my heart stops pounding in my ears, I hear it. The soft moan coming from an indistinguishable place in the freezer. It bounces off the walls, sounding like it could be coming from anywhere, even next to me, but it's too dark to see.

"Hello?" a faint, feminine voice calls out into the darkness. *"Nikolai, my family, anyone? If you can hear me, please, I'm ready to come home."*

I stiffen at the mention of Nikolai in Avery's thoughts.

I'm almost too afraid to speak. Taking a breath, I say, "Avery, I don't think that's going to happen."

"Are you kidding me?" Her voice echoes through the large freezer. *"Where is she? I'm going to kill her."*

"Calm down," I say. "You need to listen to me."

"The hell I do. Come on, where are you, Skye." She's thinking to herself. The soft thump of bare feet on metal sounds through the air, Avery now strolling around though I can't see her. "I'm listening." The footsteps send a small vibration under my own bare feet. *"Come on, say something. I know you're close. I can hear you breathing."*

I swallow the lump forming in my throat from her words. "I know you think I'm some horrible person, but whatever I did, it wasn't my doing. It was Nikolai's. We were friends."

"Some friend." She huffs. *"Of course she blames Nik."*

"Please, they're doing this for a reason. Caretaker Sienna will kill you permanently. But we can stand together," I whisper, trying my best to ignore her thoughts not meant for me.

"My family won't kill me." More footsteps.

I press into the wall, afraid of what will happen if I can't reason with her. "Nik got into your head. If he cared about you, you wouldn't be in the freezer with me."

"I'm in here as a part of my journey, and it would better serve our family if you weren't part of it. You know what happens to those who turn their backs." A loud bang erupts through the air as she hits something. "Nothing you say will work on me again, Skye."

I don't remember what happened, but I'm afraid to find out.

"It'll work." The words come from behind me, and I spin around, blinking my eyes in the bright sunlight coming in through the open window behind a glass and black metal desk.

"It'll work," I repeat, the memory rushing hot and fast over me. I stare into Nikolai's bright blue eyes. He sits at his desk, the sun silhouetting him, casting shadows across his clenched jaw, making the stubble on his cheeks appear darker.

"Avery is a fighter. She's been resisting me for weeks. You sure you're up to it?" Nikolai asks, lacing his fingers together on his desk. "It's important for her to join our family here on our terms."

I nod. "She trusts me. I can handle it."

"Good. Because I need her."

"Don't worry, Nik. You'll have her."

For what? I'm sure I knew at the time, and it's why I never asked Nikolai. The memory is strange, comforting almost.

What changed?

Luka. Luka changed things. I know that, but old me doesn't. It's not like I can travel back and fix things, though. This memory will remain the same.

Walking around the desk, I bend down and slide an arm over Nikolai's shoulder in a half hug, surprising myself. He kisses my cheek, smiling, and holds my hand while looking at me with fatherly affection lining the corners of his eyes.

"My girl. You're going to make a great leader one day. The Knezha Estate and our eternal family will thrive while the rest of the world remains lost in war. I hope you know that." He says it like I need the reminder. Maybe I do.

I hug him again. "Our journey will change things. We're already changing things, Nik. I promise I will never let you down."

He ruffles my hair. "I knew I'd always be able to count on you."

"Always." I turn away from him.

Nikolai's chair squeaks, and I glance over my shoulder, watching him watch me stroll across the spacious room to the double doors. On the other side lies a hallway that'll lead to a living room and beyond it an entire wing that I know belongs to me. Flashes of a room in light gray and white, sheer laces and light woods, flickers through my mind.

And then I see Avery.

She's waiting for me outside Nikolai's office.

The second I meet her eyes, the memory changes. I'm no longer in a warm hallway but lounging by an indoor pool. Water splashes across my legs as Avery sits next to me. Tiny drops of pool water cling to her black eyelashes, and her dark eyes trail over my glittering toenail polish.

Avery's gaze flicks up to meet my eyes. "You're not gonna swim? I heard Cooper's coming soon, and I don't want to be swimming alone. He turns me into a blabbing mess. I need you to stop me from sounding dumb."

"I'll meet you in there," I say. "And I'm pretty sure Cooper is a total mess around you. You guys are made for each other."

Avery smiles, squealing, and gets up before diving back into the water. A cell phone buzzes from the opaque glass table to my right. Hesitantly, I pick it up and glance at the text message flashing on the screen.

Nikolai: *Enjoying your swim?*

Instead of responding, I hit the call button. Nikolai answers on the first ring.

"You're stalling," he says.

"I can't do this, Nik. Avery will never forgive me. Her birthday is in a few weeks. We can wait." I glance at my friend, who swims a few laps in the Olympic-sized pool. She lifts her hand and waves at me.

"We'll still celebrate her end and beginning properly. But I need her now."

I twist the towel I'm on between my fingers. "Okay. Can I at least warn her? She loves us enough that she would volunteer."

"She won't understand until she's made the transition. Just remember, this is for our family. She'll forgive you."

"I hope so, Nik. It'd have been easier if you didn't introduce us weeks ago. She's my friend."

"You have plenty."

I huff. "Not like Avery."

He hums into the phone, causing me to grimace.

"And if I do this, you have to promise to never introduce me to a new family member again. Not until after."

"Skye, she had nowhere to go. Not everyone is lucky enough to have had an Angelica in their lives like you. I can't make you that promise unless you never leave your quarters."

My heart aches hearing him mention Angelica's name. "Okay, Nik. I understand."

"Good, my girl. Now help our family grow."

The line cuts off, and I turn my attention back to Avery in the water. She motions for me to join her. I set my phone down and stand, dropping my swimsuit cover to the ground. She poses with her hand on her hip, a smirk playing on her lips as I pretend the poolside is a catwalk just to make her laugh.

Taking a deep breath, I step into the pool. The water is perfect. The pebbly bottom shimmers under the lights from overhead, and I focus on it, not meeting Avery's playful gaze.

She swims closer, splashing me with a laugh. With a huge smile, she hooks her arms around my neck and tugs me underwater. I hover weightlessly without closing my eyes. Peace washes over me, wrapping me in a protective blanket, and then hands push me back to the surface.

I gasp for breath.

Avery stands a foot away, water dripping down her forehead, a frown marring her usual playful expression. She runs her fingers through her wet hair, shaking out her bouncing curls.

"What's wrong? You're acting weird, Skye," she says.

I frown. "Avery, I—I'm sorry."

"What?"

"I just—" I snap my mouth shut to stop myself from saying more.

"Come on, you can tell me anything. You're my best friend. You have no idea how grateful I am to be here and how nice you've been."

"Please, don't say that. I'm a terrible person. I don't deserve friends."

Avery releases a loud laugh, startling me. "Is this some weird Knezha Family thing no one's told me about? Are you testing me?"

I swallow. "No, I—"

"You're an amazing person. That's why I'm totally going to help you find your mysterious soul mate. Nikolai can't keep pretending that boy doesn't exist."

"I hope you do," I whisper. "And I hope you can forgive me. Because I'm so, so sorry."

"Forgive you for wh—"

A door appears behind her right in the middle of the pool. One second everything was normal and the next, the door.

Avery stiffens. "Skye...what's wrong? Look at me."

But I can't look at her.

My heart pounds in my ears, each beat slowing with every deep breath I take. If I could force my eyes closed in this memory, I would. I'd do everything I could to block the view of the door, to hide from what I know is coming next.

"I'm sorry, Avery," I whisper so softly she can't hear me.

Reaching into my hair, I pull out a stick—not a stick—a small blade. It nicks the side of my thumb, sending a trickle of blood splashing into the water. Avery's eyes widen, but surprise holds her in place. With a quick jab of my hand, I stab her in the stomach.

Avery screams, and an arc of red water splashes me in the face. I inhale the sour mixture of the saltwater pool and blood and choke. Nails bite into my wrists, the pain nothing but a faint memory now though everything else feels utterly real.

My ears ring with Avery's wails. She pushes me back, and a loud crack reverberates through my skull. Even injured she's strong. And she's angry. So incredibly angry. I can't blame her, though. Nikolai promised her what he had promised me—a family to care for her, to protect her. She was promised a ceremony and an eternity of togetherness, something she had never had before. And Nikolai made me betray her. He betrayed her.

I scream, releasing all my air into the water. She drags me back to the surface, and everything is so confusing.

Blurring eyes.

Gasping breath.

Blood.

Swinging my arm, I punch her in the throat. My boney knuckles slide against damp skin. Avery's fearful eyes widen, and then her face obscures with glittering bubbles as she sinks under. Her mouth opens, filling with water. The bubbles stop.

The water calms.

Slowing heartbeat.

The red door in the water swings open.

"I'm sorry…" I send the thought into Avery's mind, though I'm not even sure if she heard it in the memory.

Then I see the galaxy.

I sob, my voice the only thing I can hear through the sudden quiet of Avery's death. Her murder. She was right. I killed her. I opened a door. I pulled her into the galaxy with me and yanked her right back out. I don't know what happened after that day.

But now she's standing in front of me so close that her breath blows strands of hair from my face.

Before I have a chance to stumble back, Avery locks her hands to my shoulders and shoves me hard. I hit the freezer wall with a bang, the wind knocking from my lungs. Sinking to the floor, I clutch my chest. I don't try to move as she reaches for me again because I can't get my body to work.

But Avery's not fast either, and she's weak. She tries to lift me from the floor and fails, dropping me a few inches.

"Avery, don't do this," I say. "I remember now. I remember everything. What I did—I don't blame you for hating me."

"I trusted you and you betrayed me!" she screams. The crack of knuckles against concrete sounds in my ear.

I flinch but remain in my place without fighting back. "I was doing what I was told. Please, believe me. You were my friend."

She presses her palms to my chest and shakes me. "Stop lying!"

"Please! I'd have never done anything to purposely hur—"

Slapping a hand over my mouth, she cuts off my words. "Shut up, traitor! You ruined me. You ruined everything. Nikolai warned me about you."

And now he's pitted us against each other. And I know what's happening.

Caretaker Sienna isn't going to finalize Avery's death. She's going to push me into it.

"Stay calm and stop talking, Skye." Luka's voice sneaks into my mind.

I ignore him and rip Avery's hand free from my mouth. "Please, you don't have to do this. I'll do anything to make it up to you, but you need to stop. Don't let Caretaker Sienna win. This is what she wants."

The lights flicker on.

It's too late.

Avery's chest heaves as she glares down at me. Her rage is so intense it makes me squirm. "Make it up to me? First you made me think I was your best friend, that I could trust you. You went against Nik and took our family's journey into your own hands, and then you abandoned us. Just up and disappeared. You're a selfish psycho. There is nothing you can do to make it up to me, but I can make it up to you. This is what Nikolai wants."

"Don't," I plead. "Please."

"You don't get to beg. I begged you to stop, and you didn't. This is how I'm getting back into Nikolai's good grace."

The lights flicker overhead, the mirrored window on the side of the freezer shattering.

"No!" I yell, my voice echoing through the room. I can't let her use her ability against me.

Rushing forward, I charge into Avery. I knock her off her feet, and we land together on the freezer floor. I wrap my hands around her neck, something coming over me as natural as breathing and as dark as my worst nightmare. I squeeze as hard as I can, not even giving my mind time to process. I'm acting on adrenaline and instincts, and I know that if I don't do something, Avery will. And if Avery kills me, I can't protect her any longer. Her life will be out of my hands and who knows what Caretaker Sienna will do. She's using Avery against me because she's trying to pull information from my locked memory, except now, I can access the door.

"Skye," she says, gasping, fighting to free herself from me.

I don't listen to her plea, struggling to keep her in place, though she realizes how fighting against me was a terrible mistake. She thrashes, pulling my hair and then clawing at my face. My blood splashes across her forehead. Flashes of us together in the pool flood my mind. The crimson water. The look on her face. The quiet of her death. The memory haunts me as history repeats itself.

I knew this was a possibility—that I might have to kill her if I couldn't show her reason—but what I didn't realize was how hard it'd actually be to follow through. I wasn't counting on the feelings the memory of Avery from before stirred— friendship. Sisterly. Feelings I somehow managed to shut off to bring her into the Knezha Family. I made it look so easy before. *You thought you were doing right by her,* I think to myself.

Tears burn my eyes, my hands digging into Avery's throat, cutting off her breath. Her body rises from the ground, lifting us both into the air so high my back hits the ceiling as she uses her telekinesis to vault us around the room. There's nothing she can use against me, and I refuse to let her go, so she's using herself to try to get me away.

But I'm strong. Stronger than I realized.

"I don't want to do this," I whisper, feeling her heartbeat pulse against my fingers from the vein in her neck. I know it'll be less than a minute until she leaves this life.

Avery's eyes bulge from her head as she stares at me. *"You can do it, Avery. Break her neck."*

I clench my jaw, realizing she's trying to use her own ability against me. And I can't let her. It has to be her. I can't be the one to die and leave her open.

My head starts to twist to the side, a small pop sounding over the pounding in my ears. *"Stop!"* I scream from my mind. Avery's eyes widen, and she goes placid beneath me.

"Skye." Luka's voice cuts through my own screaming thoughts. *"Stop. You don't have to do this."*

"But I do," I think to him.

"We'll figure a way out of it. Just stop. You don't have to. You don't want to. Don't let them push you into being someone you hate. This isn't you. Nikolai can't manipulate you anymore."

"Are you so sure?" I ask.

"Yes. Just stop."

My tears splash on Avery's face, and I release her neck. She gasps, shoving her hands hard into my chest, and then we both drop to the floor. Pain erupts through me even though she cushions my fall, and I struggle to get off of her.

Avery doesn't move. Blood pours from her head.

Her wide, blank eyes stare past me.

She's dead. I killed her anyway.

Caretaker Sienna clears her throat, appearing seemingly out of nowhere, and I flick my gaze to her. I was too concerned about Avery that I missed the true monster sneaking in. She must've learned from the best. Pressing her thumb on the canister, she sprays me with the god-awful poison.

I scream.

Five.

My vision turns black.

Four.

Heat washes over my skin.

Three.

I gasp for air that doesn't come.

Two.

My heart stops.

"Time of death: Nine twenty-two P.M."

For the first death ever, I don't see the stars. I see the door. The red door that's been evading me. And then I see Avery. Standing in front of it, she raises her hand and knocks. The taps resonate through the air, sounding loud in the silence that has overtaken the room.

"What's happening?" Avery asks. She peers over her shoulder, a weird look crossing her face as our gazes meet. Her shapely brows pinch together, and she swivels to face me completely.

"I'm sorry," I say.

It's like I'm speaking underwater. The world presses against me, the air as thick as jelly. I wish I'd gone into the galaxy. Why didn't I go into the galaxy? What's going on?

"Subject two will need the healing box," Caretaker Sienna says. I can't see her on the other side of the door, but her tennis shoes squeak, and I know she's entered the freezer completely. "Head trauma."

I glance away from Avery standing in front of the door to a pool of blood crawling across the floor. It seeps from her body and into my blond hair. My blond hair? I cringe, looking at my dead body sprawled next to her, my hospital gown hiked up so I can see my plain white underwear.

"Damn it," I whisper.

"*Skye?*" Luka's voice erupts in my mind. "*Where are you?*"

"*Luka, help me. Everything is so strange. I'm not in the galaxy world, and I can see Avery. I can see my body. I'm scared.*"

He doesn't respond to any of my questions but instead says, "*Come on, Skye. Don't do this to me. Where are you? You've locked access to the galaxy.*"

"*Luka, I'm here,*" I say.

"*Come on. Open the door.*" He's not talking to me. "*Damn it, Skye. You slammed the door and locked it.*"

"*What do I do?*" I ask even though he can't hear me.

"*Open the damn door!*"

I blink once, and the closed door is suddenly wide open.

The beautiful stars call to me on the other side of it. Peace bursts from the doorway, begging me to step forward, but Avery stands in front of it, gazing at me. I don't even think she realizes the door's open.

"Skye? Skye? Can you hear me?" Luka asks. *"I can feel you."*

"Luka I'm—"

"Oh, God, Skye," Avery says, interrupting me. "You can't let me go back. He's in my head. He's broken through the block you put on me."

Shock washes over me, stealing away the peacefulness radiating from the door. "Avery, I'm so sorry. I didn't want to do this. I don't know exactly who I was before, but I'm not that girl now. I ran away from that life because it wasn't what I had expected it to be. Nikolai, he—"

"I know, Skye. I know you did what you had to do, and I know you did it for me. You did it for everyone. Nikolai ruined us. He's in my head. I can't stand it. You have to push me through the door. It's the only way."

My brows furrow. "What do you mean? What happens?"

"Please, trust me. It has to be done. I knew this moment would come. Push me through and lock the door. Hurry, Caretaker Sienna will bring me back first, and if she does—" Tears stream onto her cheeks, glittering onto her face. "I can't—"

"But that would mean—"

"Keep it locked."

I nod. She's right. I just wish it wasn't her making the sacrifice.

Sucking in a deep breath of the gelatin-like air, I thrust out my hands, connecting with Avery's chest like she's solid. Like she's alive and not dead on the floor. Her eyes widen, her lips twisting to the side, and then she stumbles back.

But I don't let her go alone.

Together, we fall through the door and into the galaxy world. Her scream rings through my mind for a second before she sucks in a deep breath of relief.

"I'm sorry, Avery," I whisper. "You never deserved any of this. Until our journey meets again."

"Skye? Come back to me," Luka calls.

I turn to the void amid the stars and follow the sound of my soul mate's voice.

Five.

My vision brightens.

Four.

A lock clicks.

Three.

Heat rushes over me.

Two.

My heart beats.

"Time of life: Nine thirty-one P.M."

CHAPTER 17

RUTHLESS

LUKA SITS NEXT to me on a double bed in a room I've never seen before. I don't know how we ended up here. Caretaker Sienna sedated me the second I opened my eyes, but I'm more unnerved than ever. She could have easily locked me back up, but now I'm alone with Luka in a room I don't think even has a camera—at least one I can't see—with a tray of food on a desk and real clothes hanging in a closet.

"What do you think will happen next?" I ask. "I think she knows I accessed the galaxy world."

He slides his arm around my back and pulls me to him. "I wish I knew, Skye. I don't even know where we are. I have never been here."

"Have you tried the door?" I stand and cross the room.

"It's locked."

I try to turn the knob anyway. It doesn't budge just like I expected. Strolling from the door, I head to the closet where the clothes hang. Luka comes up behind me, hooking his fingers onto my hips, resting his chin on my shoulder.

"Pick out something," I say.

"Think it's a good idea?" He pulls away, and my heart sinks at the sudden lack of his touch.

"None of my ideas are good, apparently." I yank a plain black shirt, one much too large for me, from a hanger. I reach around and untie the top strings of my hospital gown and pull it over my head, side glancing Luka.

He keeps his eyes trained on the clothes in the closet. "Skye, about what happened—"

"It is what it is." I shrug into the shirt and turn to Luka. "I just—" Inhaling a long breath through my nose, I force the guilt sweeping through me away.

Luka pulls me to him, wrapping me in his cool arms. Something in me breaks, like Luka poked the balloon that was containing my emotions, and a shudder rushes through me. My bottom lip trembles, and my eyes blur with tears. I can't stop my nose from sniffling even though I want nothing more than to slap myself and snap out of it.

Whatever friendship I had with Avery before, whatever I was to her, was ruined the moment I allowed Nikolai to control me. I stole her life and replaced it with one fitting of the Knezha

Family name. I was playing a game under Nikolai's persuasion, and it turned her against me, and not by her doing. I should feel better that somewhere along the line after I brought her back from death that we mended things, and that she didn't hate me in the end, but I still betrayed her. It doesn't change the fact that I obeyed an order from a man who I have mixed emotions about during a time between my first death and running away with Luka.

"Don't blame yourself, Skye," Luka whispers. "Once Nikolai gets to someone, it's impossible to save them. Avery as she was would have made things a lot worse for us."

"Nikolai's still going to," I say, wishing I could push away the thought of how he made me feel like I belonged in my memory.

"He's a powerful man. Brutal. But we can be just as ruthless. He'll see. He made that possible."

"I just wish I knew what happened so I can feel like I can live with myself. We were on our journey as a family together. I'm still having trouble believing he wasn't great or he tricked me into murdering people in the name of the Knezha Family to brainwash them. But why have me do it? He's like us."

"He's nothing like us, Skye."

"There is no one else like us, my beautiful girl." Nikolai's voice crowds my mind as Luka triggers a memory. Nikolai stands in front of me, the same height as I am, and holds me in his intense gaze.

"But he's different, Nik. I can feel it. Just give me more time," I say.

"I've given you plenty of time. You've been gallivanting around with him for weeks. It's time to bring him home." Nikolai grasps my shoulders. "You can still have your fun with him once I'm through."

Luka. We're discussing Luka.

I catch sight of my reflection in the wall mirror behind him. My blond hair hangs in my face, my lips pouty and twisted downward, but the second I feel Nikolai focusing on me, I smile. I wish I could remember the exact thoughts that swam in my mind at the time. Something's different about this memory. It reminds me of the time I told Luka to run from the diner.

"Okay," I say. "I'll bring him home tonight."

"That's my girl." Nikolai leans forward and kisses my forehead. He pulls me into a hug, making the world shake as he lifts me off my feet and spins me around. "I always knew you'd know how to pick them. Luka will be a great addition to the Knezha Family, and a great asset on our eternal journey as your guardian."

"Skye?" Cool fingers lace with mine. "Come back to me."

I gasp, clutching my chest. My heart races, thudding in overdrive against my palm. I can't believe the memory. I can't believe I had promised Nikolai to bring him Luka.

I blink the memory away and pull myself together. "I'm sorry." I try to think about what we were just talking about, but the thoughts flee from me.

Luka reaches out and brushes my hair behind my ear. "What were you remembering?"

"Nikolai," I say.

"You have to stop thinking about him, Skye," Luka says. He reaches into the closet and pulls out a pair of too big track pants for me and hands them over. "It's inviting him in."

I hold onto Luka's arm while I step into the pants and tug them up. The warm material pushes away the coolness of the AC coming in through the vent. Now, if only I could relax enough to climb into the double bed. It looks so inviting.

"I can't stop it. Everything keeps pulling these memories from me. Especially you," I say.

Luka sighs but doesn't say anything. He swipes a shirt and pair of jeans from the closet, and I watch him shrug out of his hospital gown and drop it on the floor. I drink in the sight of him, the deep bruises clustered across his side from who knows what, a jagged scar zigzagging across his chest, and the puckered skin of a bullet hole a few inches above his naval.

I point my finger at it. "That was from me."

He shifts away, hiding the scar from my view to yank the shirt over his head. "Yeah."

I close my eyes, trying to push the memory of him bleeding out on the ground from my mind. "Did you know I was still in contact with Nikolai after we ran away?" I hate asking, but he has a right to know. He has a right to see me for the monster I am, even if he can't see it for himself. Even if he can make excuses for my actions.

He doesn't say anything for a long moment as he gets dressed. I almost don't think he's going to respond to me at all, but after an uncomfortable minute, he swivels to face me.

"I did. We got as far as the gate to the Knezha Estate before you decided you weren't going to take me after all. That's when we went to the cabin in Mount Pine."

A million questions pile on top of each other in my mind until my head throbs like it's about to burst. Rubbing my temples, I shuffle from the closet and back to the bed, plopping down. Luka follows my lead and sits next to me, bouncing me into him with his weight. I don't move to put space between us. Neither does he.

"Skye, I know you don't want to hear this, but none of that matters to me. I was angry at you for lying to me and hurt that you thought you couldn't tell me, but we worked through it. We were in a good—a great place—before I went and screwed everything up." His fingers lace through mine, and he holds my hand. "You did what you thought was right until it didn't feel right anymore. You had your reasons, just like I had my reasons to forgive you."

A tear drips onto my cheek and rolls off my chin to splash onto the fabric of my long shirt. "And what were those reasons?"

"Does it really matter?"

I nod. "It does." Because if I can hear his reasoning, make sense of how and why he could forgive me for allowing myself to be one of Nikolai's little pawns, for nearly taking him to be added to Nikolai's collection, for lying and being the horrible person I know I was, then maybe I could find an excuse for myself that I can deal with. An excuse that'll make every new memory easier to live with. I'm afraid if I can't, and if more come, I'll shatter.

"Well, I'm in love with you, Skye."

I know he cares about me. I know we're soul mates. But hearing him say those words, feeling the intensity of his stare, his eyes the most honest things I can even remember—my heart nearly explodes with a mixture of fear and raw desire. It confuses me. I don't even know how I really feel. What I want to feel. I have these memories of our life together, of our past, and it's like I've messed everything up for me. That maybe my brain tried to suppress my feelings because my love is poisonous. It's not good. It doesn't lift him up or make his life better. It ruined us. It ruined him.

"And look where it got you," I say.

He shakes his head. "All you were trying to do was protect us."

"From Nikolai," I say. A glimpse of a silhouette within the pines flashes through my mind. I remember raising the gun and pulling the trigger. I thought it might have been Caretaker Sienna before, but I know it wasn't now. "He had found us. I went in the forest to get to him first." I know it's the truth in my very bones. Had Luka never followed me, I'd have used the gun against Nikolai. The memory of him in the forest outside the cabin is nothing like the rest. I'm overwhelmed with hate and fear and so much anger.

Luka runs the pad of his thumb across my wet cheek. "But then I had to go and screw everything up. No wonder you forgot me."

I bump my shoulder with his. "I should've told you."

"No, the less I knew, the better it was for me."

Grimacing, I say, "My words, right? I should've stayed with you."

"We didn't spend all that time running for you to end up back with him. Now stop thinking about things we can't change."

I lean my elbows on my knees, and Luka rubs his hand in circles on my back. Exhaustion creeps up on me, and I finally relent and lie back on the bed, keeping my legs over the edge so my feet touch the floor.

"Will you give me something else to think about then?" I ask.

Luka flops back on the bed next to me, still holding my hand. "Like what?"

Without responding, I shift to my side and close the distance between us until my lips meet his. I trace my finger along his jaw, kissing him gently, just feeling the softness of his lips against mine for a moment. He pulls me down on him with his free hand until our chests press together and my elbows rest on both sides of his head. We continue to kiss so softly, just teasing each other, testing each other. Remembering each other.

A series of fleeting moments flash through my mind, and I glimpse Luka kissing me under the covered porch of our cabin, next in a car—the same car where it felt like the storms were chasing us—and then in a room, on a bed much more comfortable. My hair veils my cheeks, my breath nearly gasping, the good pressure of his fingers digging into my sides.

Luka rolls me over until he's on top of me, drawing me back to the present. His fingers lace through mine, raising my hands over my head. He trails his lips from mine to my jaw, his warm breath tickling down my neck to brush against the collar of my shirt.

I gasp, tilting my head back with my eyes closed so I can feel like we're not in this strange room, but just together in our own world. Our galaxy.

"I love you, Luka." The words are another piece of my memory sliding into place. My voice sounds so certain in my mind. I almost can't take it, having the memory, feeling the emotions behind it, half expecting it to just disappear forever.

I draw in a long breath. "Luka," I whisper. As much as I want him to continue kissing me like I'm the best thing in the universe, I can't stop the fear from sneaking up on me. Luka might feel so, so right, but everything else in this room feels utterly wrong. He makes me let my guard down, and right now, I need a brick wall, bulletproof glass, an entire universe to surround myself to prepare for what Nikolai and Caretaker Sienna have in store. Because it can't be good.

He pulls away. "I'm sorry. It's just—"

I kiss the apology from his lips. "I know, but...if it were any other place."

He bobs his head. "Why don't we try to get some sleep then? It's been a year since I actually got to sleep in a bed."

"Okay," I say, shimmying up to one of the two pillows. I don't think I could sleep if I tried, even if I'm exhausted. My mind won't let me. Not until I figure out why Caretaker Sienna put us here.

I missed this, you know, " he thinks to me as he curls against me.

I shift and turn to face him. "*I can see why.*"

He smirks and rests his head against mine. "*You're not going to sleep, are you?*"

"*Just close your eyes. I'll make sure we're safe, okay?*"

He kisses me once more. "*Maybe you'll let me keep you safe next?*"

"*I'd like that,*" I think to him.

He chuckles. "*Liar.*"

I only respond with a shrug and adjust to wrap my arms around Luka so I can feel his warm breath on my shoulder as he hugs me. There's something about feeling it that comforts me, because I know he's alive.

The light turns off, and I tense, but Luka's already sleeping. I train my gaze on the crack of light from under the door. A shadow passes by, but the door remains closed.

"*Be patient, Sienna. Give her one night.*" Caretaker Sienna's voice creeps into my mind, and I force her voice away.

One night for what?

I guess I'll soon find out.

CHAPTER 18

THE KEY

"YOU DON'T LIKE it?" Nikolai asks, holding up a glittering gown in the prettiest lavender color. It's a form fitting dress with capped sleeves and a cinched waist that'll make me curvier than I actually am.

I stroll forward and run my fingers along the textured fabric. "I do. It's just—what if I mess it up?"

Nikolai chuckles. "Then I'll buy you another. A dozen. Whatever you want, my beautiful girl."

I grin, beaming my brightest smile and hold the dress up to myself. I don't even have to try it on to know it's the perfect fit. "Thank you, Nik. For everything you've done for me. I don't even know where I'd—"

"You'd be just fine without me. Angelica would be so proud of who you've become in such a short time. She always knew you were meant for the Knezha Family the moment she laid eyes on you. I only wish you could've come sooner," Nikolai says, hugging me.

"But Angelica thought I'd be too distracted, and she might've been right. I wouldn't have figured out how—" I pause, sadness gripping at my chest, remembering the woman who helped me when I needed it most. *"To unlock the door,"* I think to him.

"There was never any doubt you couldn't. You're the key, my girl. We have access to everything we could ever want. The things we know—people spend their whole lives looking for it. We'll build the family we want. Not even death can hold us."

Immortality. Control over people. Traveling between the planes of life and death and everything in between. Nikolai's ambitions are big, seemingly impossible. But not to him. To us. I've opened the door with Nikolai, we've entered through together and returned better than ever. Physically rejuvenated, more in control—and it's not the only thing. Opening a door gives us access to parts of ourselves we never could otherwise. Nikolai can acquire more talent that far exceeds our mind reading ability.

"A family," I say.

Nikolai bobs his head. "You'll never be alone again. They'll always protect you. I'll always protect you."

"And I'll protect you, Nik."

"I'll protect you, Nik. I'll protect you—"

"Skye, wake up." My body shakes, my words to Nikolai playing on a loop in my mind.

I snap my eyes open, disoriented and angry that I fell asleep. I should've gotten up to pace, to do push-ups, anything to keep me awake. But the darkness was too heavy, Luka's arms too inviting, the bed too comfortable.

Luka hovers inches away, resting his cheek against the pillow close enough that if I leaned forward, I could kiss him if I wanted to. But I don't. The intensity of his gaze holds me back.

I blink the dream—memory—of Nikolai away. It felt too real, too familiar to be something my mind created, but I can't know for sure. Luka wasn't there, so I can't even ask him about it, not that I want to, because something about listening to Nikolai, hearing his thoughts in my mind, feeling how much it felt like he cared about me, leaves me utterly confused. He was all I had after Angelica's murder. He got me through it. But I'm supposed to hate the man, not yearn to do everything he asks like some lonely girl starved for attention, starved for someone to replace the father who abandoned her.

"What's wrong?" I ask Luka, licking my lips to draw moisture to my mouth. It takes me a second to realize the lights shine overhead. How much time has passed? Is it morning already?

"I heard Gemma," he whispers.

I hold my breath to help me listen, but no sound comes through the door.

"Don't listen with your ears," Luka thinks to me.

Closing my eyes, I concentrate on trying to hear for someone who isn't Luka. Only the strongest thoughts around me tend to trickle through, but I know Luka can hear into the thoughts of whoever he wants as long as they don't know how to block him from probing into their heads. I'm not even sure I know how to do it now. All that I know is instinctual, and my instincts tell me to hold onto the imaginary soundproof wall I've built around my thoughts as tightly as I can.

"I can't do it." My voice is softer than a whisper. "I don't want to let her in."

"You don't let her in. Not unless you want to give yourself a massive headache. You go into her head."

"That doesn't sound any better." I squeeze my eyes closed tighter and try to imagine Gemma on the other side of the door.

Luka reaches out and cups my head in his hands, covering my ears. *"Just listen. Focus. You've done this a million times. It's how we stay one step ahead."*

Twisting my lips to the side, I grimace. I might have been able to do this before, and easily, since Luka makes it sound like doing so is as simple as breathing, but I'm hitting a wall.

"Just tell me what she's sa—"

"You are strong. You are powerful. You will not let anyone hurt you," Gemma thinks to herself. *"Skye and Luka will see to it you die. They'll pick each other."*

I try to listen for Caretaker Sienna's thoughts but can't pull them from the cacophonous noise created by Gemma's loud panic. And I'm afraid for her. I'm afraid of what will happen to her if Nikolai gets into her head, if we're forced to face each other. Nikolai used a moment of turmoil to turn Avery against me, amplifying one bad moment. And Gemma? If she acted anything like she does now, I'm sure we had a bunch.

I open my eyes to peer at Luka, who's still watching me. "Where's Caretaker—" The door swings open, cutting off my words, and Caretaker Sienna stands in the doorway like I just summoned the devil with the thought of her.

Luka flips over to face her, sitting up. He blocks me with his body so I can only see half of her. I don't move to get up. I even turn my gaze away from her. I'm afraid if I look at her long enough, she might somehow claw her way into my brain.

"Great. You're dressed." She takes a small step into the room. "Subject one, please get to your feet and hold your arms out."

Her request kicks me into action, and I scramble off the bed before Luka even rises. She holds up the black canister of poison, stopping me in my tracks a few feet away from her. The last thing I want is to be sprayed again, but I'll risk it for Luka. I'll die over and over again so he doesn't have to. It's the least I can do after everything I've put him through. I can't think of any other way to redeem myself from my horrible past.

I place my hands on my hips. "He's not going anywhere with you."

Caretaker Sienna's eyebrows shoot up from behind her protective glasses. "I'll humor you, Skye. But only because I think we can still salvage things between us."

"You think?"

"Had I known you remembered how to open—"

"Just stop. If you think your sudden nicety will change anything, you're delusional. I can't believe what you pushed me into doing," I say. I'll die before I admit that I know Avery was okay in the end, that we didn't end on the horrible terms I thought we would've.

"So, you did finalize her death? Do you know how long I tried to resurrect her? Such a waste of my time. She should've been okay."

Nothing Caretaker Sienna could have done would have brought Avery back. I made sure of it by locking the door to the galaxy world like she asked, and that I'll keep locked. She was right to make me do it. I couldn't risk the danger she put me and Luka in, especially because Nikolai had gotten into her head. Who knows what she'd have done.

"I don't know why she wasn't," I say, playing dumb.

Caretaker Sienna sees right through me, but she doesn't call me out on it. Instead, she pulls her phone from her pocket and glances at the screen. "You know, I wasn't actually going to finalize Avery's death. That was all on you." I'm enjoying how whiney she sounds. I'll do everything I can to make it hard for her. To make her absolutely miserable. But of course, this will be exactly what she'll tell Nik to put the blame on me. The traitor who will kill her own family members to protect herself.

"Keep telling yourself that," I say, crinkling my nose.

"It doesn't have to be this way."

"I don't understand—"

"There's still time. Her body is still fine."

"I can't bring Avery back," I say.

She shifts on her feet. "Then I guess I'll have to put you in the position to do it again."

I grimace. "Do what?"

"Open the door. Because the stars brought you back into our lives for a reason, Skye. There was no mistake how you ended up back in the forest. You wanted to come home, but your mind...Your poor mind."

I don't even know how to respond. She's out of her mind if she thinks I just happened to die at her feet in the snowy forest. But of course, she'd have to be a little brainwashed to keep us locked in the basement as her death-defying experiments for Nikolai as she tries to break us.

"My mind is great," I say. I turn to look at Luka who stands quietly behind me. "Right?"

Luka's fingers graze against mine. "Perfect."

Caretaker Sienna stiffens. "Skye, knock it off. I'm not stupid, and our family is getting impatient. You have to open the door."

I narrow my eyes. "Even if I could remember how, I wouldn't do it for you."

"I think you would. You've forgotten everything our family has to offer. I'm sure Nikolai realizes his mistake with Luka now."

"You can't believe anything she says. Nikolai doesn't make mistakes," Luka thinks to me.

I shake my head. "Nothing would be worth it."

"You sure about that?" She eyes Luka. *"Think things*

through, Sienna. She's volatile, especially when it comes to subject one. Threatening him will just push her farther away."

I relax a bit, hearing her sudden thoughts invade my mind. Or I'm invading her mind. Like Luka said. "What's that supposed to mean?"

"Don't you like all the time you get to spend together?" she asks.

"Tell her you don't care about our time," Luka thinks to me. *"Tell her I'm just a distraction."*

Even if I say the words, it's hard denying the emotions I wear on my face in the form of a scowl so heated I can barely see past my eyelashes. "Of course I do, but it's not worth playing these games."

She shakes her clenched fists out. "This isn't a game!"

"You're right. It's my life."

Turning on her heels, she spins and leaves, slamming the door behind her. I release a shuddering breath and swivel on my feet to fall into Luka's arms. He holds me against him, and I bury my face into the cotton of his shirt.

Then I hear it.

A light hissing sound comes through the only vent in the ceiling too high for even Luka to reach to cover it. The room grows hazy as Caretaker Sienna fills it with gas, and not even gas that'll send us to the galaxy world where we can at least get a few hours of sweet reprieve.

"She's going to separate us," Luka says, wobbling on his feet.

I nudge him back to the bed. "I'm sorry I've failed you."

He tightens his hold on me. "Don't talk like that. You didn't fail. It's not over until it's over, and even then, who's to say we've failed? You found me. You always do."

I blink my tears away and just lie with Luka without another word. The haze continues to thicken, making my head spin with a thousand images I can't seem to grasp or keep. The only thing I can hold onto is Luka. But even this can't last.

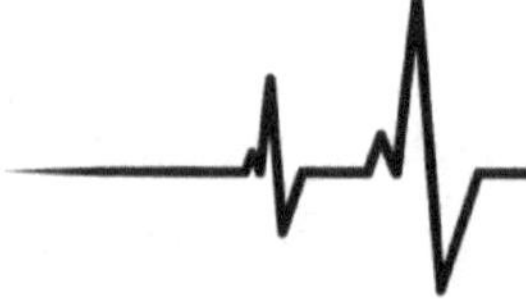

CHAPTER 19

BROKEN

"**O**H, MY GOD. *She's waking up. Nikolai can't do this. Oh, God, please help me. I don't want to do this. This isn't part of my journey.*"

I fly to my feet, and a scream rips through the air, pushing the foreign thoughts from my head. I gasp, my chest heaving with each breath. My first instinct is to fight any possible threats now and then think about the consequences later, but Gemma sobs uncontrollably. The feeling of danger coursing through my blood eases the more I get my bearings together.

I draw my attention to Gemma standing in the corner of the empty room. Her auburn hair hangs half in her face, but she peers through the knotted strands in my direction. She reminds me of the panicking girl I first woke up to in the basement, desperate and afraid, praying for things that won't change by thoughts alone.

The sparkle of a knife glints from her hand, and I take an automatic step back. Clearing my throat, I say, "Hey, Gemma. It's okay. Calm down."

She doesn't respond with her voice. *"God, please forgive me for this. I don't want to die. I've learned my lesson. Please, Skye is my friend."*

I tense at Gemma's thoughts. She takes a step closer, the knife shaking in her hand. Glancing around the room, I search for anything I can use to protect myself. I don't have to be a psychic to know what Caretaker Sienna is doing. She's trying to push me into doing something I don't want to do, something I'll have to if Gemma tries to fight. Because I'm pretty sure she's been given an ultimatum, and people do crazy things out of desperation, crazy things to protect themselves. I should know.

"I don't know what Sienna told you, but you don't have to listen to her," I say. "It's all part of a twisted game."

"Make her stop talking. It's making it worse. I have to do this." Gemma takes a step closer. "You don't think I know that?"

"Then don't do this." I say.

"I've failed. I'm so sorry. But you've failed me, too." She freezes, tears blurring her eyes. *"Now, please. Do it. Do it now. You're running out of time."*

I back into the wall. *"Running out of time for what?"*

Gemma responds by screaming out and rushing me. My body kicks into action before my mind has time to process, and I dodge out of her way. Swinging out my arm, I punch her in the shoulder, throwing her off. She hits the wall but doesn't drop the knife.

Loud sobs escape her mouth, and by the way she holds herself, I know she doesn't have the same training my body accesses from muscle memory. Maybe she's never had to fight before. I doubt she's ever used a knife for anything other than cutting food in the kitchen. But she's terrified—her thoughts scream a million things to me at once.

"Skye, please. Hurry. He broke the block you put on my mind. He'll find out what you did."

I put distance between us and raise my hands up. "I won't kill you, Gemma. Please, you have to listen to me. This is all just a game."

"You're dead, Skye," she says, her voice lowering though her thoughts scream. *"This is the only way. You have to do this. We've always protected each other. It's my turn."*

"We did?"

Gemma rushes me, slashing the knife, but again, I'm too fast. I spin out of the way. *"My journey would always end with you. Now, please. Don't let him access the door. Don't let him use me against you. He broke Avery. He broke me. If I survive, I'm lost. Don't let that happen."*

"We'll figure this out," I say out loud.

"It's you or me," she says. *"It has to be you who survives."*

"Skye? Skye can you hear me?" It's Luka.

Gemma charges me again, and I grab her wrist, twisting her arm behind her back. She tries to swing the hand with the knife behind her, and I ram my free hand between her shoulder blades and slam her into the wall. I need her to stop fighting me. I need her to see reason. It doesn't have to be her. It doesn't have to be me. We can still fight. I can't do this. I can't be forced into doing what she wants.

The knife drops from Gemma's hand, and I kick it out of the way. I race for it before she even has a chance to realize that she dropped it.

"Skye?"

"Luka, I'm kind of in the middle of something."

"I know. You have an audience."

I glare at the camera and hold the knife up to it. "You can't make me do it."

"Skye, I heard Gemma. She's right. This has to be done," Luka thinks to me.

Hands lock into my hair, pulling me away from the camera. I let my guard down, and now I'm paying for it as Gemma scratches her nails across my cheeks. I jerk my elbow back and clock her in the clavicle, using all my weight to shove her into the wall behind us. She loses her footing, and we both fall to the polished cement floor. Pain sears through my hip as I land hard on my side, but it only stops me for a second. I roll away until I hit the opposing wall, and then I force myself to get to my feet.

The knife sparkles from the middle of the room. I'm too slow to grab it, and Gemma lunges for it.

She charges me, swinging her arm out, trying to gut me.

She nearly stabs me, but the knife catches on my baggy shirt instead, and it flies from her grasp. The second she looks at the discarded weapon, I slam my palms against her chest and knock her off her feet. She collides with the floor, her scream cutting off as she hits the concrete hard. She gasps and coughs, her eyes bulging from their sockets.

"Skye, please. Don't make me do this," Gemma thinks. *"I can't stop. He's in my head."*

Oh, no. Her words sink into me, and I realize what's happening. It's not that Gemma is trying to push me into killing her, it's that Nikolai is pushing her into killing me. He's in her head, controlling her like he controlled Avery. He's trying to force me to be the monster he spent all that time drawing from me by playing with my head.

Gemma stumbles to her feet and back toward the knife. *"Skye, please. I can't do this."*

"Skye," Luka thinks to me. *"You have to."*

I tense, bracing myself, too many thoughts coming into my head, making it hard to concentrate. Gemma rushes me, and I falter. She buries the knife deep into my stomach, and pain explodes through me, my legs giving out from under me. Gemma doesn't stop. She pulls the blade back and stabs me again. And then another time.

Blood gushes from my stomach, coating my hands as I touch the wounds. Gemma's screams rip through the air. I blink the haze from my eyes and watch her scramble to the corner of the room where she slides against the wall. Blood coats her hands, and she continues to sob without looking at me.

"God, Skye. What have I done? Forgive me. Please, forgive me."

I open and close my mouth, the air hard to suck in. "It's o-okay," I manage to mutter.

"Why, Skye?" Luka thinks to me, filling up my thoughts with his voice. *"Why did you let her stab you?"*

"Because it had to be me or her, and she doesn't deserve this."

"But Skye—"

"Luka," I whisper. I can't even think anymore as my body succumbs to my wounds.

Five.

I shiver, ice coating my very soul.

Four.

The sound of Gemma's screams disappear.

Three.

I close my eyes.

Two.

My heart stops beating.

"Time of death: One fifty-three P.M."

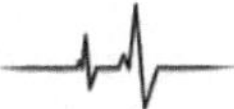

"You shouldn't be here, Luka," I say, turning on my side.

He hovers next to me amid the stars, and they bounce off his brown eyes. "What did you expect? There was no way I was going to sit back and do nothing as I watched you get stabbed to death."

I grimace. "I'm sorry she made you watch."

Reaching out his hand, he locks his fingers to my dangling arm and pulls me to him. "Probably not as bad as experiencing it. I just wish you hadn't let Gemma do that. She's broken, Skye. Because she forced you to open the door. Nikolai used her against you."

I close my eyes. "Oh, no. But I—Luka, I can't do it again."

"You must."

"I can't kill her. Don't make me." Even if the door remains open, I'm not sure I have it in me to let Gemma sacrifice her life for a world I still can't seem to grasp.

"It's the righteous thing to do, my girl." Nikolai's voice cuts through my mind as a memory crashes over me.

I groan. "How come it doesn't feel that way? They put up such a fight."

"Facing death is the most difficult task in our existence. Once they realize it isn't the end and all the gifts we bestow on them, they forgive you."

"I broke my neck last time."

"It's a good thing you can heal yourself."

I wring my hands together, staring out the window at the fountain sparkling in the rose garden below. "I don't know if I can continue, Nik."

"Is this about the boy?" Nikolai rises from his desk, drawing my attention away from the sunlight bouncing off the rippling water in the fountain outside.

"It's about me."

"This is your purpose."

"How are you so sure?"

"You doubt me? Look what we've accomplished in our few months together. Angelica would be so proud of you. I'm proud of you," Nikolai says. "Now, come on. The new recruits are waiting for you to lead the morning vows."

I stiffen. "Cover for me? Just for today?"

"You said the same yesterday before you disappeared."

Disappeared? I wish I could remember where.

I turn to face him, and he rests his hands on my shoulders, staring at me with his vibrant blue eyes. I hadn't noticed before but looking at them leaves a chill in my stomach. They lack the warmth that laces every word he speaks to me. I can't tell if it's because I'm remembering with a new perspective or if I just ignored it before. Either way, I wish I could turn away, but the old me has fallen under his charm.

"I'm sorry. I promise it won't happen again. Just today. I need some time to myself."

Nikolai stares at me for a long moment. "If you plan to leave, take a guardian with you. It's dangerous out there."

I smile. "Of course."

"And I want you to open the door for me right now before you go."

The world turns dark as I close my eyes.

"Good girl," Nikolai says. "Now go on."

I snap my eyes open to watch the red door swing open. But something's different. I can't see my galaxy. All I see is a black void. The void swallows me and spits me out on a busy street corner. I glance over my shoulder, searching for something or someone I no longer recollect. A car horn blares, and Luka jumps out from the passenger seat of another young guy's car. They bump fists, and he smiles and waves as he approaches me.

"You made it," I say.

"You make it hard to resist, Skye," he says, closing the distance between us. Without hesitating, he wraps me in a warm hug. "I was surprised to hear from you. You said you didn't want to see me again."

I pout my bottom lip out. "Of course I wanted to see you, but it doesn't mean I should. You see—" My phone buzzes from my hand. I look at the screen to see Nikolai calling. Paranoia rushes over me, stealing away the excitement coursing through the memory.

"Is that Nik?"

I peer over my shoulder. "I shouldn't have come. I'm sorry I have to go."

Before I have a chance to dash away, Luka grabs my hand. "Wait, you just got here."

I tug my hand away. "I'm sorry. It isn't safe for either of us. If Nik found out I was here, he'd get to you."

"I'm not afraid of Knezha." It's the first memory I have of Luka's voice in my mind.

"Well, I am. As long as I'm in his care there's nothing I can do."

"Then maybe you shouldn't be."

"Are you serious? You want me to run?" I ask out loud.

He shrugs. "You seem like you want to."

I press my lips together. "What about you?"

He shrugs again.

"You could come with me," I say. "I could protect you."

"Can I think about it?" he asks.

I nod.

"Skye." Luka pulls me from the memories of Nikolai and him. It's in this moment that I know why I did what I did for Nikolai. He would've killed people regardless, playing a game of fates. He's done it before. The man who killed me and brought me into the Knezha Family's daughter faced that fate for the chance. I did what I did to save people despite the consequences. But it became too much. Luka put the idea of running in my head, and I went with it.

Tears blur my vision. It takes me a moment to respond to him. "I don't want to go back. I'm going to lock the door now."

"Don't leave me," Luka says. It's different from all the other times he's begged me to return to the living world. Something hitches in his voice, burying deep inside me.

"But if I stay—Luka, I can't let them die. I can't."

Guilt and heartache sneak into the galaxy world. The sudden dark feelings slither around me and rip me from Luka's arms. My head spins, pain bursts from my core, but I don't fight the pull dragging me back to life, back to everything horrible I'm capable of in a world that doesn't want to let me go.

Five.

Ice flourishes in my chest.

Four.

A scream rips through the air.

Three.

My eyelids turn red.

Two.

I gasp, my heart pounding in my ears.

I snap my eyes open. Blood covers the floor and wall next to me. Pain burns in my stomach, and I lift my shirt to look at my wounds. My fingers slide across my slippery, blood-covered skin, but I don't seem to be bleeding anymore. I'm healing. The memory of Nikolai triggered something in my mind, and I realize I can rejuvenate my body. I can withstand any damage done to me.

"No!" Gemma yells, pulling me from my thoughts of the red door. Of Nikolai. Of a bunch of unfamiliar faces that flash through my mind. Of phantom pain I've experienced with death. I don't even have a chance to get to my feet before Gemma's on top of me, sliding her hands around my throat to squeeze the air from me.

"Fight, Skye! Lock the door." Her thought hits me in the mind, and I jerk my head back, sending starbursts through my vision.

I try to open my mouth to tell her to stop, but the words never come. *"Stop!"* I push my own thought into her head as fast and as loud as I can manage, not even sure if it's possible or if it will work.

She freezes, though her hands remain tightly around my neck.

"Let go!"

Gemma releases me, and she holds her hands in the air without moving. Her wild eyes bore into mine, and I thrust my arms out and knock her off me. Scrambling to my feet, I search the bloody room for the knife and scoop it up. She was right. Luka was right. I don't have a choice. I'm not sure I ever had one. But it doesn't mean I won't try.

I aim it at Gemma. "Sienna! Sienna, open the door now! If you make me do this, I'll lock the door forever."

"No," Caretaker Sienna says through the speaker overhead. "You won't do it. You don't have it in you."

Gemma wails at the sound of Sienna's voice. And Caretaker Sienna might be right. Because Gemma is one step closer to Luka. I'd gladly return to Nikolai and continue on my journey with the Knezha Family if they figure out how to break him.

"Luka?" I project my thoughts out, hoping for a response.

Nothing comes. He hasn't returned. I've left him behind.

Maybe this is it. We can all be the stars. It might be my last chance.

I inhale a shuddering breath. Looking at Gemma, I whisper, "It's going to be okay." I get to my feet, still holding the knife, and straighten my shoulders.

"I know," she says, her voice hitching.

"I'm sorry."

She doesn't have a chance to get to her feet. She doesn't even have a chance to scream.

"I'm sorry," I whisper again.

Then all I see are stars.

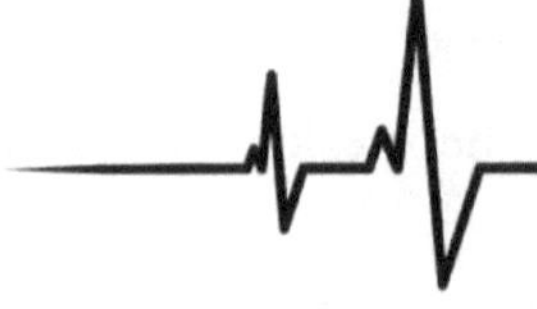

CHAPTER 20

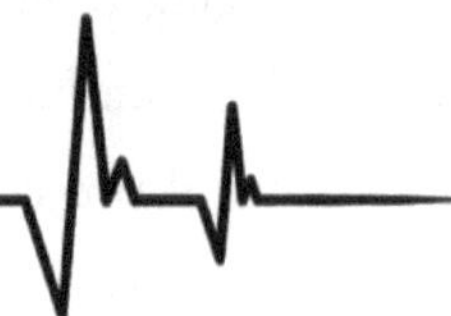

FAILURE

WATER RUNS FROM my hair and into my teary eyes. "I'm sorry. I'm so, so sorry."

Soft sniffling sounds from beside me, but I don't open my eyes to look. "Why did you do this to me? I thought you were my friend." The feminine voice stirs something familiar in me.

"It couldn't wait." I finally open my eyes. It's Avery. "Nikolai sai—"

"You ruined everything."

"I—"

"Skye, please meet me in my office." Nikolai's thoughts sneak

into my head.

"Just give me a minute, please. She's taking it hard. I told you—"

"Let me handle Avery, okay? You need your rest."

He's right. I need rest. I need to go to sleep and forget everything I've done. Nikolai will help me. He always does. He's always been here for me, even when I mess up. He forgives me.

And I manage to forgive him.

We're family.

"Skye!" It's Luka. *"Skye you have to come back. Don't leave me."*

"Come on, Skye. You have to lock the door," Gemma says, her voice cutting through the air, pulling me from my memory and from Luka.

"I have to go back."

A wave of sadness rushes over me, but it's not mine. It's Gemma's. "You can do it from here. Lock it. Please."

"Gemma, I can't!"

"Damn soul mates. You always choose him. It's what will destroy you, you know."

"Skye!" Luka's voice rips me from Gemma and the stars.

The void swallows me, and for the first time ever, I don't count down to my time of life.

An alarm blares through the air, startling me. I jolt upright, disoriented about where I am, and then scramble to my feet. Water sprays from the sprinklers overhead, creating a pool of red water around me because Gemma's body blocks the drain on the floor.

Rushing forward, I kneel in front of Gemma and flip her over. I pull her into my lap, holding her like it'll somehow make up for the fact that I murdered her. That it was me who brought this mess upon her.

"I'm sorry," I whisper. I could apologize a million times, and it would never be enough. "I'm so sorry."

Gemma's eyes snap open at the sound of my voice, startling me. She thrashes, grabbing at my sopping hair. She leaves me no choice but to push her away before she tries to gouge my eyes out.

"*Skye, no,*" she thinks to me.

Screaming, she splashes water, searching for the knife we both used to kill each other. The lights flicker overhead, and then they cut off completely, leaving us in the dark apart from the red blinking light from the camera.

Glass shatters, and I glimpse a spark above me. Gemma wasn't supposed to come back, which means I didn't lock the door, and now I've given Nikolai access to her. To the stars. To Luka and me. With Gemma's life, I've failed. And a violent death seems to have affected her like always as her telekinesis flares.

"*Stop, Gemma!*" I force my thoughts into her mind. "*It's over. I've failed you again.*"

"You didn't fail me, Skye," Gemma says out loud. "I've never felt so alive."

The alarm cuts off, but my ears continue to ring with the sound. "But—"

Gemma smiles, releasing a laugh. "Don't you get it? It's going to be okay. Like you said, it's over."

"Subject four and three, please raise your arms above your heads," Caretaker Sienna says through a loud speaker, cutting off Gemma's conversation.

I don't raise my hands. We were wrong. It isn't over.

The sprinklers cut off and lights flash back on. Stars dance in my vision, and it's like nothing horrible happened in the room. All the blood that once coated the walls and floor has been washed down the drain. The only signs of violence are the stains covering the fronts of both mine and Gemma's clothes too blood-soaked to be washed away so easily.

I meet Gemma's green eyes from feet away. She keeps her hands on her head, but I refuse to raise my arms. The knife is clear across the room, and even if I ran to grab it, Caretaker Sienna would kill me before I got the chance to try to attack her. She'd be expecting it. I need to wait until I can surprise her. Because I'm over this. All of it.

The door swings open, and Caretaker Sienna hovers in the doorway, the harsh light from the hallway silhouetting her in an ethereal glow. Her eyes crinkle in the corners, and if it weren't for her medical mask, I'm sure I'd be able to see her wide smile. She looks like she's had a breakthrough, a miracle even. I just wish it didn't involve me.

"Skye, raise your hands. I will not ask again," she says, motioning to me with her black canister of poison.

I relent and raise my hands without a word.

Caretaker Sienna steps into the room and closes the distance to Gemma first. With a quick flick of the wrist, she grabs

Gemma's shirt and raises it to reveal three stab wounds on her stomach, but they're no longer bleeding. The blood coagulates like my own wounds. I don't need to be a medical professional to know they're already healing. That dragging Gemma in and out of the galaxy through the same door I remember from a vision with Nikolai has healed her. It was different from the times Luka pulled me back to life in the galaxy. This was my doing.

With the thought of Luka, fear clenches my heart. *"Luka?"* I project my voice out.

He doesn't respond. My worst fear comes to life. Nikolai's getting into his head. I know it. Bringing Gemma back left the door open, and I'm not so sure I can shut it. Not without doing it when I'm here. Alive.

"I'm so proud," Caretaker Sienna says, drawing my attention away from my thoughts. "I don't think you're going to even need stitches. This is miraculous. Better than ever."

"You did a great job, Gemma. Your journey will be so rewarding. But for now, you need some time to rest." Caretaker Sienna motions to the door, and Gemma doesn't even put up a fight. I can't tell whether she's too scared to try or if the circumstances extinguished whatever fight she had left in her. Whatever the case, it buries beneath my skin to my soul. I feel responsible. I *am* responsible.

"Wait," I say, taking a step forward. "You can't leave me here."

"Have some patience, Skye," Caretaker Sienna says, tightening her hold on the canister of poison. "We're not quite finished here yet."

"But—"

"Skye..." Luka's voice drifts into my mind, stopping me from arguing with Caretaker Sienna. She takes my sudden silence as surrender and ushers Gemma from the room before locking the door behind her.

"Luka, where are you?" I ask.

"In my room. I saw Nikolai, but he left."

"So, he already knows."

"Skye, this is bad."

"You think?"

"I'm sorry, it's just—"

His thought cuts off, and I feel utterly empty and hopeless as I pace the room. It smells like wet cement and something gross, maybe mildew, and I want out of here. I'd gladly return to the others if it meant I didn't have to be alone to replay what I've done over and over in my mind. Sure, Gemma's alive. But the fear in her eyes. Her screams. The blood. I wanted so badly to stop. But I couldn't. And then I failed anyway.

"Luka?" I ask after what I feel like a minute passes.

"Skye, are you hurt?" Luka switches from worry to panic. His voice rushes into my mind so hot and fast that he could explode through any mental barricade I put up.

"I'm healing, why?"

"Because of the door."

Uh oh. *"I had a memory about Nikolai. He reminded me I could."*

"Skye, you have to block yourself. He's getting in. He's breaking through faster than me. Lock us both out."

"I don't understand."

"I'm sorry. I should've told you." So, I was right. Luka's triggering the memories. He's pulling them for me. But so is Nikolai.

"Why didn't you tell me you could do this?" I could've let him in, and he could've brought everything back to me. I could've known what I was planning. Why I ended up here. How I was going to fix it.

"I'm not some cure to your amnesia, Skye. I didn't want to risk undoing whatever it is that's blocking you from your memories. I was just poking the surface to help. I knew you'd ask me to dig deeper, and then what? Nikolai's stronger than me."

"Maybe I'm stronger than him. You should've just let me try."

"I was protecting you. But my mind isn't as strong as yours. I can't put you in any more danger. You have to close yourself off. Shut me out."

"Luka..." His words stir something dark within me, but I can't shut him out. He's my soul mate. *"I don't think—"*

"Come on, Skye. You have to trust me. If you don't, it's going to get worse. Believe me—" His words cut off.

It's not that I don't believe him. I just—I don't believe me. I don't believe how much I'm hesitating to do something I know I should do.

"Darlin', if you can't believe in yourself, then how do you expect me to believe in you?" Angelica's words wrap me in a comfort I didn't know I needed until the memory broke free from the prison my mind kept it in.

"I don't," I say, peering into Angelica's dark eyes.

She sits across from me on the floor of the apartment, holding my hands in hers. We sit cross-legged, our knees touching, with the soft sound of music coming from an old stereo. Black curtains hang over the windows, blocking the sun so that only a beam of sunshine lights the place.

Angelica laughs, her voice husky, pleasant, something I could listen to all day. "Oh, you need to knock that shit off, Skye. I know you think I'm some crazy lady with her head in the clouds, but you gotta trust me. I didn't just stumble upon you fishing for change in that fountain. The universe led me right to you."

"Are you sure you didn't accidentally take a wrong turn?"

She rolls her eyes, and I smirk. "I guess we'll find out soon, won't we? Nikolai is almost ready for us, then we can say bye to this crappy place. You'll have your own bathroom and everything."

"I like it here," I say.

"But you'll love the Knezha Estate. There's even a chef."

"I like your cooking, too."

She shakes her head, laughing, and happiness courses over me. The memory of Angelica reminds me of how some of the memories of Luka make me feel. Completely different than the new ones of Nikolai.

"Now, darlin', try again. Close those pretty gray eyes of yours and open up your mind. I'll show you the door, so when the time comes, all you have to do is unlock it and step through."

"Skye? Did you hear me? Skye, I'm injured."

I blink my eyes, pushing the memory of Angelica away. Something about it settles deep in my core, but I don't know why it was so important. If I could just remember...

"Skye, brace yourself. Caretaker Sienna—"

The door to the room flies open, banging against the wall. I jump, startled by the sudden intrusion and tense. Trailing my gaze around the room, I spy the knife in the exact spot where I left it next to the drain. I race forward and scoop it up to hold out.

But I'm not met by a threat. Caretaker Sienna doesn't push Gemma back into the room. She shoves Luka forward. I don't even have a chance to process anything before Caretaker Sienna rushes out, closing and locking the door behind her.

I fly from my spot. "Luka? Luka, are you okay?"

Luka's beautiful dark eyes harden, glassing over. He lowers himself to the floor and lies down, like it's too hard to stand. His eyes roll around a moment before he shuts them and then stops moving all together. I shake him and force him onto his side. Warm liquid coats my fingers, and I gasp at the sight of Luka's blood covering my hands.

He's injured. Worse than injured.

He's dying.

"Oh, my God," I say, pressing my hands against his stomach like I can somehow make a difference. I don't know first aid. I don't know how to help him. The only thing I'm good at is hurting people. This is the forest all over again.

"Luka? Please, you have to wake up," I think to him. *"Please. I can't go through this again."*

He doesn't respond, igniting fear into my thrumming heart.

"Skye, it's time to end your games. The door is open. Take him through properly," Caretaker Sienna says from the speaker overhead.

This has gone from bad to awful. Now that she knows I can access the door, that I took Gemma through, she knows I won't slam it shut on Luka.

"I can't," I say. If I take him through and he returns, I'm afraid of what will happen to us. Nikolai's already seeping into my mind. And I know it's only a matter of time that he'll figure out whatever I did before to keep Luka safe. If only I could remember to repeat it.

Static buzzes through the air. "You can. This can all end here. Make the right choice. Follow the journey the universe intended for you."

I jerk my head to glare at the camera. "I can't! I won't! He's mine. I won't let you have him."

I shove my fingers into my hair, yanking it from my face. The only way I can even attempt to heal Luka is if I open the same door I dragged Gemma through, but if I do, it will ruin him.

"Please, don't do this. Just help him. I'll do anything. I'll be the good little girl you want. I'll follow whatever path you put in front of me. Please, just leave Luka out of it. You don't need him." I'm willing to give up every bit of my freedom, my life, my existence as long as I don't have to take Luka through the door.

No one responds to my pleas.

"Skye." Luka's whispered voice enters my mind, causing me to gasp and pull him onto my lap. *"You have to shut me out. Slam the door. Lock it shut."*

Tears burn my eyes. *"What?"*

"Please, you have to do it. Nikolai will break you. I can't let that happen. Let me protect you."

"Luka, I can't. You're my soul mate. Don't make me."

"I won't let you lose yourself, be turned into the person you can't stand to live with, just so I can follow. I love you. Now, do it. Shut me out. Slam the door. Lock it."

I sob, pressing my hands into his cheeks, willing him to open his eyes. "Luka, I will find you."

He doesn't respond. His heart doesn't beat.

I see the door, glowing with a million stars. But I can't see Luka.

He is now the stars and the stars are him.

"Until we meet again," I think to Luka. But he doesn't answer once more, leaving me alone with the empty shell of my soul mate. A life I couldn't save. A journey come to an end.

"Skye!" Caretaker Sienna yells.

I don't respond. All I do is hug Luka to me, holding him in my arms, listening to my own heart beating. There's nothing but the silence of his death, one I can't bring him back from.

The door to the room swings open, and I meet Caretaker Sienna's narrowed gaze. Jumping to my feet, I rush the woman, fury pushing me forward. She scrambles back into the hallway, hitting her back to the wall. I aim the knife at her, ready to gut her for putting me through this, for putting everyone through this. For making me kill Avery. For taking Luka in the first place. For murdering him.

The blade sparkles in the harsh lighting.

I hold up the blade, pushing away everything good that was ever in me into the open door of the galaxy.

Caretaker Sienna screams.

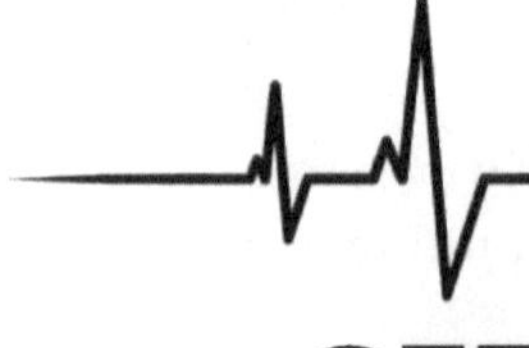

CHAPTER 21

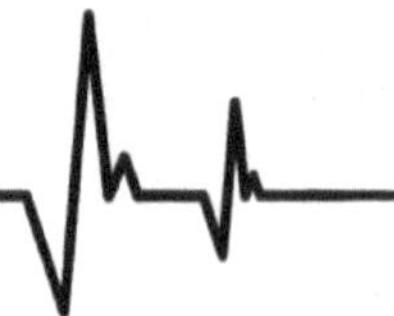

MONSTER

"SKYE NO!"

I lock my fingers on Caretaker Sienna's shoulders, spinning her around. Pushing her forward, I make her face the galaxy world through the open door.

This is all Nikolai's fault. Had he just left us alone, Luka would still be alive. I wouldn't have had to abandon him to die in the forest. Or now. But I can't stay with him. There's nothing I can do except follow through with his request. And Nikolai's forcing my hand. He doesn't think I have it in me. That I can do such a thing. But Nikolai is the one who made it possible. He took every broken piece of me and arranged them so the sharp edges could do more damage. His pretty doll now a monster.

"Luka," I whisper into the galaxy world. "I'm shutting you out now."

I push everything from my mind, sealing me off with metal and moats and bulletproof glass. I steel myself from everything, locking away all that's left of me.

"Please, don't shut me out." My own voice trickles to my ears, pulling me away from the galaxy world. I stare at one of the pictures of Luka and me together he had framed for Christmas. "You have to answer me. Why can't I find you?" The memory hits me so fast, pulling a moment from the time after he died in the forest. One I wish would stay locked away.

I'm greeted by nothing. I can't hear Luka's thoughts. I can't feel him at all.

He's gone. Like he's gone now.

A knock resonates on the door, and I snatch my gun off the carpet next to me. Without getting up, I train it on the door of the cabin.

"Skye, you're not really going to shoot me, are you?" Nikolai's voice intrudes my mind.

I cringe. I accidentally let my guard down. Luka's death chipped away at my protective armor, leaving me vulnerable. But what's the point now? Luka is gone, even his blood disappeared from the melting snow.

Scrambling to my feet, I rush to the door and fling it open. My hands shake as I hold my gun up at Nikolai. I blink tears from my eyes, more angry than upset at the man I've given everything good in my life to.

"You have five seconds to leave before I kill you," I say.

"Oh, come on, Skye. You don't have it in you." Nikolai squares his shoulders, daring me to pull the trigger. "But you can stop playing these games. It's been two days."

It takes everything in me not to shoot him. "I don't deserve this. I've done everything—"

"You've done nothing!" Nikolai yells, making me wince. "You've made battles out of disagreements, and I won't let you ruin everything I've worked hard to acquire."

I sob. "Please, give him back to me."

"Not until you give me what I want."

I shake my head. "No. You can't."

"You were doing so well. What changed? What turned you from our path?"

"Luka," I say. But something doesn't feel right about the words.

He glowers. "It's more than that. You've locked me out."

I'm sure he's right.

Nikolai studies me for a long moment, and I can feel pressure build up in my ears. He's trying to glimpse into my mind. He's trying to see what I see. But my guard has been built up so high, so impenetrable, it'd take a missile to shatter through the barrier that protects me.

"You know, it hurts me so deeply that you've just thrown everything away and shut me out without even talking it through with me. You know how dangerous the world is and why we need our family—" He stops talking the moment he sees my bottom lip tremble.

"I'm not afraid of danger. I'm afraid of you," I say, trying to harden my words by lowering my voice. "Now, please. Give him back to me and forget we exist. You can find another key."

"You are my key. You are so strong and beautiful. Don't throw this away and burn our bridge. Not everything can be repaired, Skye. Some things remain broken. But you can make this all possible. Just imagine the wealth involved in immortality."

"But we're not immortal. We age. We die. Not everyone can unlock the door."

Nikolai rests his hands on my shoulders. "And you're not everyone."

"It should be locked. Our journey isn't supposed to stay here forever. You taught me that."

"Things change."

I lower my hand, pointing the gun at the floor. "And so do people."

"They don't have to."

"But I do. Give him back, Nik. I mean it. Don't make me—"

The world shakes around me, and I pull myself from another memory, one so intense it felt real. It felt like Nikolai was here, standing before me, trying to show me his reason. He was in my head, sneaking his way in the opening left behind by Luka.

And I can't let him do it again.

Pressure builds in my head, like a balloon is expanding in

my mind. Caretaker Sienna's boney fingers dig into my arms, trying to pry herself from me. But nothing she does makes me turn away from the open door, staring at the stars that were always mine—the stars Nikolai's been trying to take.

But he can't have them.

I shut the world out. I slam the door shut. I lock it, separating me from the galaxy world, away from the place I've abandoned Avery. The place Angelica showed me how to access. The place I first met Luka, the place he is right now.

Even if the door is locked, freedom is now within my reach. Nikolai can't get into my head. He can't keep me locked away.

I'm locking the world out. I'm silencing it off. I'm sealing away the memories.

It's why I had forgotten. It's why there was nothing left except for the death that led me here. Nikolai can't take what I don't have. He can't use my mind against me.

Hands grab my hair, Caretaker Sienna fighting, knowing that it's all she can do now. I push her away, and she skids across the floor giving me the chance to get to my feet.

Charging forward, I run out the door and into the same corridor that'll take me up the stairs to another door. The stairs Caretaker Sienna had pushed me down. But I have no choice. If I can't access the galaxy world, then I'll try to get out another way. This is my last chance. I didn't give up everything for nothing. To stay imprisoned. To let Nikolai try to get into my mind.

My bare feet pound the cold floor and an alarm blasts

through the air, ringing in my ears. I expect the place to flood with people hell-bent on keeping me locked away, to glimpse the faces of my supposed family—though I wouldn't be able to put any names to their faces. I expect an army to get in my way. Because even though I've never seen anyone beside Caretaker Sienna, I know she's not alone. Nikolai is never alone.

But me? Without Luka, I'm lonelier than ever.

"Skye, stop!" Caretaker Sienna yells from behind me. "We can work things out. The universe sent you back to us for a reason. We can make you see."

But the universe didn't send me to her. The universe sent me to Luka. It always sends me to Luka. I could slam a thousand doors shut, I could board them up, seal them off, destroy them altogether, and the universe will still give him to me. Our journeys are together.

I know he wanted me to shut him out, slam the door, close it off so he could protect me, but I know deep down, that's not how it works. I protect him. I face the world for him. I can never abandon him.

"Luka," I think. *"Help me find you."*

At the top of the stairwell, an unfamiliar blue door appears in front of the tan one that leads to who knows where. My breath heaves as I race up the last flight and to the door that I know will take me to where I belong, maybe it'll finally allow me to leave this life to enter the next, to see where the universe is supposed to take me. I just need to open a door one more time and seal it off with me in it. Because if I don't, I'll never escape Nikolai. He'll always try to break me. It never should've been Luka in that door, with me shutting him out, slamming it shut. He should've done it to me. Because I'm the reason he's broken. I'm the reason nothing can ever be fixed.

"Skye!" Caretaker Sienna screams again.

Taking a deep breath, I step into the doorframe, curling my bare toes over the edge. *"Luka? Luka are you there?"*

Silence.

A deep ache clenches my heart, stealing my breath away. Tears pour down my cheeks, and the sudden relief the galaxy world brought to me seeps away, leaving agony in its place. The feeling is enough to make me take an automatic step back. Something's terribly wrong. My instincts scream to slam this particular door shut and lock it. This isn't the door I know how to open. This is one I should never be near.

But I don't get the chance.

A body collides into mine, propelling me forward, and the stars shimmer around me, lighting my skin. A thousand unfamiliar thoughts cross my mind, fogging my head. The voices press down on me, threatening to consume my very essence, and there's nothing I can do to stop them.

The stars grow brighter and brighter, burning my eyes, warming me from the outside in until I feel like I am a star glowing in the vast universe full of everything wrong in all of existence.

Five.

My vision blurs.

Four.

The voices in my head quiet.

Three.

A scream comes from nowhere and everywhere.

Two.

The strange door opens again.

One.

Darkness consumes me.

Bolting upright, I gasp, sucking in freezing breaths of air that burn my lungs. The cold, frozen ground seeps through the hem of my shirt, and I shiver. Thousands of stars glitter through the dead branches of trees, but it's not my galaxy world. This is life. Where? I have no idea.

I dig my fingers into the snowy ground, scraping my hands on sharp pieces of gravel. Pain slices through my palms, but I don't let it stop me from pushing to my feet. A soft groan sounds from behind me, and I spin on my feet, catching sight of Caretaker Sienna lying in the muddy snow a few yards away.

She did this. She pushed me through a door that my mind screamed to stay far away from. But why? I'm free from the prison she locked me in. Even though the freezing air burns my lungs, it's utter bliss to gasp in fresh air. And the pain? It means I'm alive. I'm free.

Searching the area, I grab a heavy branch from the ground and hold it on my shoulder like a bat. I step forward in the snow toward Caretaker Sienna and jab her with the branch without getting too close.

"If you try anything stupid, I will kill you," I say.

Caretaker Sienna's shoulders shake, and my brows pinch together as she silently sobs—no—silently laughs. She rips her mask free, tilting her head toward the sky and releases a long, manic laugh that stirs dread in my soul.

"You did it, Skye!" Caretaker Sienna yells. She smacks her palms on the ground, hollering with excitement, confusing me. "He said you would and you did."

Slowly backing away, I put distance between us. Her elated reaction was the last thing I expected after yanking us through a world meant for neither of us.

What have I done?

"You opened the door, Skye," Caretaker Sienna thinks to me.

My breath quickens as she continues to laugh, to shout, to throw her hands toward the glittering night sky.

"I knew you could do it, my beautiful girl." Her thoughts in my mind send fear crawling from my heart to my feet. She doesn't sound like the woman who's been killing me over and over, forcing my hand to do the unthinkable. She sounds like Nikolai.

And the door? The strange, new door? It's the one Nikolai wanted open all along. It's the one he wanted me to travel through.

Breaking into a sprint, I run away from Caretaker Sienna and deeper into the wintery forest. My breath fogs in front of me, each gasp leaving my head spinning. I can't get away fast enough. Branches snap from behind me, and a crack echoes through the air, nearly sending me out of my skin. A massive pine crashes in the distance, blocking my path. I spin on my bare feet, now numb from the snow, and turn to face Caretaker Sienna.

"You can't run from us, Skye," she says.

I hold my hand up. "Stay away from me."

Another tree snaps, shaking the ground beneath my feet.

"Don't you see? This is the universe's doing. It brought you back empty so we could fill you up," she says, cautiously closing the distance.

A sob breaks from my mouth, tightening my chest. "Shut up! This isn't right. Where is he? Luka!"

She raises her hands up. "It's going to be okay."

I shake my head. "No. I can't be here."

Caretaker Sienna narrows her eyes. "Calm down, Skye. Just listen."

"No. You killed him," I say. "You killed him over and over. You took him from me. You destroyed my life. You destroyed the one place that felt like home to me. The universe didn't send me to you to help you. It sent me to him to destroy you."

Caretaker Sienna flicks her hand, and the world falls out from under me. The wind knocks from my chest, and I can't even scream. Twigs rain down on me, pelting me hard enough to cut open my skin. Drops of blood blend with the snow around us.

"Stop!" I send the burning thought to her.

Caretaker Sienna freezes, and the world suddenly falls silent. Scrambling back to my feet, I close the distance between us and get into her face, staring at her wide, unblinking eyes. I brush my hand along her cheek, and her nostrils flare, but still, she can't move.

"You're done controlling me," I think to her, pushing my

way into her head.

"Help me," her thoughts whisper to me. *"Help me."*

"It's too late," I think. *"I'm in your head. There's no escaping now. You can't run, because I'll always find you."*

"I'll always find you this way, okay?" I say, staring into Luka's dark eyes. "You can always find me, too. We just have to let each other in." The memory washes over me in a wave of warmth that sends the chill of the winter forest away.

As quickly as it comes, it fades. And now I know how to find Luka. How to get the universe to reunite us like it did after our first death and then again when Caretaker Sienna brought me right to him.

Drawing my attention back to Caretaker Sienna, I meet her saucer eyes straight on. She's the reason I was forced to close my mind off to Luka, because I accidentally allowed her into my head to ruin everything. But she doesn't have control anymore. Nikolai can't control me either. I do. I've had control all along.

"This ends here," I say to her. "You end here!"

With a silent scream, Caretaker Sienna falls from my grip and hits the snowy ground hard, the thud of her body resonating through the hushed forest. Blood flows from her head, staining the frozen ground crimson. The whole world quakes under me, and I imagine the galaxy world breaking through to life to swallow me whole.

My head spins, my eyes blurring, and then my bare knees hit the ground. Pain explodes through me as I blow up the walls I built around myself.

"Luka," I think, calling into the universe. *"Where are you?"*

My back hits the ground, and I stare through the bare trees at the stars shining above. Pressure expands in my mind, edging my vision.

"Skye?" a voice sounds out through the thudding heartbeat in my head. "Skye, stay with me, okay?"

But I can't stay.

I must go.

I must let it all go.

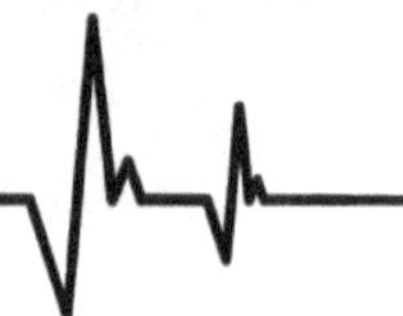

CHAPTER 22

BELONG

A RHYTHMIC HEARTBEAT thumps against my ear, drawing me from my thoughts. I snuggle my face into the soft cotton of a shirt covering taut muscles of a chest that feel so familiar. Groaning, I squeeze my eyes shut tighter, trying my best to ignore the throbbing headache threatening to knock me out.

"She's waking up, Nik," a deep, smooth voice says. My heart picks up speed, pounding in overdrive.

"Here, give her to me." I tense at the sound of Nikolai's voice. He shouldn't be here with Luka. They shouldn't be talking like they're friends. They've never even met.

Digging my fingers into Luka's shirt, I cling on for dear life the second he tries to let go of me. I release a small cry, burying my face into his neck, but I can't manage to form any coherent words.

"Skye, it's okay. You're okay. You're safe." Luka's voice swirls through my mind, calming the fear encasing my heart.

"And you're alive," I think to him.

"Of course I'm alive. It's you we've been worried about."

My blood cools at his thoughts. What does he mean by that? *We* as in him and Nikolai? I don't understand.

Snapping my eyes open, I meet Luka's dark gaze. His eyebrows pucker together with worry, half hidden under a black beanie. I reach up and run my fingers over his clean-shaven jawline, and he smiles at me, showing off his straight teeth.

"I think she's confused, Nik," Luka says, speaking out loud again instead of in my mind. "She was hit on the head pretty hard. I think she's going to need stitches."

"Let me take a look at her," Nikolai says. Gentle fingers touch the back of my throbbing scalp, and I thrash in Luka's arms. "Settle down, my girl. I'm trying to—"

"Where is she?" I ask, finally finding my voice. I wriggle in Luka's arms until he has no choice but to set me back on my feet or risk dropping me. Spinning around, I search the forest for Sienna. When I take a step forward, I realize I'm wearing boots. And jeans. "What's going on? What happened to my clothes?"

Nikolai reaches out his hand and grips my arm. He turns me toward him and forces me to meet his blue eyes. "I was hoping you could tell me what happened, my beautiful girl. You were only supposed to bring Sienna Thomas in, not kill her."

My bottom lip trembles. "She's dead?"

Nikolai wraps his arm around my shoulders. "Come on, Skye. Let's get you home so I can take a better look at you."

Uneasiness washes over me, freezing me in place. I'm so confused. "We have to find Gemma. She needs our help."

Nikolai tilts his head, his brows nearly touching together, and then he turns his gaze to Luka. They share a silent conversation I'm not a part of, and it gets under my skin. Luka hates Nikolai. I kept Luka away from him as best as I could because I didn't want Nikolai to...

"Skye, look at me," Nikolai says. "Gemma chose a journey apart from ours. She ran away. We were left no choice but to sever our ties to her."

I hold his gaze. "No, you're lying."

Something's incredibly wrong.

"You made Sienna do this," I say. The words come rushing out my mouth, like if I don't say them out loud, I'll suddenly forget them like all my memories from before. The ones still begging to break free.

Nikolai's jaw tightens as he presses his lips into a thin line without saying anything.

"Sienna kidnapped Luka after you showed up at our cabin to take him away," I add. I swivel to glance at Luka. "And you were there for almost a year."

"Skye," Luka says. "Come on, Nik's right. Let's go home. We can talk about everything there."

I shake my head, tears burning the backs of my eyelids. "Home? With Nik? You hate him."

Luka steps closer to me. "Where is this coming from? Nikolai's given us a home. He's done nothing but treat us like family."

"You've never even met!" My voice screams through the air. Confusion ties around me, squeezing me harder and harder. It was bad enough losing my memories once, waking up in a scary place with no idea what was going on. But now? Waking up to have the boy I'm most connected to, the boy who shares a soul with me, tell me that what I experienced, what I know I've lived through, wasn't even real is too much. I know I didn't imagine it. I know Caretaker Sienna killed us over and over again.

But why am I dressed? Why am I in the same forest I know I died in to get to Luka?

I couldn't have imagined it all, could I have? I think back to the time before waking up in the room, to Luka, to Angelica, to Gemma and Avery, to Nikolai—every memory I have. Fear trickles through me when I realize that I don't remember much from the time I shot Luka to the time I found him. Almost a year of my life still missing.

Hugging myself, I step back to put distance between me and Luka and Nikolai. "I want to see her."

"Sienna?" Nikolai asks.

I nod. "Let me see her body."

"But Skye—"

I knew it. Nikolai was trying to get in my head like he got into Luka's. This was his plan all along. "Where is her body?"

My voice echoes through the forest, startling Luka.

"Please, don't let her near me." Caretaker Sienna's thoughts intrude on mine, but she's not talking to herself. I can feel it.

"She's alive?" I ask.

One look at Luka confirms she is.

"Where is she?" Both Nikolai and Luka cringe at the pitch of my voice.

A small whimper sounds through the air, and I shove both guys out of the way to rush in the direction I heard the voice. A few yards ahead, just off of the trail and next to a tall pine stands Caretaker Sienna. She uses the tree to half block herself, and all the fight and authority she once had is lost on her frightened expression. Her nose crinkles, her eyes glistening under the light of the bright moon.

"Where is it?" I ask, pointing at her. "Where did you keep us?"

She remains silent apart from her sniffling.

"Tell me or I'll kill you."

Slowly moving from behind the tree, she takes a few steps out into the open. Her boots crunch the icy ground, sending my heart sliding into my stomach. I've never seen her in boots before. Or without all her medical gear. Now, she just looks like a frightened woman. Helpless even. Not the psychotic monster who forced me to kill Avery, who murdered Luka, who knocked us through a door I wasn't familiar with.

"I don't know what you're talking about, Skye," Caretaker Sienna says.

I clench my fingers into fists. "Liar! You said the universe brought me to you. You forced me here."

"I didn't find you. You found me," she says. "You murdered me."

"Because you killed me," I say.

Her hand flies to her mouth. "I'd never hurt anyone."

Covering my face with my hands, I gasp in deep breaths. The sincerity in her voice burrows into my skin and stabs at my insides. It's so convincing I almost believe her. Because I know I've killed people. I know I've taken them into the galaxy world to turn them into something for Nikolai to acquire. To bring them into our little family.

I'm not innocent.

Arms slide around me, and I collapse against Luka as my mind spins out of control. I'm not even sure if my memories are real or not. I'm not sure about anything anymore. I suck in a ragged breath, filling my lungs with icy air.

"What's happening to me, Luka? I'm scared," I think to him.

"I'm here. You're safe. We'll figure it out."

"But I don't even know what's real anymore."

What if I'm not really here? What if this is all in my head? What if I'm trapped in some weird memory to protect myself from accepting that Luka is dead and gone from me forever. What if all I have to do is wake up?

I pinch my arm. "Wake up."

"What are you doing?" Luka asks.

"I'm trying to wake up."

"You are awake, Skye. What if you just dreamed all that other stuff?" he asks. "Have you thought about that?"

I swallow, trying to process everything. "No, it was real."

"This is real," he says.

"But it's not. You don't know Nikolai. We were on the run until I shot you and Caretaker Sienna took you from me. We were apart for almost a year," I say.

"Not true," he says. "I can prove it to you."

Digging into his pocket, he pulls out a cell phone, one I've never seen before. He taps the screen and holds it out for me to look at. It's a picture of me and Luka standing in front of the fountain outside of Nikolai's office at the Knezha Estate. The time stamp is from what I think would be two weeks ago, before I ended up with Caretaker Sienna. But how?

The edges of my vision darken. "That can't be right."

"Just take a deep breath."

"Don't tell me what to do," I snap.

"Do you always have to be such a pain?" he asks, a lightness to his voice that reminds me of the first few days we were with Caretaker Sienna. It reminds me of the cabin, too.

"Luka," I whisper. "Something's wrong with me."

"What do you mean?"

"I can't remember taking that picture. I can't remember anything."

"But you remember me," he says.

My heart clenches in my chest. "I don't know if my memories are real."

He holds me closer and kisses my forehead. "Do you remember what you told me a few weeks after you showed up at my door and asked me to run away with you?"

I blink tears away. "That you were my soul mate."

"Yup, and you said to trust you."

"Do you still trust me?" I ask.

He laughs. "Of course I do. But I want you to trust me, too. Trust that I'm here, and I'll keep you safe. Trust that I'll help you figure things out. Trust in Nikolai, too."

I slowly nod my head even though my heart's not in it. "I do. It's just—"

"Come on, you two. We're going to freeze to death if we're out here any longer. Let's go home," Nikolai says. "And don't you worry, my beautiful girl. We'll get everything sorted out. Promise."

I let Luka tug me with him. He wraps his arm around my shoulders and hugs me against him. His familiar touch ignites a feeling of peace and love, of everything good in the universe. I soak in the feeling, pushing all my confusion away.

A car idles on the dark stretch of road that'll take us back down the mountain, and I try my best not to glare at Sienna as Nikolai gets her settled into the front seat of the sedan. Luka holds open the door for me, but I hesitate getting in. Instead, I tilt my head up to glance at the sparkling stars overhead.

"What is it, Skye?" Luka asks.

I lick my chapped lips. "Just thinking about something."

He studies me a long moment and then whispers, "You're shutting me out."

I nod. "I'm sorry. I have to."

Sadness lines his eyes. "But—"

Nikolai catches my gaze from over the roof of the car. A

small pinch behind my eyes makes me jump, and it takes everything in me to hold a straight face. Nikolai's trying to get into my head. Luka's upset I won't let him in. And Careta—Sienna, stares at me like I'm the worst person in the universe, and I can neither confirm nor deny it. I can't do anything but get in the car.

Luka laces his fingers with mine and smiles at me despite my frown. I should be happy to be out of that dank basement trapped by chain-link and plexiglass. I should be relieved Luka is alive and well and holding my hand. I should be ecstatic the worst moments in my life might not have happened at all, and that I'll be returning to whatever life I had before I died in the forest and returned in Sienna's care.

But I'm not.

I feel trapped in the car. Suffocated. Betrayed by my own mind or someone else. It's like I traded one prison for another, even if Nikolai doesn't chain me down or hide me away. It's far worse. He's put a lock on my mind, and I can't open it, because he's broken the key. He's broken me. I just know it.

Luka presses his lips to my temple, and I can't resist cuddling close. It's less scary with him by my side, even if he's not my Luka, the one who reminded me of the stars, who died with me so I'd never do it alone, who did everything he could to try to protect me, even if I failed to protect him all along. And I'm still failing.

We'll never be free in this life, maybe not in the next either, because Nikolai managed to get in my head...or he's been there all along.

I inhale a quiet breath. *It's going to be okay. It's not that bad. You've escaped once before. You can do it again.*

Nikolai smiles at me in the rearview mirror, and I blink my thoughts away. It's hard not to get wrapped up in his charm and familiarity. Because it's not so bad being with him if I'm to be honest with myself.

"All set?" Nikolai asks from the front seat. "Ready to go home?" His eyes never waver as he directs the words to me.

I glance away and say, "I guess so, Nik."

"Good, because that's where you belong."

I blink away the foreign thought in my mind and pretend I didn't hear Nikolai's voice in my head. He might think he's winning this dangerous mind game, but now I know the rules, and I'm going to break every last one.

My name is Skye Stone. I'm seventeen years old and from Los Angeles, California. I've died before, but now, I'm more alive than ever.

In this second, in this life, nothing else really matters.

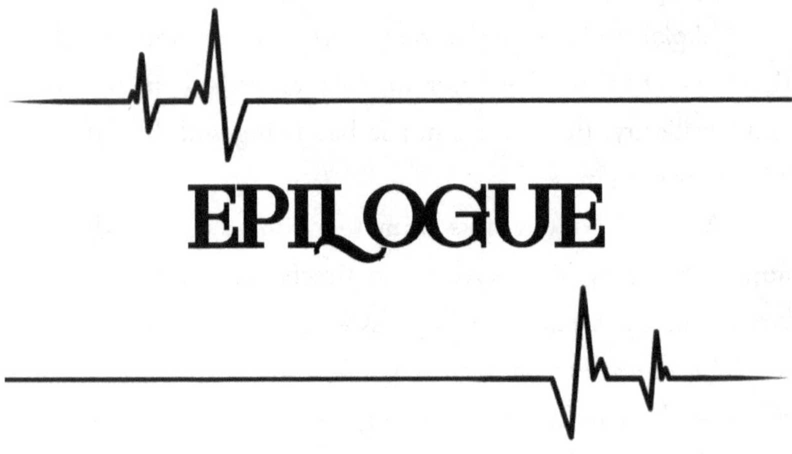

EPILOGUE

BREAK FREE

BREATHE IN. BREATHE out.
One heartbeat.
Breathe in. Breathe out.
Two heartbeats.
Breathe in. Breathe out.
Three heartbeats.
Breathe in. Do it now.
Silence.

Opening my eyes, I stare at the white door before me. "Damn it!"

It flies open, and Luka stands in the doorframe, pressing

his hands on both sides so I see the muscles in his arms flex. His damp hair hangs on his forehead and a towel drapes over his bare shoulder.

"What are you doing?" he asks. Peering over his shoulder, he glances into the empty hallway behind him before shuffling inside.

I motion for him to close the door. "Trying to escape."

I haven't been able to open a single door into the galaxy world since waking up in the forest. Whatever happened between the moment I was in the basement and then lying in the snow keeps the door shut. Gone. Maybe for a reason.

Luka chuckles, crossing his legs to sit next to me. "Without me?"

I shrug. "Depends. Would you come?"

The smile on his lips disappears as he thinks about my question. I don't know if it's the intensity of my stare or the closeness of my body, but it's the first time since the basement that he's looked at me like that, all brooding and serious. It's a shadow of the boy from my memory, and I want so badly to hide in his shadow like it'll keep me safe and protect me from the world.

His gaze trails from my eyes to my mouth, and he sucks in his bottom lip for a moment. "What kind of question is that? If Nik fo—"

I cut off his warning with a kiss. *It was a hypothetical question.*

He wraps his arms around me, pulling me closer. *"I'd follow you anywhere."*

I break away from him with a smile. *"Good, because I'd never leave you."*

After kissing me once more, he pushes to his feet and picks up his wet towel off the floor. "I should go before a guardian catches me in here."

All I do is watch him go, my heart racing the moment I lay my eyes on the tattoo on his back. The one that goes with mine. The heartbeat to my heart. I can remember getting it now, how it itched like hell for a few weeks after, how I barely slept because I like to sleep on my back. How Luka traced his fingers over the simple lines when he could finally touch it without annoying me. The memories I know are real. The memories that break free one at a time, one by one, as my mind puts itself back together again.

I startle when Luka shuts my bedroom door, but not because of the sound. Only feet away, right in front of my white-painted door is a bright red one. It taunts me, a vivid contrast to the muted colors of my room in a mansion that feels more like a prison.

But now, as I stare at the door, I know it's time.

I'm ready to be free.

To be continued...

ACKNOWLEDGEMENTS

THIS BOOK WOULDN'T have been possible without a few important people in my life and career. Thanks to Jan Moran, for listening to me work through plots out loud on our morning walks. I'm so lucky to have such a talented, caring, cheerleader as my mother-in-law. Another thanks goes to both Sarah and Katie, who've read and polished a dozen plus books for me. You girls are rock stars!

A huge thanks is owed to my sister, Tami, for letting me write this book at her kitchen table while I was transitioning from Texas to California. You're seriously the best in the world, and I can only hope to be a fraction of who you are—empathetic, kind, generous, and my personal motivational speaker. Another thanks is owed to my parents for your love and support, your constant enthusiasm, and for your ability to give me hope in times where all felt hopeless.

Lastly, infinite thanks to my husband, Eric, for your unending support and love. I'm pretty sure our souls collided when we met, and I couldn't have found a better soul mate.

ABOUT GINNA MORAN

GINNA MORAN IS a writer from sunny Southern California. She started writing poetry as a teenager in a spiral notebook that she still has tucked away on her desk today. Her love of writing grew after she graduated high school, and she completed her first unpublished manuscript at age eighteen.

When she realized her love of writing was her life's passion, she studied literature at Mira Costa College in Northern San Diego. Besides writing novels, she was senior editor, content manager, and image coordinator for Crescent House Publishing Inc. for four years.

Aside from Ginna's professional life, she enjoys binge

watching television shows, playing pretend with her daughter, and cuddling with her dogs. Some of her favorite things include chocolate, anything that glitters, cheesy jokes, and organizing her bookshelf.

Ginna Moran loves to hear from her readers so visit her online at www.GinnaMoran.com. You can also find her on Facebook, Twitter, Instagram, and Snapchat (@GinnaMoran). To stay up-to-date on new releases, sign up to her newsletter. You'll not only get a FREE story, but you'll be able to participate in monthly giveaways!

Ginna Moran is currently hard at work on her next novel.

OTHER YOUNG ADULT SERIES BY GINNA MORAN

PARANORMAL

Destined for Dreams Series

Demon Within Series

Finding Nate Series

Spark of Life Series

Going Ghostly Series

When Souls Collide Series

Demon Watcher Series

CONTEMPORARY

Falling into Fame Series

STANDALONES

Life After Lila

www.ingramcontent.com/pod-product-compliance
Lightning Source LLC
Chambersburg PA
CBHW051645180726
48284CB00006B/1870